'I don't see why the men should have all ...' laughed Tracie, moving to the door and sliding the bolt shut. 'It simply isn't fair.'

'You don't mean . . . ?' said Pauline.

'I certainly do,' Tracie replied eagerly, tugging once at her wraparound top and then dropping it on the desk by way of confirmation. Her button-up mini-skirt followed suit within seconds, leaving her standing directly in front of Pauline, tall and proudly naked except for her high-heeled shoes. 'You can see I came prepared,' she breathed . . .

Also available from Headline Delta

The Perils of Pauline Peach
Prisoner of Desire
Secrets
The House on Punishment Corner
Gigolo
Amateur Nights
Amateur Days
Naked Ambition
The Casting Couch
Return to the Casting Couch
Bianca
Compulsion
Two Weeks in May
The Downfall of Danielle
Exposed
Indecent
Hot Pursuit
High Jinks Hall
Kiss of Death
The Phallus of Osiris
Lust on the Loose
Passion in Paradise
Reluctant Lust
The Wife-Watcher Letters
Three Women
Total Abandon
Wild Abandon

The Taming of Tracie Trix

Alison North

Delta

Publisher's message
This novel creates an imaginary sexual world. In the real world,
readers are advised to practice safe sex.

Copyright © 1998 Alison North

The right of Alison North to be identified as the Author
of the Work has been asserted by her in accordance with
the Copyright, Designs and Patents Act 1988.

First published in 1998
by HEADLINE BOOK PUBLISHING

A HEADLINE DELTA paperback

10 9 8 7 6 5 4 3 2 1

All rights reserved. No part of this publication may be
reproduced, stored in a retrieval system, or transmitted,
in any form or by any means without the prior written
permission of the publisher, nor be otherwise circulated
in any form of binding or cover other than that in which
it is published and without a similar condition being
imposed on the subsequent purchaser.

All characters in this publication are fictitious
and any resemblance to real persons, living or dead,
is purely coincidental.

ISBN 0 7472 5777 9

Typeset by CBS, Felixstowe, Suffolk

Printed and bound in Great Britain by
Mackays of Chatham plc, Chatham, Kent

HEADLINE BOOK PUBLISHING
A division of Hodder Headline PLC
338 Euston Road
London NW1 3BH

The Taming of Tracie Trix

Dear Alison

I've just finished your account of my recent adventures and I'm speechless – well, almost. You don't pull your punches about a girl's most intimate moments, do you? I know I told you every little thing about what I'd been up to but seeing it all in print makes it all so much more *lurid*! And exciting, too. I admit I got a bit turned on reading about me and my wicked little urges. I bet there'll be more than a few stretched trouser-fronts and creamed panties when this hits the book stalls!

All I can say is, you'd better watch out, Alison North. You're not such a goody-goody yourself when you fancy a bit. One day maybe I'll put down on paper what happened when you took the coach with the cricket team last summer. There are a few people out there who might like to read about how you let that long blonde hair down when you play away!

So just remember, you owe me. In fact, there's a night next week when Peter's away and you could come round to my place and start to repay your debt . . .

Kiss, kiss

Tracie

Prologue

It was Thursday morning at the office.

Tracie Trix, tall, slim, ravishing (and frequently ravished), sat in front of her word processor, her jet-black hair cropped short in a sort of urchin cut that perfectly suited her beautiful but decidedly mischievous face. An education spanning twelve years at a fee-paying convent school for young ladies of breeding had done nothing to curtail the wild and wilful spirit that dwelt inside her.

'Eureka!' she cried to the empty room. She'd finally cracked it, she told herself happily. She'd finally solved the problem that had been grating on her all morning. Inspiration had come out of the blue, right in the middle of tapping this long, hugely boring contract into the word processor. The answer was so simple. All she'd have to do was to make one short phone call, then she'd be home and dry. Well, not so dry, if she managed to have her wicked way. Which she was confident she would.

Her husband, Peter, had been a pig towards her earlier that morning. A real pig, and as stubborn as a mule, despite the fact that she'd done her best to put him in a good frame of mind. She'd made love to him before getting up, lying on top so he could watch her bottom in the wardrobe mirror, as he always liked to do. Not that she blamed him for that. She was only too well aware of the way men regarded her randy little rear end. Then she'd started to get dressed in front of him, very slowly and slinkily, whilst he'd been sprawled out on the bed studying her every move.

Wearing nothing but a frothy, plumply filled bra, she'd looked back at him over her shoulder and asked innocently about the dates of the Torquay conference the following week.

'Why do you want to know?' he'd asked, staring suspiciously at her bottom as she wriggled it sexily into a pair of G-string knickers.

'I'd just like to make some plans, that's all.'

'Who with, exactly? One of those horny buggers from the office who're always trying to get between your legs?'

Tracie looked back at the screen of the word processor. Of course, Mr Jealousy Bollocks had been absolutely one hundred and ten percent correct! She was certainly hoping to make some plans, either with George Franks or Jim Browne, or preferably with both, since the conference would take Peter away from home for two nights. Two whole, wonderful nights of glorious sexual freedom!

But which two nights would they be? That had been her problem. Without that knowledge there was no way she could make any arrangements at all. And if she left it too late, both George and Jim might well have other plans. Mind you, that would still leave Young Harry, Mr James' trainee. There were many worse ways of spending the night than curled up in bed beside him. Or rather, underneath or on top of him. The only slight drawback there was that it would have to be her place, as Harry still lived with his parents. It was never quite as relaxing, rutting and raving in the matrimonial bed, with the half-thought at the back of your mind that you might hear the latch key turn in the front door just as you were about to be shot full of lovely hot spunk . . .

Peter had remained extremely dogged and unhelpful, so after the very expert blow job she'd given him by way of reassurance, she'd slipped downstairs in her undies whilst he'd still been in bed and hunted high and low for his diary, but without reward. Obviously the ultra-suspicious so-and-so had hidden it somewhere.

She supposed she knew why poor Peter was so untrusting. It was a result of that really bad business last year. What a crying shame that he'd decided to take a walk round the block at precisely the wrong moment. At precisely the moment that Martin, or Raymond, or David, or whatever his name had been, had just started to shag her silly on the front seat of his car. Peter had strolled past the car, tickled pink to observe that some couple were having it off nineteen to the dozen inside. He'd been less tickled twenty minutes or so later, however, when, on the way back, in the sodium light from the street lamp, he'd recognised his own wife clambering out of the passenger door and tugging down the hem of her miniskirt.

Yes, Tracie thought ruefully, that had been a very bad business indeed. Peter had been far from the most trusting of souls beforehand, but he'd been considerably worse ever since. Not to mention the painful fact that every night for the next week he'd put her across his knee and painted her bottom bright red with hard smacks, as well as the backs of her thighs. He'd flatly refused to believe her (rather feeble) excuse that she'd simply been giving the driver directions. Anyway, to cut a long story short, he'd become so unbearably jealous and inquisitive that she'd often had to go as long as three or four weeks without getting her end away elsewhere. And with a tail such as hers that needed constant diversification, three or four weeks was an intolerable length of time.

But now she had the solution to the problem of the Torquay conference. It was really simple in the end. All she had to do was ring Peter's company and say she was from the central clearing agency for Trust House someone-or-other, and then ask them to confirm the details of their bookings for the conference because her computer had gone a bit wobbly.

It was a great shame that this year they'd cut the conference from three nights to two, which meant she could only keep two men happy. Obviously George and Jim had to be given the first option, as they had prior claim by dint of precedence. Both of them had had her before she'd been with the firm for a week. But it would have been really nice if she'd been able to accommodate Young Harry as well. After all, they could easily have booked into a small hotel somewhere, rather than sleep at her house. Well, she'd make him first reserve, as it was always possible that one of the others might have another commitment. She knew that George, at least, wouldn't object.

As Tracie reached for the telephone, Kevin, the office boy, was busy in the stockroom moving huge cartons of headed notepaper from one end to the other. His objective was to clear sufficient floor space to enable two people to stretch out in comfort.

He was feeling lucky, he told himself, as much in hope as genuine expectation. After all, it was about time it happened to him. Hell, he'd be seventeen next week! He didn't want to end yet another year without having lost his virginity.

But at least he felt that he had some sort of a chance with that slinky Mrs Tracie Trix, old Davis-Davies' sexy, long-legged secretary. Everyone at the office knew that she put it about quite a bit. It was common knowledge that Mr Franks and Mr Browne had definitely been getting their share of her. And there were rumours about most of the other men, too. Certainly Harry Hotspur, Mr James' trainee, had come close at the office disco last week. Harry had told him that she'd sat on his lap for almost an hour, wriggling her plump little bum and letting him finger her as hard as he pleased. And Harry wasn't the sort of guy to make that up. Apparently, when he'd asked her if he could take her home, she'd told him she'd love to say 'Yes' but that her husband was so suspicious of her that he'd be meeting her off the mini-bus. There'd be hell to pay, she'd told him, if she wasn't on board. Then she'd furtively slid her hand down the front of his trousers, squeezed his overstretched cock, and told him in a giggle that he'd simply have to be patient. After that, she'd closed her eyes and allowed Harry's fingers to bring her off, even though several of the other secretaries had been sitting nearby and must have been able to guess what he was doing to her under cover of the table top.

Carefully, Kevin inspected the bolt he'd recently fixed

inside the stockroom door. So Harry was confident about Mrs Trix, he pointed out to himself. Harry was sure he'd have his leg over there. And if Harry could score, then why couldn't he? Okay, Harry was twenty-one and had already screwed half a dozen girls or more. But everyone had to start somewhere.

Kevin thrust his hands into his pockets and thought deeply about his wretched state of celibacy. Surely Tracie was just the right type to give him his start in life. And she'd definitely been very amenable towards him of late. In the last few days he'd taken to patting her bottom whenever the opportunity had arisen. There'd been not the slightest hint of protest from her, of course. Just one of those knowing grins of mock reproach and some vaguely suggestive remark. Indeed, once or twice she'd even patted him back.

So that was it, Kevin decided at last. Next time he was alone with Tracie he'd definitely press the point and see what she did. After all, she could only say 'no'. That would be disappointing of course, but it wouldn't be the end of the world. It wouldn't make him any more of a virgin than he already was. And if by some chance she'd said 'yes' . . . !

'Mr Davis-Davies can wait. This photo has really stirred me up, Pauline.'

'Pardon?'

'I don't see why the men should have all the fun,' laughed Tracie, moving to the door and sliding the bolt shut. 'It simply isn't fair.'

'You don't mean . . . ?'

'I certainly do,' Tracie replied eagerly, tugging once at her wraparound top and then dropping it on the desk by way of confirmation. Her button-up mini-skirt followed suit within seconds, leaving her standing directly in front of Pauline, tall and proudly naked except for her high-heeled shoes. 'You can see I came prepared,' she breathed, gesturing down at her firm bare breasts and dark triangle of pubic hair. She reached out for the well-filled top of

Pauline's dress with the lightest of touches. 'Don't you like me enough?'

'Tracie, I . . .'

'Don't you fancy me at all?'

'. . . It's not that . . .'

Slowly and lovingly Tracie ran a finger through Pauline's long blonde ringlets. 'You're so beautiful,' she whispered, leaning a fraction forward and kissing her fleetingly on the lips. 'So incredibly beautiful.'

The shape of Pauline's nipples was now clearly visible through the lightweight fabric of her summer dress. Tracie continued fondling the ringlets, but at the same time she began brushing the back of her other hand against the tip of each thrusting breast in turn. Brushing so lightly that Pauline almost cried out at the sudden spark of electricity created by the other girl's touch. Tracie smiled into her eyes and then kissed her gently on the lips once more. This time she lingered several seconds longer than before, each girl savouring the sweetness of the other. Pauline stood stock still, trying not to give any indication of the intense sensuality she felt. Tracie ended the kiss and began using her fingertips to trace the outline of both nipples, very delicately, making them so hard that they felt as if they'd soon fragment.

Tracie smiled again. 'Haven't you been made love to by a girl before?'

'Not very often,' she stammered.

'Did you enjoy it?'

'Oh, well, er, in a sort of a way, I suppose . . .'

Tracie began stroking and squeezing Pauline's breasts, so tenderly that Pauline felt that she was going to swoon away. 'You're so fuckable!' Tracie breathed hotly, feeling her vaginal juices starting to run down her thighs. 'So soft and blonde and fluffy. So hot and moist and sexy, and unable to say no.'

'Tracie . . .'

Tracie kissed her again, this time using her tongue, briefly but oh-so-lovingly. 'I bet you've been spanked by a girl, haven't you? I bet you loved every moment.'

'Oh, well, er . . .'

Tracie reached behind Pauline and started to unzip her dress. Pauline raised a hand to stop her, but it was guided gently back to her side. 'The men don't deserve to have you all to themselves,' said Tracie, before kissing her again. 'You're far too gorgeous for that,' she added, when she was through.

Thirty seconds later Pauline's clothes were on the floor around her feet, leaving her as naked as Tracie. 'Oh, I love that shaven pussy!' enthused Tracie. 'How long have you had it bare?'

'Since I got married.'

'It's lovely!' cooed Tracie, running a fingertip over the outer lips. 'So plump and pretty. And so incredibly smooth.'

'I use a special cream on it.'

Pauline closed her eyes as Tracie's arms wrapped round her waist and she felt Tracie's hot hard tongue slide deeper and deeper into her mouth. Involuntarily, she slipped both hands round Tracie's bare bottom, reflecting momentarily on the stark contrast between those smooth round cheeks and the usual hard male haunches. In their high heels the girls were almost exactly the same height. Whilst Tracie's tongue pushed even deeper, Pauline sighed with pleasure as she felt a pair of pointed, rock hard nipples begin gently teasing her own. The effect on Pauline was instantaneous. She could feel herself melting into her companion's soft, smooth body. Then a bush of springy pubic hair was pressed firmly into her groin. Expertly her clitoris was located and worked upon by Tracie's pubic mound.

'Ohhh!' groaned Pauline, squeezing the firm, creamy smooth cheeks she held in her hands and starting to come at once. The sort of soft, slow, dreamy orgasm she could never have had with a man.

Slowly Tracie withdrew her tongue from the warm succulence of Pauline's mouth. 'You're incredible!' she whispered in admiration, as Pauline continued the long, gentle climax, completely oblivious to her surroundings. 'Utterly incredible!' she added, sliding both hands down round Pauline's bottom.

Tracie kissed her again, even deeper and more passionately than before. 'How can anyone come so easily?' she wondered aloud.

They stood locked together, mouth to mouth, nipples to nipples, groin to groin, and hands cupped lovingly round each other's honey-smooth bare buttocks. The two girls stood like that for several minutes, kissing passionately, whilst Pauline quivered and quaked in the throes of the most sustained and deliciously delicate orgasm she'd ever known in her life.

Later, as Kevin fastened the bolt on the inside of the door, Tracie pulled her short skirt up to her waist and stepped nimbly out of her tiny knickers. Kevin gazed in awe at her luxuriant bush of jet-black pubic hair. His penis seemed to stretch even further, causing it to ache with genuine pain.

'We'll have to be quick,' whispered Tracie, unzipping him and taking his urgent erection in both hands. She lay on the floor, drawing him down between her legs. Then she slid him inside with practised ease.

Kevin gasped in wonder at the incredible sensation. A sensation that was entirely novel to him. He couldn't believe how good it felt. He'd often tried to imagine how it would be, but the reality far outweighed any of his fantasies. The glorious wet warmth and pliable tightness of her quim were a marvel to him.

'You don't have to be that quick!' she panted, as he flew in and out of her at speed. 'You can make it last a bit longer, if you want.'

Kevin slowed down. 'Sorry,' he muttered breathlessly. 'It felt so nice I just got carried away. I just couldn't get enough.'

'You youngsters are all the same!' she giggled. 'Wham! Bam! Thank you, ma'am!'

Kevin concentrated on keeping the pace as slow and easy as his over-excited tackle would permit. 'That's much better,' she sighed happily, as he slithered and slid back and forth along the full length of her vagina. 'Now you're starting to make me come!'

Kevin wasn't exactly sure what she meant, but he was enjoying it, whatever it was. And he could see from the look on her face that Tracie felt exactly the same. Instinctively he began prodding her more sharply, and was delighted with the effect produced. So he kept on doing it, making her squeal with pleasure and wriggle her hips underneath him as hard as she could. But now he found he was unable to revert to a slower speed. He was unable to prevent himself poking her harder and faster with every thrust of his groin. He tried to slow down the pace, but he couldn't control the manner in which he was stoking her with all his strength. The delicious sensation was becoming more and more delicious with every stroke. Harder and harder he poled her, until his sperm suddenly exploded into her with a velocity that neither of them could believe. 'Geronimo!' she gasped, wrapping her legs round him and then thrusting up with her bottom in order to force him as far inside as he'd go.

'You certainly seemed to enjoy that!' laughed Tracie, when he'd finally finished emptying himself into her womb. When at last he'd concluded the very important business of shedding his wretched virginity.

'It was my first time,' he groaned, trying desperately to recover his breath as he lay beside her.

'Well, it certainly won't be your last. I shall see to that. Right now, in fact!'

So saying, Tracie lowered her mouth to his groin and sucked in the whole of his sticky, half-hard cock. The effect was immediate. Instantly he started to expand in her mouth. So quickly that she gasped in admiration. She lay back and in a flash he was between her legs and solidly inside her again. He could feel much of his own recently sewn seed being forced out of her as he pushed all the way up to the top of her tight little passage. 'Kevin!' she gasped happily. 'I'm as full as ever I've been! And it must be years since I was gorged with virgin meat.'

He slid a hand underneath her bottom, relishing the silky texture of the flesh. 'I'm not a virgin now,' he muttered, pumping her with all his might.

'I suppose not,' she panted, thrusting her groin up to meet him.

He pulled her top open and was delighted to find that she wasn't wearing a bra. Clamping both hands back round the cheeks of her bottom, he sucked greedily at one erect nipple and then the other, making her squirm and groan.

This was the life, Tracie told herself. This was what it was all about. How could anyone in their right mind expect you to stay faithful to one man when there was all this fresh young meat to be had? All this prime, but not at all tender, young pork?

As the waves of climax built up, Tracie reminded herself to telephone her husband's company after lunch. She must ascertain the dates of the conference as soon as possible, in order to ensure a continuing supply of her favourite form of protein.

PART 1 – WILD

Chapter 1

Harry

It was later on Thursday at the office, and Tracie was back at her desk.

She looked down at her lap and sighed deeply. God, she was feeling so horny! Far too horny to be able to type. First there'd been that truly wonderful session with Pauline. With hardly any effort at all she'd been able to make that beautiful blonde climax time after time. How satisfying it had been to do that to her! And how wonderfully well Pauline had then set about gobbling pussy! Clearly she'd done it many, many times before. Tracie had almost swooned with the pleasure of Pauline's lips and tongue working away inside her. And when she'd finally been brought to the boil, what a mega-special orgasm she'd had! One that had lasted and lasted, and made every nerve in her body throb with delight. Just like the time that Peter, at her suggestion, had used the buckle end of a belt on her bottom, before shafting it all the way up to the hilt.

Then, of course, there'd been Kevin. Almost immediately after Pauline had finished eating her alive, Kevin had arrived on the scene. Her pussy had still been purring with happy contentment when Kevin had offered it something much more substantial than a tongue. Twice in a row he'd stretched and then swamped it, opening her almost as wide as she'd ever been opened before.

Afterwards, she'd deliberately avoided paying a visit to the ladies, with the result that her knickers were now soaked with his lovely thick virgin come. She just loved that sensation. The sensation of slowly leaking seed. Whenever possible after sex, she'd leave it all inside her and let it find its own way out. The only problem was that it made her randier than ever – the feeling of yet another sticky dollop oozing its way through saturated knickers and gumming the tops of her thighs together even more. Just as Kevin's was doing to her now.

Tracie slid her hand inside her skirt and cupped it round the sopping wet crotch of her panties. Slowly she began to squeeze and tease. Christ, she was as horny as hell! Every time she touched her swollen clit, it sent shock waves racing right through her. Peter wouldn't know what had hit him tonight. She'd rape him as soon as he got in the door. She'd tug his trousers and pants down to his feet and then gorge herself on him for ages. First in her mouth, and then between her legs. That was one thing she could say about him, he was always up and ready for that sort of thing. He could keep it going all night if she needed him to. Which she had to admit she often did.

Sod it! This was no good at all! This hand job was only making things worse. It was bringing her off – sort of – but there was no real pleasure or satisfaction involved. It was just making her feel randier and randier. She definitely needed some more of the real thing. And she couldn't possibly wait until evening. She'd die of frustration long before it was time to go home and hump her husband. If only she could get her hands on Pauline. That would really be good. She could sit back in comfort and let that lovely lady eat pussy till it came out of her ears. But the gorgeous strumpet had already left the office. So there was no relief to be found from that particular quarter. And both Jim and George had taken their long, smooth dicks out of the office for a couple of hours.

Suddenly Tracie was struck with an idea. Why not? It was her lunch hour, after all. She punched a button on the intercom beside her desk.

'Hello,' a male voice said in response.

'Harry,' she said softly down the line. 'Is Mr James in there?'

'No. He's just gone out to a meeting.'

'Will he be very long?'

'Well, a couple of hours or so.'

'Great! Stay exactly where you are. There's something I want you to do for me.'

Tracie whipped off her soggy black knickers. She fisted them into a ball and used them to effect running repairs between the tops of her legs. Then she dropped them into the drawer of her desk. She'd screw Harry with the rest of Kevin inside her, she decided. It was fun doing that. It always gave her that extra thrill . . .

Thirty seconds later Tracie slipped into Mr James' room, braless and knickerless, just as she'd been for Pauline earlier that day. 'Who's a lucky young lad?' she cooed as she walked over to Harry, who was seated at his desk.

'What are you doing?' he gasped in surprise as she knelt on the carpet in front of him and then reached out with both hands for his zip.

She didn't reply. She didn't feel it was called for, nor indeed possible, because seconds later his rapidly expanding erection was filling her mouth. Slowly and expertly she started to suck him, covering him with saliva and stroking his testicles with her free hand. He reached forward and unwrapped her top, leaving her naked above the waist, as her head worked up and down.

Harry glanced across the room at the wall behind where she was kneeling. There in the glass-fronted cabinet was the perfect image of her saucy little bottom peeping out from under the hem of her skirt. Peeping out at him so cheekily – smooth, round and beautifully bare. He gazed hungrily at the reflection. First Pauline, and now Tracie. Both in the space of a couple of hours. This was surely his day. Today he could do no wrong.

Harry could see the cheeks of her bottom joggling in time with the rise and fall of her head. It was a wonderful sensation, feeling her mouth working away on his bulging member, whilst at the same time being able to lean back in the chair and stare at her prettily bared behind. Her skirt was so short that, as she knelt forward, almost all of her bottom was exposed to view. He'd spent the last six months watching those self-same cheeks wiggle and bounce their way around the building, respectably clad in short skirts. Watching them and knowing that his elders and betters, Jim Browne and George Franks, were regularly stripping them bare and taking their fill. Now it was going to be his turn to participate in what must be her husband's most favourite feature. His turn to have a slice of that gorgeous, pert little bum.

At length Tracie lifted her head. 'You taste of pussy!' she giggled, holding his hot, upright penis against the side of her face. 'I suppose it's that Pauline Peach?'*

'That's right,' he breathed, as she started to rub him.

'Was she good, Harry? Was she as tasty as she looks like she'd be?'

'What do you think?'

'I think you enjoyed her so much you really pigged yourself on her,' she said, unbuttoning her skirt and tossing it aside. 'Exactly as I'm going to pig myself on you!'

Tracie reclined the armchair and then knelt on it, facing Harry, her legs straddling his. Fascinated, Harry stared at the glass-fronted cabinet, watching her sink slowly down onto him, watching the reflection of her pouting bare buttocks lowering themselves towards his groin as she speared herself deeper and deeper on his rigidly upthrust column of flesh. 'You'd better have plenty left for me!' she said fiercely, delighting in the way she could feel him opening her wider and wider until he was pressing firmly against the neck of her womb. His tool was every bit as large as Kevin's, she sighed happily to herself. It was parting and probing her just as extensively as that young lad's had so recently done.

Harry gazed at the image of her bottom as she started to work up and down. He watched the reflection of his left hand as it squeezed each cheek in turn. He could even see the fleeting white mark that it left behind. And he could also see his own erection vanishing into her hot little chasm

---

For a complete account of Pauline's deplorable behaviour see The Perils of Pauline Peach

every time she bore down on him. Her hot, wet little chasm, he said to himself. In fact, her incredibly wet little chasm. As she shafted herself on him with gusto, he could feel her juices running out of her and trickling over his. In far greater quantity than normal, it seemed to him.

Tracie closed her eyes and continued to pump lustily up and down. This was just what she needed – spiking herself on Harry as hard and as fast as she could.

Harry was still enjoying the show. Still appreciating the reflection of her sweetly bouncing bottom as she rode the full length of his stalk. It was a truly enthralling sight. Suddenly Tracie sensed his interest and paused to peer back over her shoulder. 'You're enjoying that, aren't you?' she murmured, biting the side of his neck rather hard. 'Watching my bum in the glass, I mean.' Slowly she lifted her hips and stared back at the sight of his long, gleaming wet shaft disappearing into her body. 'Doesn't that look nice?' she breathed.

He took a fierce two-handed grip on the cheekiest part of her bottom and tugged her back down, jamming himself deep inside her once more. Then he slapped her, playfully but quite sharply, causing her to jerk and force him even deeper inside. 'Do that again!' she gasped. 'Only harder.'

He was delighted to do as she'd bid, several times, loudly and enthusiastically, hammering her harder and harder onto the point of his erection with each stinging slap. Almost immediately he felt her climax flare up. 'Oh my God!' she shrieked. 'That's beautiful! Keep doing it as hard as you can.'

Whilst her smooth little bottom quickly changed colour, Tracie wriggled and writhed on his lap in wild, uncontrollable climax. Each smack seemed to drive him even further into her, stretching her and making her squeal and squawk with delight.

Slap! *Slap*! *Slap*! *Slap*! 'Jesus, that's good!' she groaned. 'You're making me come so hard.'

'I know,' he replied. 'I can feel it.'

Eventually it was over and she collapsed forward on top of him, her breasts pressing warmly into his chest as she panted and puffed. 'That was lovely!' she sighed into his ear. 'Really, really lovely.'

'Your bum's going to be sore,' he said. But she wasn't listening. Already recovering, she was going back into action.

Tracie adjusted her position on top of Harry, stretching her legs out behind her so that her toes were now firmly on the floor. This gave her the extra purchase she'd need in order to pick up the pace. And pick it up she certainly did, the cheeks of her bottom flying wildly up and down as she impaled herself on him for all she was worth.

At last Tracie decided on a change of routine. With some difficulty she slithered herself free and returned to her former position on the floor. She swallowed him greedily once again, relishing the mixture of tastes, the cocktail of different flavours. She rather wished now that she'd taken the opportunity of getting her mouth into Pauline. There was nothing more delicious than this delightful combination of his and hers. She and her best friend Jackie used to spend ages enjoying each other after a night on the pull. And sometimes they still did.

Harry stretched back in luxury, still gazing at the image in the glass. The picture was even prettier now. The picture of her nicely reddened bottom joggling gently in time with her head. Slowly but surely he could feel his climax approaching.

Tracie could feel it too, and doubled her efforts, going down on him much more quickly than before, and pampering his swollen testicles in the palm of one hand. At the very last moment, just as he was about to erupt in her mouth, she disgorged him and hopped back onto the chair, kneeling over his groin once again. She squeezed his penis hard in her right hand, holding it between the very tops of her thighs so that it was brushing lightly against her wide open lips. 'What will you give me if I let you back in here?' she teased.

'Anything!' he gasped desperately. 'Absolutely anything in the world!'

'Will you love me for ever and fuck me five times a day?'
'Yes, yes!'
'And you'll never fuck anyone else?'
'No, never!'

Suddenly she pushed down with her hips, enveloping penis with pussy all the way up to the hilt, and causing Harry to buck wildly in the armchair. 'You men are all the same!' she giggled, as she felt him begin to spurt. 'You'll say anything to a poor girl, just to get into her hole!'

Tracie lay curled up and content on top of Harry, his penis slowly shrinking inside her. 'How long will Mr James be gone?' she asked.

'At least another hour,' Harry murmured breathlessly. 'Probably longer.'

'Then there's plenty of time for another!'

'I'm knackered. I'm not sure I can raise a gallop.'

'Rubbish!' Tracie snapped firmly. 'Wait till I use my mouth to revive you.'

Two minutes later she was kneeling on the floor yet again, Harry's sticky, flaccid end inside her mouth. Slowly she began to frig the tip in and out, simulating the act of intercourse on his sadly wilted organ.

Harry closed his eyes and brought to mind the delightful sight of her plump little bottom as it worked up and down on his lap. He recalled the sensation of slapping it – of slapping it hard whilst she climaxed so fiercely. He remembered how it had turned such a pretty shade of pink. He remembered, also, how nicely it had then joggled and bounced whilst she'd fucked him with all her might.

Surely enough he started to swell in her mouth, prompting her to work on him even harder. Less than a minute later he was fully erect. Tall, hard and proud, despite the rigours to which he'd been subjected. Tracie lapped at him greedily, delighted at the response she'd provoked. He had a really beautiful dick, she said to herself. Long and smooth and wonderfully stiff. And incredibly resilient, too. How was he able to perform so well with her, after he'd just sorted out Pauline?'

'How many times did you squirt?' she asked, lifting her head and holding the hot, round knob of his penis against her lips.

'Eh?'

'Into Pauline, I mean. How many times did you plant something sticky inside her?'

'Three,' he said without having to think.

'Jesus!' she whistled, impressed.

Tracie returned to the giving of head. She'd keep him in her mouth, she decided. This time she wanted him to ejaculate in there. She wanted to taste his fluid. She wanted that very much. She could feel his first load starting to dribble down her thighs, mingled with Kevin's. She wasn't doing as well as Pauline, but she wasn't doing too badly, either. She'd be very nicely seen-to by the time she headed home to hubby for more. And Jim Browne was due to bed her tomorrow, as well. So she was getting plenty of the wholesome nourishment she needed to stay in fine tune.

Harry couldn't believe how stiff she was making him. And just as it had been with Pauline, the sight of her pretty mouth swallowing him whole was so erotic that he could feel himself stretching and straining at the leash. Both girls were incredibly skilled in the way they were able to take all of him down. He'd never had that done to him before. Their husbands must be very happy men. But did either of them ever suspect that this particular intimacy might sometimes be practised on somebody else?

Suddenly they heard a footfall outside the door and a familiar cough that could only have belonged to the firm's senior partner, Mr Fennell. Tracie jerked up her head. 'Christ!' she squawked in panic, letting go of Harry and allowing his penis to slap hard against his stomach. 'I don't think I locked the door!'

'Get under the desk!' he hissed.

Grabbing her skirt and top, Tracie scuttled into the well of the desk on all fours, her nicely reddened bare bottom disappearing from view in a trice. Fortunately, there was a modesty board on the front, so she was safely hidden from view. As the door handle started to turn, Harry pulled himself forward on his chair and jammed the lower half of his body under the desk. Then he leant as far forward as he could and started to pray. Now Tracie and half of Harry were crammed tightly into the relatively small space under the surface of the desk – Tracie stark naked and leaking heavily, Harry unzipped and still extremely erect. Far too erect for comfort, since the swollen head of his member was pressing painfully into the underneath of the worktop. He managed to adjust his position and lean even further forward, thus alleviating the pressure. To his surprise, his penis showed no sign of wilting or waning, despite the impending danger. It continued to point stiffly up at his chin, although, fortunately, out of sight.

Mr Fennell stepped into the room. 'Good morning, Harry,' he said pleasantly.

'. . . Good morning, sir,' Harry managed to reply. His throat felt tight and his voice sounded weak and croaking.

'Is Mr James around?'

'He's in a meeting, I'm afraid.'

'Will he be long?'

'About an hour, I think.'

Mr Fennell sat down on a chair in front of the desk. 'Perhaps you can help me, Harry. Have you read the Talbot file yet?'

Harry opened his mouth to respond, but just at that moment he felt a hand wrap itself firmly round his erection. 'Garrh!' was all he could say, as the hand tugged at him so hard that he was obliged to slide forward to the very edge of his chair.

'Pardon?' enquired Mr Fennell, seeming not to notice the very unnatural position in which his employee was sitting.

'. . . Y-yes, I h-have, sir,' Harry stammered, Tracie's warm wet mouth having settled round him and resumed work as before.

'Have we exchanged contracts yet?'

'I d-d-d-don't th-think that we have.'

'Would you mind getting the file for me, Harry? I'd just like to check a couple of points.'

Harry grew even redder in the face as Tracie continued to suck lustily and long. 'I'll bring it to your room, Mr Fennell,' he managed to croak in reply.

'That's all right. It'll only take a couple of minutes, if you could find it for me now.'

Harry groaned inwardly. Surely he could have expected Tracie to possess the good sense to stop what she was doing and tuck him back into his trousers? But she was obviously not going to do so. She was obviously intent on finishing the job that she'd started, come what may.

'I c-can't do that, sir.'

'Why on earth not, Harry?'

'I'm . . . I'm . . . I'm . . .'

'Are you all right, young man? You seem rather hot and bothered.'

'I think it might be the flu.'

'You'd better go home, then. And get into bed. Ah! Here's the file, anyway. Right on top of Mr James' desk. I'll just skim through it while I'm here.'

'Y-yes, sir . . .'

Whilst Mr Fennell read through the papers on his lap, Tracie continued to give head to Harry under cover of his desk, very enthusiastically and effectively. Try as he might, he couldn't prevent his breathing becoming increasingly heavier and more laboured. He stared hard at the file immediately in front of him, pretending to study it carefully, whilst at the same time trying desperately to ignore the very expert way in which Tracie was attending to him below the belt. Trying desperately, but failing, nevertheless.

Mr Fennell glanced up from his own paperwork. 'You don't sound at all well, Harry,' he said with concern. 'Very chesty indeed. And you look quite feverish, as well.'

'. . . I'll be . . . okay, sir,' he could only just manage to rasp. Tracie's hot little mouth had cleverly built up a rhythm that was now bringing him closer and closer to the point of no return. If he ever got out of this situation alive, Harry said to himself, he'd put that wicked minx over his knee and make sure that she couldn't sit down for a week. He rather suspected, however, that the little hellcat would probably enjoy every moment. She was definitely that sort of girl.

Harry buried his face in his hands and started to pant. This was it! He couldn't hold back any longer. Any second now he was going to shoot his lot! With the senior partner of the firm sitting just a few feet in front of him! Both he and Tracie were history. They'd be down at the Job Centre before the day was out.

Start coughing! screamed a voice inside his head. *For God's sake start a coughing fit as soon as she brings you off! That way you might have a chance.*

Seconds later Mr Fennell looked up, a worried frown on his face. Harry had suddenly been convulsed with a wracking cough. He was wheezing and spluttering loudly as he rested his head on the desk and shuddered and groaned. Under the desk, Tracie opened her mouth as wide as she could and allowed his scalding hot seed to race over her tongue and down her throat. Quite deliberately, she pulled back her head and let him splash her face. Then she took him back in her mouth once again, relishing the feel of his sperm trickling warmly down both cheeks as well as gushing into her mouth. With one hand she reached down to the junction of her legs, and immediately her own orgasm started again. Fiercely she stoked it up with her fingers and thumb, until she was shaking and shuddering every bit as much as Harry. *This is definitely the life!* she told herself happily, swallowing as fast as she could.

At last the coughing ceased, leaving Harry gasping for breath. 'I'm sorry, Mr Fennell,' he croaked, tears rolling down his face. 'I don't know what came over me.'

'You're not at all well, young man. Take the rest of the day off work. I'll tell Mr James I gave you authority. Go home and have a jolly good rest in bed.'

'Thank you, sir. I think I might well take your advice.'

Tracie crawled out from under the desk, grinning broadly at Harry as he clambered to his feet. 'You witch!' he hissed angrily, glaring down at her naked nether regions. 'If I had a cane, I'd lay it right across that fat little arse as hard as I could!'

'If you had a cane, this fat little arse would love you to deal with it that way. Six of the best from you would really give it a treat.'

'That's just as I thought,' he muttered, carefully easing his much used equipment back inside his pants.

She buttoned her skirt around her. 'I must go,' she murmured, looking at her watch. 'The Welsh Weirdo will be after my arse himself, if I don't catch up with his work.'

'Let's hope he gets it,' Harry said with feeling.

She wrapped her arms round him and snuggled her still bare boobs against his shirtfront. 'That's not very nice,' she pouted sexily, kissing him lightly on the lips as she spoke. 'It was only a bit of fun, after all. Aren't you glad you've come in my mouth?'

'I suppose so,' he sighed, already feeling softer towards her.

'And we didn't get found out. I thought you were brilliant, Harry. Coughing away like that and pretending to be ill. And I never expected you to come so much. Not after everything you've been up to today. You must have more balls than anyone I've ever known.'

'You can twist a man round your little finger,' laughed Harry, squeezing her bottom affectionately. 'You'd better go before they start working again.'

Chapter 2

Payment In Kind

It was still Thursday. Tracie looked up at the clock on the wall.

Three o'clock. Time for her to pop along to George's office for their afternoon kiss and cuddle. And maybe a little bit more, if he wasn't too busy. Should she tell him about Kevin and Harry? Should she tell him that both of them had dicked her during the course of the day? He wouldn't mind, of course. He knew only too well what she was like. He wouldn't get jealous or anything like that. But they were supposed to be lovers, after all. She and George, she meant. Very casual lovers, maybe. But lovers, as opposed to mere fornicators, nevertheless. Ought she to tell him, before he found out in some other way? Or should she take the view that it was really none of his business?

She supposed, if she were honest with herself, that she sort of wished he would show just the tiniest bit of jealousy whenever he learned she'd been had by someone else. Just the very tiniest sign of concern. But he never did. Never in the slightest. He was more than happy for her to shag her husband night and morning, and then anyone else she pleased. He was never put out when she slid out of her knickers for Jim Browne or whoever else she fancied. Provided he had his fair share of her, George was perfectly happy for others to have the same. She supposed it was nice in a way. But it might be even nicer if, just occasionally, he got a little bit miffed at the way she was letting other men have a slice of the action – a share of her hot little hole.

What a difference between George and Peter! Poor Peter simply couldn't stand the thought of her being unfaithful.

Of course, he must suspect that sometimes she was. Especially after that business last year. But, thankfully, he had no idea of the scale. It was strange, really. It was strange how she still thought so much of him, despite the number of other men she'd had in two years of marriage. Perhaps that was why? Perhaps she felt guilty about cheating on him . . . ? No. Not really. She couldn't, in all honesty, claim that. It was simply what she'd already told herself hundreds of times that she couldn't exist for only one man. She could love Peter, but she couldn't prevent herself opening her legs for others whenever the urge was upon her. And she knew from bitter experience – or should that be sweet? – that the urge was there almost all of the time.

Why was Peter so jealous and George so much the opposite? Why couldn't Peter bear the thought of her being mauled about and bonked stupid, when George didn't give a monkey's what she got up to? Was it simply because she was Peter's wife that he felt that way? Would George act any differently if she was married to him? She really wasn't too sure, but she rather suspected that the answer to both questions was no.

But never mind all that for the moment. Was she going to tell George what she'd been doing that morning? Was she going to try, once again, to see if she could detect just the tiniest reaction? Perhaps the fact that she'd got herself shagged by someone as young as Kevin might make a difference?

No, she wouldn't say anything about her exploits that Thursday. It was nothing to do with George, even if the two of them were supposed to be a kind of part-time couple. She didn't want him to think that she felt anything for him other than a strong physical attraction. She didn't want him to believe that she was interested in anything other than his superbly responsive cock. Even if, sometimes, she was. And even though it would be nice to see just the slightest twinge of envy on his part.

George Franks removed his tongue from the succulence of Tracie's mouth, as well as his hands from the lightly clad cheeks of her pouting rear end. 'I need your help,' he said to her, slowly running a fingertip down the side of her pretty face as she stood there in front of him, tall and very upfront in her willingness to resume their embrace and allow it to progress all the way to full sexual union behind the privacy of his locked office door.

'In what way, George?' she asked, hoping it might be his way of suggesting a quickie, bottoms up, across his desk. Just as they'd done at half past eight that morning.

'Sir Roland is almost on the point of putting a lot of business our way,' he replied, thereby dashing her hopes.

'Sir Roland Rayke? The tycoon with all the hotels and casinos?'

'Yes, that's right. He's a very wealthy man indeed. And I've almost persuaded him that we could handle a lot of his legal work at a fraction of the cost he pays those city slickers who rip him off left, right and centre with every job he sends them.'

'That would be great, George! A real feather in your cap. Your standing with the firm would go through the roof if you got Sir Roland Rayke on board.'

'I know. That's why I'm doing it, of course. Old Fennell could never refuse me a full equity partnership then. But Sir Roland is a difficult fish to hook. As well as a great big fat one. That's where I'm hoping that you'll come in.'

'What on earth has it got to do with me? I'm only a humble secretary.'

'He needs a little inducement. A sweetener, you might say.'

Tracie stared him coolly in the eye. 'You want me to fuck him?' she said quietly, after a pause. 'You want me to fuck him for you?'

He held her gaze for several seconds. 'In a word, yes,' he finally replied.

'What would that make me, George?'

'Happy, I'd have thought. You've never tried to hide the fact that you like plenty of variety.'

'I prefer to know a man before I get out of my knickers for him,' she responded, blushing slightly.

'You won't have any problems with Sir Roland, Tracie. Honestly, you won't. I wouldn't suggest it otherwise. He's one of the old school. A gentleman, in every sense of the word. He's just a randy old bugger as well. And his particular delight is to shag another man's wife. He's not after a regular mistress or girls on the game. He much prefers a genuine housewife who has to go home to hearth and hubby and keep quiet about what she's been up to. He simply relishes the thought of sending her home soundly shagged.'

'Don't most men feel that way?'

'I suppose so. But Sir Roland has the money to indulge himself in that pleasure. That's the difference, I guess. He has the power and the money that's needed to guarantee an endless procession of nubile young wives stepping briskly out of their knickers.'

'Doesn't his wife know what he gets up to?'

'Yes. But I don't think that makes any difference to him. He's sufficiently wealthy to be able to do just as he pleases, whatever his wife might think. After all, she knows on which side her bread is buttered.'

She looked at him intently. 'You really want me to do this, George?'

'It would make all the difference with Sir Roland. I know him well enough to say that much. I'm almost certain he'd come over to this firm if you'd exercise your very considerable charms on him.'

'How often?'

George looked slightly uncomfortable. 'Oh, just every now and then, I suppose.'

'Starting when?'

He looked at the clock on his desk. 'You've got at least half an hour to nip home and get yourself all twanged up in stockings and suspenders and so forth.'

'Half an hour!' she gasped in surprise.

'And then join him for a drink in the penthouse suite at the Royal Hotel. He owns the hotel, of course.'

'Of course.'

Tracie stepped out of the private lift that opened directly

into the enormous living room. She was dressed for the occasion, a short but very smart black cocktail dress, silk stockings, and the most alluring white lingerie imaginable. In her three-inch high heels she was exactly six feet tall – a veritable vision of raven-haired carnality, dressed to be undressed.

'You must be Tracie,' Sir Roland Rayke said pleasantly, standing up from the leather armchair without delay.

'Compliments of George Franks,' she replied, reddening slightly.

'It's very good of him to share such breathtaking beauty with his friends,' he murmured, gallantly allowing his gaze to wander up and down her lithe young body. 'You're very lovely indeed.'

'Thank you,' she said softly, relieved to find him as charming as he was good-looking. Good-looking in a tall, distinguished way. And he wasn't nearly as old as she'd expected, she thought to herself. About forty-five, she'd imagine. With iron-grey hair and a close-cropped beard that suited his strong, handsome features to perfection. And she could see the sparkle of humour in his eyes, in addition to the very obvious gleam of virility. The very, very obvious gleam.

'Would you care for a drink?' he asked politely.

'Not really, Sir Roland, thank you. It's a bit early in the day for me.'

'Let me show you around, then. You might be interested in some of the views. At this height you can see right across town to the countryside beyond.'

Tracie stood in the master bedroom, gazing out of the vast panoramic window at the scenery below. The room was luxury itself, with mirrored walls and a huge circular bed in the middle that could comfortably have slept four. Sir Roland stood close behind her, his arms loosely round her waist and the side of his face brushing lightly against her jet-black hair. 'This is my favourite view,' he told her. 'With the ruined abbey on the crest of that hill above the river.'

'It's wonderful,' she said truthfully, allowing the softness of her buttocks to nuzzle against his groin. He was fully erect already! She could clearly feel the heat and the hardness of his cock against her bottom, even though she was exerting only the very gentlest of pressures. And what a cock it was too! He was massive! There was no disguising that fact. Despite the thin layers of clothing that separated him from the cheeks of her bottom, she could tell at once that he was much more than just handsomely hung.

Tracie took a deep breath and savoured the way in which she was lubricating so delightfully. If George wanted her to fuck for his sake, she was going to make absolutely sure that she enjoyed every single moment. And she'd also make sure that George knew how much she had.

'You feel very good,' she whispered, slowly wriggling her hips against the enormous pole of a penis he harboured inside his trouser fronts.

Sir Roland ran his lips over the long, graceful curve of her neck. 'So do you,' he breathed, biting her very, very gently and leaving no mark. Tracie closed her eyes and continued to wriggle her bottom. This was going to be good, she decided. An older man, such as he, always knew how to make her feel extra special. And added to that was the exceptional power she could feel in that glorious part of his person against which she was still rubbing the cheeks of her oh-so-randy rear end.

Now his mouth was on her throat, causing her to pull back her head as far as it would go so that he could explore the soft, sensitive skin to the full. Oh God! She wished he'd bite her hard enough to draw blood! She could easily understand the cause of the vampire myths and legends. There'd be nothing more delightful than having his teeth sinking into her throat. The very thought was enough to make her clitoris throb and ache. But he was being so tantalisingly gentle. Consequently, her whole body was now tingling with lustful expectation. But her throat! How she longed for him to hurt her there!

Sir Roland tightened his hold round her waist, with the result that his burning hot erection was pressed firmly against the plumpest part of her bottom. The crotch of her tiny G-string knickers was now soaked through and she could feel her internal juices starting to trickle down her bare upper thighs. She was as oiled and as slick as she could possibly have been, she said to herself, eyes tightly closed. Which was just as well, bearing in mind the obvious size of the weapon she would shortly have to confront.

Still standing behind her, he used one hand to turn her face towards his own. Then he kissed her on the lips. Eagerly she accepted his tongue deep into her mouth, at the same time thrusting back with her bottom and squirming it from side to side. His hands settled lightly over her breasts, instantly detecting hard, pointed nipples. Carefully he began to massage them between forefinger and thumb, making her moan with pleasure at the delicacy of his touch.

Now her pussy was positively on fire. It yearned and burned with the urgency of her desire. She could tell that the lips were curled right back in a wide open smile of welcome. And she could feel her love juices pouring down the inside of each thigh as far as her lace-topped stockings. George Franks, eat your heart out! This was going to be far and away the best dicking she'd had in many a moon.

'That was lovely!' she sighed happily, when he eventually vacated the sweetness of her gorgeous mouth.

Still embracing her from behind, Sir Roland eased her away from the window and guided her towards one mirrored wall. There they stood facing it, staring into the reflection of each other's eyes. 'Will you unzip me?' she whispered, blushing despite herself.

'My pleasure,' he chuckled, stepping back and then running the zip slowly but steadily all the way down to the small of her back. Then he held the dress whilst she wriggled out of it. Whilst he folded it over the back of a chair, she stood there, still staring into the mirror, but now clad in just the ultra skimpy, snowy-white undies and stockings she'd donned such a very short while before. A fluffy little half-cup bra and G-string knickers, lace-topped stockings and equally lacy suspenders, all were revealed to the light of the day. Tracie could feel his eyes roving all over the pouting pink cheeks of her blushing, almost bare bottom, just as surely as if they'd been his hands. Then he moved up behind her and slipped his arms round her waist once more. 'You're gorgeous!' he breathed thickly, looking over her shoulder and studying her in the mirror. 'Absolutely stunning!'

She followed his gaze as it travelled down from her face – as it moved slowly down over her cleavage, suspender belt and stomach, before finally settling on the area of smooth bare flesh that lay between the plumply filled crotch of her tiny G-string and the tops of her stockings. The copious quantities of expensive handmade lace in the stocking tops exactly matched the straps and belt of the suspenders, as well as her bra. Tracie began to lubricate even more freely at the way he was staring at her so appreciatively. She parted her legs a fraction, in order that he could see for himself just how she was aroused. 'How rewarding!' he whispered into her ear, staring at the trickle of liquid down her thighs.

'You've made me as wet as I've ever been,' she told him truthfully.

'Perhaps I should do something about it?'

'Yes please, Sir Roland,' she replied.

Still standing directly behind her, and still looking at her in the mirror, he slipped quickly out of his clothes. He was totally naked, but she could only see the reflection of his head and part of his shoulders. She looked him in the eye, in the mirror, and he smiled so sexily that she felt her insides churn. Then he reached out and drew her back against him. In her high heels, she was almost exactly his height. Tracie gasped as she felt the length of his scalding hot penis being pressed firmly into the cleft between her buttocks. The long, deep cleft that divided one saucily dimpled cheek from the other. All the way into the cleft he pressed it, so that she could feel him there, rigid and upright, burning her, so tall that the tip was poking stiffly into the base of her spine. She squeezed the cheeks of her bottom together, gripping him in there, feeling every inch of him. Feeling him so hot and hard, so vibrantly pulsating with life. Her vaginal juices continued to flow like a river in flood, streaming down her legs as far as her stockings. It would ruin her expensive lace stocking tops, she said to herself with a happy sigh.

He unclipped her bra at the front and removed it, laying it on top of her dress. Firm, round breasts were revealed in the mirror, with nipples that stood out proudly, pointing straight ahead. Very slowly and lightly he ran a fingertip round and round each nipple, making them swell and bulge even more. And making her throbbing, soaking wet quim open wider than ever. Without disturbing him between her buttocks, she eased the lacy little G-string down to her knees. Now she could feel him better than ever, and shivered with pleasure. Both of them stared down at the mirror image of soft, wispy pubic hair and pretty pink lips below. Pretty, plump lips that were glistening wet and wide apart. Now he could see exactly how ready she was for him. As she looked into his eyes in the mirror, once again, she slipped her hand down to the junction between her legs and gently squeezed the plumpness around her over-swollen clitoris. Immediately she started to orgasm, still holding his gaze as she did so. She always loved to do that. To look deep into the face of the man who was making her come. He stared back, clearly feeling almost as much pleasure as she was.

The giant horn of flesh between her buttocks seemed to stretch even further, expanding in length and girth as she held it there and squeezed. Then both of them looked down at her fingers as they worked away inside her, a few inches below the frothy white lace of her suspender belt. They were dripping with her juices as they slid slowly in and out of her tight little opening. Another mini-orgasm made her shudder, and gush even more. She loved the way he was taking his time and allowing her to indulge herself. But she guessed, quite rightly, that very soon he'd want to get inside her. She could feel the need in his penis. She could feel the way it was yearning to be put to use. Faster and faster she worked her fingers, resting her head back against the side of his face as she felt herself starting to spasm much more strongly than before.

When it was over she bent forward from the waist, at

Sir Roland's instigation, resting the palms of her hands on the mirrored wall and presenting him with a wide open target. Then she arched her back in order to grant him even easier access to the much-sought-after part of her person that now craved his attention so greatly. Fleetingly she twisted her head and peered back over her shoulder, instantly reassured that he was every bit as big as he'd felt.

'Fuck you, George!' she gasped to herself, as Sir Roland gripped her waist in his strong, warm hands and entered her hard from behind. It was a delicious sensation, being taken in that position by someone so splendidly endowed. She could feel herself straining to accommodate him as he slithered and slid all the way up to the hilt. She closed her eyes and held her breath, savouring the pleasure of that first powerful thrust into her willing wet softness. Oh God! He was one hell of a tight fit. She was packed to capacity! Skewered from middle to mouth! He was stretching her and opening her so wide – much further than she'd comfortably go! She could feel him pressing powerfully against the neck of her womb.

'Ohhhhhh!' she groaned painfully, as he tightened his grip on her waist and then pushed forward into the springiness of her bent-over bottom in order to stretch her as far as he could.

'Are you all right?' he asked considerately.

'Yes,' she only just managed to croak, tears starting to trickle down her face. 'It's lovely! Fuck me as hard as you like!'

He took her at her word and started to shaft her, sharply and stiffly, whilst she stood there in just her frilly white suspenders and stockings, plus her sopping wet G-string panties decoratively around her knees. Now her juices were pouring down her legs in even greater quantity than before. Pouring down them and soaking into the stocking tops that adorned her long, perfectly rounded thighs. But she was no longer thinking about how much they'd cost. She was far too preoccupied for that. Her whole being was concentrated on the iron-hard rod of flesh that was scouring her insides so incredibly well. She listened with fascination to the regular slap, slap, slap of his groin against the soft bouncy cheeks of her upthrust bottom, coupled with the slurp and squelch of his erection slithering so powerfully up and down the full length of her channel.

She knew he was huge anyway, she said to herself, as he ploughed on and on and on. She'd seen it for herself. But wasn't it an undoubted fact that being taken from behind your back always made a big man seem even bigger? That certainly seemed to be the case, she was totally delighted to say.

So there she stood in her high heels, stockings and suspenders, bent right forward, boobs joggling wildly, enjoying the knowledge that Sir Roland would be enjoying the sight of his gleaming wet stalk working industriously back and forth between the cheeks of the pert bottom she was tilting up at him so saucily. Peter always liked doing it to her that way, she reflected. From behind. He was always telling her that her bottom was so sexy that its only possible purpose in life was to be fitted snugly into a rampant male groin. Saucy devil! It was just as well he didn't know quite how many organs onto which it had, in fact, been fitted!

Sir Roland was indeed enjoying himself. As he continued to shaft her with long, even strokes of awesome length and force, he gazed down with approval at the spectacle of her pretty, pert little bottom, bent over so cheekily and framed so delightfully in snowy white lace. Framed at the top and sides by her suspender belt and straps, and below by stocking tops that exactly matched. And added to that exquisitely erotic picture was the sight of his huge, overheated weapon disappearing and then reappearing between those honey-smooth cheeks. Cheeks that were gaining in colour with every loud slap from his groin. Pretty pink cheeks that grew pinker and pinker as the lovemaking proceeded at pace. Now their hue was almost a red, the hot, nicely spanked bottom contrasting enchantingly with the frothy white lace with which it was surrounded. Harder and faster he worked, gripping her tightly around the waist and glorying in the power he could feel in his erection as it parted pussy with consummate ease.

Tracie jerked back her head and goggled wide-eyed at the ceiling. This was definitely one of the best she'd ever had! Not only was he hung like the proverbial donkey, but his stamina was incredible too. He was now bonking her so fiercely that she was being lifted right up onto tiptoes with every forward thrust. It reminded her very much of that glorious time when Peter had bent her over the back of the settee and screwed her violently after suspecting, quite rightly, that she'd spent the evening in bed with Jim Browne. And talking of Peter, she'd really make it up to him tonight. She'd really give him a treat to make up for the way she'd been so unfaithful. She'd ask him to spank her in these gorgeous stockings and suspenders. She'd come downstairs in just her high heels, stockings and suspenders, and ask him to put her over his knee. That would do the trick. He'd want to spend the rest of the night hammering away inside her. And she'd want him to, as well. There was nothing like a good spanking from your husband to make you want to shag until you dropped.

Slap! Slap! Slap! went groin against soft bare buttocks. *Ohh! Ohh! Ohh!* gasped Tracie, as the oversized organ bonked her from one climax to the next. *Squidge! Squelch! Squidge!* squeaked her vaginal juices, almost as if her insides were protesting at the mammoth scale of the invasion. On and on he shafted, pillaging and plundering pussy with all his might. Pussy, he thought to himself, that would be as reamed out as ever it had been by the time she trundled it back to her good husband later that day.

Tracie closed her eyes at a series of particularly violent thrusts from behind. This was unbelievable, she gulped to herself. This was truly incredible! There was no feeling to equal it in the world. He was shagging her with such ferocity! And his tool was so enormous she was surprised she couldn't feel it in the back of her throat. She was so full of him that it was a wonder she still had room left in her torso to draw breath!

Slap! Slap! Slap! Ohh! Ohh! Ohh! Squidge! Squelch! Squidge! Yard after yard ran through her at pace, making her writhe her hips against him and groan with delight. And still yard after yard ran through her, followed by yard after yard after yard.

But at last Sir Roland paused for breath, savouring the silky-smooth texture of the plump little bottom jammed hard and fast against his stomach and groin, and the heat of the sweet little pussy he was stretching as tight as a drum. Slowly he withdrew, watching his long, dripping wet tool as it eventually voided her completely. He stared down in fascination at the redness of her buttocks, due undoubtedly to the ferocity of the treatment they'd been receiving from his groin. Unfortunately for him the combination of pink/red bottom and lacy white suspenders and stocking tops was very much his undoing. Suddenly he was struck with the realisation that he was unable to hold back any longer. There was nothing he could do to avoid it. Matters had come to a head much earlier than he'd have wished.

Sir Roland reacted quickly, not wishing to waste a drop of the very special gift he'd been storing up for this lovely young wife. Fortunately she was so open and ready for him that full re-entry was effected just in the nick of time. As his bulging, bursting erection slid all the way up to the top of her vagina, he closed his eyes and with a groan of despair he started to squirt. Feverishly he rammed his groin even harder against the bounciest part of her bottom, wanting to bury himself as far inside her as he could, wanting to implant her just as deeply as he was able.

Tracie felt the first rush of scalding hot seed. Liquid fire burning its way into her womb. Immediately her climax was renewed, as was almost always the case. With each fresh squirt her vagina tightened greedily around him, as if it was trying to milk every last drop. Rock-hard though he was, her spasms were so powerful that he could actually feel himself being compressed. He tried to force himself even deeper, and she responded by thrusting back against him. By lifting her bottom and jamming it into his groin, and then wriggling from side to side. She, too, was determined that he should impale her with every millimetre at his disposal. Determined that he should spunk her as thoroughly as humanly possible. So as a result of their joint efforts, he was embedded in her to his absolute maximum. No matter how they wriggled and pushed against each other, there was simply no more cock to go in. Which was probably just as well, she said to herself, as she huffed and puffed. Bearing in mind that her poor pussy was already extremely replete.

And still Sir Roland continued to gush. One long fierce spurt after another, with intervals of about a second between. 'Yes!' she squealed as she felt each hot fresh salvo squirting powerfully into her womb. 'Oh, yes! Yes! Yes! Yes!'

Sir Roland gritted his teeth and continued to pump, his penis wedged far inside her, jammed solid and tight whilst it spewed and spewed and spewed. He savoured the thought of his sperm flooding the sweet little opening he was occupying to the full. Tracie could also picture it sluicing around inside her, a turbulent torrent of come swirling first this way then that. The greatest flood since Noah took to his Ark. Already she could feel the hot sticky surplus seeping out of her overstretched pussy. Never had she known such a spillage so soon. Never in her life had she been so copiously implanted. And she could tell that he still had more to provide. Her insides sucked at him harder than ever, wanting it all in one go, wanting to gorge on him even more.

But eventually all good things must come to an end. And surely enough the invidious insemination of yet another lovely young housewife was at last approaching its close. Tracie was still wriggling her hips in delight, but the well was starting to run dry. The eruption was almost spent. She felt the flow of molten lava begin to subside and then, suck as she might with her vaginal muscles, it slowed and turned to a dribble, before finally ceasing completely.

Tracie lay on her back on the bed, exhausted but happy, enjoying the feel of his seed as it continued to ooze out of her. Sir Roland settled himself beside her and kissed her with his tongue, sweetly and gently, hardening her nipples almost at once and making her ache at the join of her legs with fresh desire. She reached down to his groin and was delighted to find that he was already starting to harden. His dick was almost as lively as Peter's, she thought to herself. It was no more than two minutes since it had shot forth its lovely thick load. Yet here it was, stiffening by the second in her hand!

Without breaking the kiss, he rolled on top of her and she spread her silk-stockinged legs in delight. Away they went again, his long thick organ charging in and out of her overflowing vagina as if there were no tomorrow. She pushed up with her breasts, feeling her sharply pointed nipples burning and boring their way into his chest as he continued to kiss her so tenderly, whilst, at the same time, driving in and out like a man possessed. He slid his hands underneath her, cupping them round the cheeks of her sticky bare bottom and then pushing a fingertip inside. Tracie gasped and squirmed with pleasure. Oh God! That was nice! Her bottom had always been incredibly sensitive. But it was much more so since Peter had started probing her in there.

Tracie wriggled as hard as she could against the intruding finger, spiking her bottom up and down on it until she felt herself starting to climax all over again. What a glorious sensation! His tongue in her mouth, his colossal cock pounding her quim, and his finger jammed in her bottom almost up to the knuckle! What more could any girl ask?

She'd definitely tell that bloody George Franks all about it. She'd tell him all the intimate details of the way she'd let herself be laid for his sake. Would that, perhaps, give him something to think about? Would that shake up the rotten so-and-so and make him go green with envy? No, she knew deep down that it wouldn't.

Tracie's climax continued to rage. One long, continuous climax that thudded right through her body, crashing through every cell. It didn't even try to abate. It just stayed there, unending, making her wriggle and writhe with the pleasure she felt. And each thrust from Sir Roland seemed to increase it, until she had to break off the kiss in order to fight for breath. Harder and faster he drove into the tightness of her vagina, bouncing her wildly up and down on the bed whilst she lay there in her stockings and high heels, completely passive, letting him service her just as he chose. Finally another tidal wave of sperm engulfed her, almost as profusely as before. Pint after pint of the stuff, or so it seemed to her. Once again she started to spasm, as was so often the case when she felt the heat of her favourite substance scorch the inside of her womb. She jammed her clitoris hard against the root of his organ, and thought she was going to die.

Tracie lay on her side, curled up in a ball, her face just above his sad sticky member as it rested on the flat of his stomach, completely lifeless and limp. 'May I?' she giggled, lifting it between finger and thumb and then opening her mouth in anticipation of his reply.

'Please do!' he chuckled happily, gazing at the reflection of her bottom in the mirror as she swallowed him whole.

'Oh, brother!' she mumbled thickly, surprised and delighted to feel him start to harden at once. Seconds later he was fully grown and Tracie was again relishing the delicate flavour of his and hers. He was far too big for her to take down into her throat, so she was obliged to attend to just the huge, swollen tip and part of the shaft. Up and down she worked her head, slowly but steadily, making him groan and writhe on the bed. After a while she lifted her face, holding him against the side of one cheek, hard, scalding hot and dripping with her saliva. 'Pussy or mouth?' she asked with an impish grin.

'Your mouth is wonderful!' he gurgled.

'You'll last a bit longer down below,' she told him wisely.

'Just for a while, then. But I want to finish off in your mouth.'

She knelt over him, her legs straddling his stomach and groin. As he watched in the mirror, she lowered her hips very slowly so that he sank into her an inch at a time.

At last he was all the way home, and she could feel him

pressing as firmly as ever against her womb. 'Jesus, you're big!' she breathed, wriggling her bottom in appreciation. 'I hope your wife understands what she has here.'

'You'll be able to ask her. I've taken the liberty of suggesting she might join us later. I hope you don't mind?'

'It sounds like great fun,' Tracie replied truthfully.

Half an hour later Tracie lay on the bed, sperm now dribbling from one side of her mouth as well as her lower opening. 'I'm Janet,' Sir Roland's dark-haired wife said with a sexy smile, closing the door behind her and then immediately reaching for the zip at the side of the black silk trousers that were stretched snugly but elegantly across the trimness of her hips.

'I'm glad,' Tracie said simply, unsurprised by the fact that there were no knickers underneath the expensive black trousers. She was delighted to see that Janet was young, as well as vivaciously attractive. Obviously his second wife, she mused to herself. Or his third, or fourth.

Janet perched prettily on the side of the bed, naked and naughty. 'Have you ever done it with a girl?' she asked eagerly, stroking the back of her hand over Tracie's raven-black hair.

'Yes.'

'Often?'

'Yes,' Tracie said once again.

To Tracie's amazement, Sir Roland was ready for more. Whilst Janet lay on her back beside her, he mounted his wife in the good, old-fashioned missionary position and began shafting her just as sharply as he had Tracie. Janet turned her head and looked knowingly at the raven-haired girl. Understanding exactly what she was wanting, Tracie leant over and kissed her briefly but passionately with her tongue.

'That's lovely!' murmured Janet, enjoying the salty-sweet taste of Tracie's mouth.

So Tracie kissed her again. A long, lingering kiss, her tongue deep in Janet's mouth as they shared the flavour of freshly shot seed. Janet reached out, sliding a hand between Tracie's thighs just above the tops of her stockings. 'Oh, yes, please!' groaned Tracie, savouring the delightfully gentle touch of fingertips exploring her soaking-wet groin. As she felt two fingers delicately entering her, Tracie pushed up so that her clitoris was now pressed against the heel of Janet's palm. Slowly Janet began moving her hand, pushing her fingers in and out of Tracie and, at the same time, rubbing back and forth over the swollen clitoris.

Tracie resumed the kiss, enjoying the feel of the fingers and palm, combined with the sound of penis in pussy. Both girls climaxed together, Tracie softly and sweetly, Janet with far less control. But still they held their kiss, Tracie's tongue hot and passionate, Janet's mouth succulent and sweet. And still they held it, even when Sir Roland vacated his wife and rolled over on top of Tracie. And even when he rolled back on top of Janet a minute or so later.

And so it proceeded, the girls mouth to mouth whilst Sir Roland moved from one wet, wide-open quim to the other. A few sharp thrusts into Tracie, and a few more into his wife.

Fuck, fuck, fuck into Tracie. Then fuck, fuck, fuck into his wife. One after the other, stretching both of them in turn. Thrust, thrust, thrust into Tracie – thrust, thrust, thrust into his own gorgeous young wife. First one and then the other, powerfully and forcefully, mingling his seed and their juices inside each of them.

Tracie could feel that his fourth climax of the afternoon was rapidly approaching. Quickly she broke the kiss with Janet. 'Not in me,' she panted, as he bounced her up and down. 'Into Janet. She hasn't had any yet . . .'

Sir Roland was perfectly happy to oblige, even though he was aware that her motives were not entirely selfless.

Then, when he was through, and at Tracie's suggestion, the girls turned on their sides, in the 69 position, and began the delicious process of delicately eating sperm-soaked pussy. Sir Roland sat beside them and watched in fascination, wondering vaguely whether the highly erotic spectacle would be sufficient to inject a further supply of lead into his currently useless pencil. Somehow he rather suspected that it might. Even if it didn't, he told himself happily, this incredibly insatiable young lady had more than earned the diamond bracelet he'd earlier told his wife to choose for her. Not that she'd be able to wear it when her husband was around, of course. But he'd leave the receipt discreetly in the bottom of the box, so that she'd be able to convert it back into cash. As, he imagined, did most of the young wives who left here with sticky knickers and a handbag containing jewellery worth more than a thousand pounds . . .

Chapter 3

Disappointment

'One thousand and fifty pounds,' said the man behind the jewellery counter at Crofter's, handing the notes to Tracie with a knowing leer. 'Lady Rayke chose the bracelet herself. Didn't you like it?'

'Yes. But I thought the money would be better spent on something my husband could appreciate as well.'

She turned and swished her way out of the shop, knowing that his eyes would be glued to the cheeks of her sexy rear end as it slid from side to side under cover of her slinky black dress. She was quite unconcerned at the thought that he'd be well aware of the fact that those same cheeks had been reposing, naked, on Sir Roland's huge circular bed for most of the afternoon. Let the nasty little man think his nasty little thoughts, she told herself, clutching her handbag firmly in her right hand. She'd pay the money into her building society account tomorrow. And next month she'd buy something really special for Peter's birthday. Perhaps that CD player for his car that he'd been admiring in Hughes last week.

But tonight she'd concentrate on making things up to him in bed. After he'd put her across his knee, of course. After he'd turned her ruttish little bottom all kinds of colours and made her shriek and howl. God, he was going to enjoy spanking her in her stockings and suspenders! And she'd enjoy it too. She was really looking forward to it. And to the lovemaking she knew would follow. She was really ready for that. She was as hot and horny as hell! It was always the same. She always found that a bit on the side made her randier than ever. And today she'd had considerably more than a bit on the side. In fact, she'd had considerably more than a lot on the side! With the result that she was just itching for more. She'd have Peter's trousers off him within seconds of him walking through the front door. She'd have a quick stand up shag in the hall. Then, after he'd had his dinner and was sipping his coffee, she'd nip upstairs and change into just her stockings, suspenders and high heels, ready to fold herself over his lap in such a way that her plump bum was peeping nervously up at him, literally right under his nose.

Tracie looked at the clock on the dashboard of her car as she pulled away from the pavement. It was nearly seven o'clock. But that didn't matter. It was Thursday, so Peter wouldn't be home for another hour. She'd have plenty of time to change out of these clothes and have a bath.

Brother, was she feeling horny! Her pussy was wet and throbbing with lust. She could really do with Peter right now. But she'd have to be patient. She could get through the next sixty minutes if she reminded herself how good the rest of the night was going to be.

That was the big thing about Peter. No pun intended, of course. He might be an ultra-suspicious sort of so-and-so, but he could certainly do the business on her. He was always ready to poke her, anywhere at any time. She certainly couldn't deny that fact. And he was incredibly good at it, too. He could keep it going all night, just one fuck after another. If only he wasn't so jealous of her. Then he'd have been just about the perfect husband. After all, his bank balance was almost as swollen as his oversized dick usually was.

She supposed she shouldn't really have married him, knowing how obsessively jealous he was. She supposed she should have married Steve. Steve, who'd always been more than happy to share her with one or more of his mates. But she'd married Peter instead, basically because she'd fancied him that little bit more. He was kinder and better-looking and, as she'd already said, he had enough balls for three men.

Oh, God! She was getting randier and randier by the

second. She supposed it was due to the way she kept thinking about what she intended to do with Peter. Perhaps, when she stopped at the next set of traffic lights, she'd be able to slip her hand up her dress, very furtively, and give her pussy a good enough tweak to bring herself off just a little.

'Bloody hell!' gasped the lorry driver, goggling out of his side window at the open-topped car that had stopped at the lights beside him.

'What is it?' asked his mate, craning his neck to peer in the same direction. 'What's happening?'

'Down there!' cried the driver, pointing to Tracie's flame-red MG Midget. 'There's some stalky young bird behind the wheel, jerking herself off as hard as she can!'

Both men stared into the car that was stationary in the middle of three lanes of traffic. Several others in the queue stared as well. There was Tracie, slumped back in the driver's seat, stocking tops and tiny white knickers on show, her head thrashing wildly from side to side and her hips writhing in ecstasy as her hand worked rapidly back and forth at the junction of her wide-apart thighs. The lights changed but nobody noticed. They were far too engrossed in the sight of a highly overwrought young lady masturbating herself for all she was worth.

At last she opened her eyes, perspiration trickling down her forehead as she gazed blankly around. Oh dear! How embarrassing! All those people watching what she'd been doing! She hadn't meant it to happen that way. But the second she'd touched her painfully aching quim, she'd been consumed with an uncontrollable spasm that had simply demanded further attention. A spasm so powerful that she'd had no option but to obey.

She'd better pull down her dress and drive off as quickly as possible. Hopefully there was no one she knew in any of the surrounding cars . . . Oh dear! Surely that wasn't Peter's boss over there?

Another set of lights turned red. This time the lorry driver was ready with his window wound down. 'Excuse me, miss!' he called out.

Tracie twisted her head and looked up at him. 'What is it?' she asked, blushing brightly.

'We couldn't help noticing you at the last lot of traffic lights.'

'I see.'

He pointed. 'We're taking this load into that warehouse over there. You could always follow us in. If you're still in need, me and Bill, here, would be pleased to help out.'

She stared at him, still blushing. 'I don't think I've got enough time.'

'Don't worry, love. We'll be as quick as you like.'

Tracie parked the car in her driveway and raced to the front door. Peter would be home any second. She must get out of this kit before he got back. There was no way she'd be able to explain why she was decked out in her most expensive cocktail dress and fanciest underwear. She must also hide all that money.

Oh, mother! She was still so horny she could die! All that cock and lovely sweet pussy, yet she still felt as randy as ever! But help would soon be at hand. Peter would soon be there to provide what she craved. She really must try to have a little more control in the future. But it wasn't her fault the way she was made. She couldn't help the way her pussy ruled her life. She couldn't help the fact that the more it got the more it urgently demanded. She'd been like that as long as she could remember. So it was small wonder she was in such a state now, bearing in mind all that she'd had since leaving home that morning. Jesus, what a day it had been!

Tracie closed the front door behind her and slid home the bolt. She didn't want Peter walking in on her until she'd changed into daytime clothes and stuffed these spunk-soaked knickers and stockings into the washer. And concealed her ill-gotten gains. Fortunately, she had an identical pair of silk stockings she could wear for the spanking. How pretty her bottom would look when it was tucked snugly over his knee, the lacy white stocking tops setting it off to perfection, no more than a couple of inches below the crease between buttocks and thighs! She couldn't wait for the way her red-hot bottom would provoke both of them into fucking the night away.

Tracie threw the smart black dress on the bed and then peeled off her stockings and underwear. Wasn't it strange, the difference? The difference between the way he'd spanked her in anger last year, and the way he now spanked her in fun? Of course, it hurt just as much either way. But that was the only similarity. She'd hated being over his knee when he'd been punishing her for getting herself shagged. It hadn't been the least bit enjoyable. It had just hurt like hell, without any of the warm, sexy glow that always accompanied that sort of treatment whenever it was done for pleasure.

Last year, after she'd been caught in that car, she'd set off for work every morning for over a week with her bottom and the backs of her thighs still sore and angrily discoloured underneath the smart blue trousers she'd been obliged to wear in order to conceal her plight. Mind you, the tight-fitting trousers had been a big success. Both George Franks and Jim Browne had admired them greatly, in the same way that they'd later admired her poor little, sore little bum. Of course they'd just considered it a hell of a laugh. Her sore little bum, that is. There'd been no sympathy from that quarter. None at all. 'Very right and proper, too!' George had said, gazing in fascination at the result of Peter's handiwork. 'I'm delighted to see that your good husband is exercising his marital rights and striking a blow for the entire male race.' She hadn't taken that lying down, of course. Or even bending over his office desk. She'd picked up one of his heavy law books and shied it right at his head. Then she'd yanked up her trousers and told him, in no uncertain terms, to stuff his prick back into his underpants and forget all about the fuck he'd been looking forward to.

Dressed now in a T-shirt, mini-skirt and a tiny pair of white bikini knickers, Tracie hung the cocktail dress back in the wardrobe and hurried downstairs to the utility room, sopping wet G-string and lace-topped stockings in hand. She wouldn't have to wait long. Peter would soon be home. And his lovely thick dick would soon be wedged tightly inside her, soothing the oh-so-urgent desires of her hot little hole. How lovely that was going to be! She was so desperately in need of husbandly attention. She'd get him to do it just inside the front door. She'd just stand there in her clothes and pull the crotch of her white cotton panties to one side to let him in. He always appreciated it when she was so desperate for him that she wanted to do it there and then. There and then, standing on the doormat, the very moment he came home, without any form of preparation, not even a kiss. Just, 'Shag me, Peter. I'm as wet and open as can be.'

She giggled naughtily. It was just as well that he didn't know why she was sometimes so desperate for him! It was just as well he didn't realise that it was often because somebody else's cock had made her yearn and burn for more! Well, it wasn't her fault her insides felt like that. There was nothing she could do about it. Nor could she do anything about the way she needed other men. It was simply how she'd been put together. All she could do was try and make sure that poor Peter remained blissfully ignorant of her extra-marital antics. And also pray that never again would he walk past when she was next being poked purple on the front seat of someone's car.

Tracie checked the lamb casserole and then closed the oven door. Peter was late! Even on a Thursday he should have been home by now. It was almost half past eight. And her poor pussy was almost as hot as the dinner. If Peter wasn't able to plug it soon, it might well self-ignite.

The answer-phone! Perhaps there was a message from him on the answer-phone? After all, he always rang if he was going to be late. But, she'd been out of the house until nearly eight o'clock. So he may well have rung before then and left a message.

She pressed the replay button. 'Hi,' said Peter's voice.

Did he sound slightly miffed, she wondered. Slightly suspicious of the fact that she wasn't home to take the call? Slightly suspicious that she might – just might – have been spread across the bench seat of a Volvo lorry, obliging first the driver and then his mate?

'I'm sorry, Tracie,' continued Peter. 'I'm going to be late tonight. Very late, I'm afraid. Not before two o'clock, at least. This new contract's come up, and it all has to be sorted by morning. Sorry. Keep it warm and juicy till I get back. And you know I don't mean the dinner. Bye for now.'

'Oh, Peter!' she groaned in dismay, clamping her thighs together and almost doubling up with the sudden shaft of white hot pain in her groin.

Peter Trix pushed the file of papers to the side of his desk and picked up his cup of lukewarm coffee. Why hadn't she been home when he'd rung? She should have been back from the office a good two hours before. Had she stopped to see her mother? Or Jackie? Or had she been . . . ?

No. He must try not to think of that sort of thing. He must try not to be so suspicious. It only harmed their marriage when he was like that. It really pissed her off when she could see those kinds of thoughts in his head. But how could he change how he felt? He was a jealous sort of person by nature. And the fact that he thought so much of her only served to make matters worse. If only he could shrug his shoulders and say, 'So what?' If only he could accept that there was nothing he could do about it, should she decide to slip into bed with someone else. But he couldn't. He agonized about it almost all the time. He absolutely detested the thought of some other sod taking a slice of what was rightfully his. Did most men feel the same? He really wasn't too sure.

But he knew only too well how he felt. He simply loathed the thought of someone else pulling her about and then poking the hot little honey pot she was supposed to keep just for him. It almost made him physically sick to recall how, last year, she'd been dicked to death in that car, just fifty yards from their front gate. And if she'd done it that

once, wasn't it more than likely that she'd done it before
... and after? Wasn't that almost certainly the case? Wasn't
it almost certain that she was still stepping out of her
knickers for another man? Or several other men?

Oh Christ! Why did he have to torture himself like this?
It couldn't do any good. It couldn't keep her inside her
knickers, tormenting himself this way. Why couldn't he
accept that he was powerless to prevent her shagging
whoever she wanted, and concentrate, instead, on making
sure that she viewed him in the best possible light? If only
he could show her that he was no longer so obsessively
possessive, then she'd feel much better disposed towards
him. He knew that, but he couldn't do anything about it.
He couldn't help questioning her about where she'd been
and who she'd seen.

Why did they still love each other? Why did he love her
after what she'd done and what he suspected she still did?
Why did she love him when he made it blatantly obvious
that he didn't trust her an inch? He had no idea of the
answer. Not a clue. Not a single, solitary clue. Perhaps it
would be better for both of them if they fell out of love?
Perhaps their lives would be happier if they split up? But
no, not from his point of view, at least. He couldn't face
the thought of not having her at home, even if she was
getting herself laid by anything that moved.

So what was the solution? Well, there wasn't one, he
supposed. You just made the most of what you'd got, that
was all. You tried your best to stop worrying about someone
else's cock encroaching on your preserve, and made certain
that yours was in there as much as possible.

Jesus, she was such a horny bit of goods! The more he
fucked her, the more he seemed to fancy her. And the more
tender he felt towards her, as well. And also, unfortunately,
the more he fretted about some third party plundering all
she owned.

Peter lit a cigarette and inhaled deeply. How many men
had had her in their two years of marriage? How many
men had had every inch of her during that time? Was it just
that so-and-so last year? Or had there been two or three or

four? Or twenty-two or three or four? How many times had she been implanted by someone else? How many times had some other bugger flooded her with spunk? And why, in God's name, did he agonize so much about it?

He supposed he was so jealous because he felt for her so strongly. Never had any other girl got right under his skin this way. Not even Jane. Jane, who'd been shagging her boss at work throughout the six months of their engagement. No, he'd never loved anyone to anything like the same extent as he loved Tracie. He positively worshipped her, even though he was well aware of her weakness for a bit on the side. A weakness which he'd convinced himself would finish once she was his wife. Of course he should have known far better. A leopard doesn't change its spots – to add another cliché to his thoughts. He'd been daft to think that a band of gold on her finger would be capable of keeping her knickers in place. If only he could learn to just live with the knowledge of the sort of person she was!

How bad he'd felt that time when he'd realised she was the girl he'd seen about half an hour earlier, in the orange light from the street lamp, getting herself so well and truly trunked on the front seat of that car! His insides had turned to ice when he'd recognised his own wife clambering out of the passenger door, adjusting her tiny mini-skirt around her hips. Suspicion was bad enough, but when you were suddenly confronted with certainty! With the undeniable fact that your wife had just been screwing! And not only that. As he'd stared in horror at Tracie, he'd recalled how, thirty minutes earlier, he'd stood there on the same spot for a good sixty seconds or so, chuckling to himself at the sight of some character's overstretched dick dripping with juice as it hammered in and out of a wide-open pussy. The same wet, wide-open pussy, he'd thought to himself with a groan, into which he dipped every night! The same wet wide-open pussy that was supposed to keep itself only unto him!

Yes, there was one hell of a difference between wondering whether your wife fucked other men, and knowing she did. One hell of a difference between wondering, and standing there on the pavement remembering how you'd actually been watching her on the job.

Was that the only time it had happened? Was that the only time she'd been unfaithful? Was he ever going to stop asking himself that question? Was he ever going to allow himself some peace?

Of course she'd denied it. 'Honestly, Peter,' she'd pleaded desperately. 'I was only giving the driver directions.'

'So who was the girl I saw earlier? The one with her skirt round her waist and her cunt full of cock?'

'I don't know!' she'd cried, as he'd draped her over his knee and held her fast. Then he'd flipped up her mini-skirt and turned down the seat of her tiny pink knickers, thereby exposing her plump, adulterous bottom to view, whilst allowing the crotch of the knickers to remain in place.

'It wasn't me!' she'd protested in alarm.

'Don't lie to me!' he'd snarled, having carried out his own research by pressing his fingertips against the nicely filled knicker crotch. 'Your knickers are already soaked through!'

'I'm wet because I've been thinking about you.'

'Liar!' he'd shouted, bringing his hand down across her prettily upturned left cheek with all the strength he could muster. 'Liar!' he'd shouted again, treating her right cheek to exactly the same.

'Peter! You're hurting me!' she'd shrieked, as he'd proceeded to blister each saucy little mound in turn. *Slap! Slap! Slap! Slap! Slap! Slap!* On and on and on, the loud ringing crack of hand on bouncy bare bottom echoing throughout the house. One loud ringing crack after another, the irrefutable proof of her guilt leaking steadily into her knickers whilst he punished the same bare bottom that, minutes earlier, had been bouncing merrily up and down in the car.

'I'm sorry, Peter!' she'd sobbed, half an hour later, squirming her hips in discomfort. 'It'll never happen again.'

Which probably meant, he'd said to himself at the time, that she'd make sure she never got found out again.

So that had been the first time he'd ever spanked her.

But not the last. Every night for the following week he'd repeated the process, making her yip and yelp in distress. It had made him feel a bit better, he supposed. He'd enjoyed the feeling of power as he'd stared angrily down at those bouncing, bright red cheeks. But the feeling of sadness had been ever present. The sense of loss. The sense of loss that had never since left him, despite the way he'd welted her cheating, pert little bum.

A couple of months later, after he'd forgiven but not forgotten, she'd surprised him by asking him to spank her again. This time in love, not anger, she'd said. This time as part of their lovemaking, not as a punishment. 'Have you done something else to deserve it?' he'd been unable to stop himself asking. Immediately he'd regretted his words, as tears started to run down her face.

Oh God, how much he loved and fancied her! If only he could come to terms with the thought that, on occasions, he might be sharing that smooth little, sweet little bum! But he couldn't. He'd tried his best, but it was simply impossible. It was anathema to him. There was nothing he could do about it. He was still as fiercely jealous as ever. Maybe without any reason? Maybe it really had been the first and only time?

Chapter 4

Pavement

The phone rang just a few seconds after Tracie had been listening to Peter's message. Eagerly she snatched up the receiver, hoping it might be him. 'Hello, Tracie,' said George Franks. 'How are you?'

'Fucked to a frazzle!' she snapped. 'You'll be more than delighted to hear.'

'I take it Peter isn't at home?'

'That's right. He's stuck at work.'

'So you'll be feeling desperate for a bit more of the same? Do you want me to come over and oblige?'

'Not if you were the last man in the world, George! It's over between us. I don't know why I've been so daft as to let it continue this long. I've done exactly what you wanted this afternoon, but now you can bugger off and leave me alone!'

'Tracie! You're not feeling yourself.'

'Well, I'm not feeling you again, George. That's for sure.'

So saying, she banged down the phone.

Of course that bloody George Franks was quite right, she groaned to herself. She *was* desperate for a little bit more. Indeed, she was desperate for a whole lot more. If only Peter was home! That was what she really wanted – a good, stiff, husbandly bonk. But he wouldn't be back for hours. So she was going to have to find someone else to take his place. Anyone would do, apart from George, of course. There wouldn't be any real problem finding a replacement. She'd just make a phone call or two from the little black book she kept well and truly hidden upstairs. That would do the trick. She'd soon find a surrogate penis. One that would keep her going until Peter came home from work. Bless his little cotton knickers! She was feeling particularly tender towards him. Partly due to guilt, she supposed. But she'd just have to keep reminding herself that what he didn't know couldn't hurt him. And also that she couldn't change the sort of person she was. She couldn't quench the fire that raged continuously between her thighs

Now, where was that notebook? Taped to the underneath of her knicker drawer, she was sure. Relief would soon be at hand. Or wherever . . .

But she was wrong. Twenty minutes later she was standing in front of the telephone, the notebook and telephone directory exhausted, yet still without a date. 'Tomorrow would be fine,' Jim Browne had told her. 'But I just can't make it tonight.'

'Harry's training at the Rugby Club,' his mother had advised her.

'Kevin's gone to the cinema,' his mum had said.

Her gym instructor was taking classes all evening. Steve was spending the night with his new girlfriend. Steve's friend, Richard the Dick, was away on holiday. Steve's other friend, Mighty Mike, was with him. And John Harris, from the office, the man with the world's largest tool, wasn't answering his phone.

Peter's friend, Poke Anything Paul, was already booked to poke someone else.

And, finally, her boss from her previous job was newly remarried and would be very grateful if she'd forget his number for a month or so at least.

In desperation, Tracie peered out of the living-room window. Damn! The wife's car was parked in the drive of the house to the left. And the neighbour on the right was a really nice man, but it took about twenty minutes' sucking to get him the slightest bit hard, and then he always shot his lot before she had time to transfer him down below.

She supposed she could always phone Jackie, or one of her other girlfriends, but it was cock, not tongue, that she needed tonight. Oh Peter, why aren't you home?

Trevor Daniels, Tracie said to herself. Trevor Daniels from the office. The practice manager. It was about time he gained some carnal knowledge of her. And she of him. She'd been teasing and flirting with him for ages. And he'd had his fingers inside her, as well. But they hadn't yet got round to going all the way. Their mutual admiration had still to be consummated in full. She'd ring him now and give him the chance of final refusal.

And, unfortunately for Tracie, refusal it turned out to be. 'I'd love to,' he groaned down the phone, clearly speaking the truth. 'But I'm seeing Sandy in less than half an hour.'

'Sandy? Who's she?'

'My new girlfriend. I only met her yesterday, but we got on fantastically well.'

Tracie giggled. 'You mean you planted something sticky inside her within ten minutes of asking her out?'

'Er, not exactly.'

'But something along those lines?'

'Well, yes, sort of, I suppose.'

'Is she that friend of Julie's with long black hair and legs all the way up to her teeth?'

'Yes, that's right.'

'You've done very nicely for yourself, Trevor. She's a lovely girl. But then again, you're a lovely lad.'

Tracie sat down beside the telephone table and sighed in despair. 'Renta-Dick,' she said aloud, staring at the Yellow Pages directory. 'It's a pity there's nothing in there as useful as that.'

Then she was struck with an idea. An idea, she suddenly realised, that had been at the back of her mind for ages. An idea that had been buried there for years, right at the back of her mind. But did she have the courage? she wondered. Did she really have the nerve?

There was only one way to find out. Tracie ran upstairs to the bedroom and began fumbling through the wardrobe until she found the clothing she'd been looking for. Her smallest mini-skirt and matching halter top, made from a stretch material so that they fitted her like a second skin. A tiny, incredibly sexy mini-skirt, the effect of which was enhanced by a huge leather belt that wasn't a great deal smaller than the skirt itself. It was the outfit Peter had loved when he'd first started dating her, but banned as soon as they'd got engaged. In those early days, she'd been prepared to listen to him.

Tracie lay the skirt and top on the bed and stared at them thoughtfully. Did she really have the courage, she asked herself again. Did she really possess the daring?

One hour later she knew the answer. She was standing nervously in Hovells Lane, the brightly lit service road that gave access to the nearby industrial estate. Although the hour was early, three other girls stood there too. And business was remarkably brisk. The large black Volvo that had been there a quarter of an hour earlier pulled up and returned a fifth girl to the post at which she'd previously stood. A sixth girl was then deposited back on the pavement. She'd been there twice during the course of the previous twenty minutes, Tracie noted. The girl next to Tracie in the tight, bright red trousers was whisked away in a van. She was replaced in less than a minute by a blonde girl in white hot-pants and knee-length boots. Then that girl was gone again.

'That was one of Nicola's regular dates,' the nearest girl said to Tracie.

'Oh?'

'Every Monday and Thursday he comes for her at this time of night. Borrows his firm's van, you see.'

'Oh?'

'He doesn't think it right to do it in the family motor.'

'I see.'

'Quite considerate, really.'

'Yes, I suppose so,' murmured Tracie.

'I haven't seen you here before, have I?' asked the girl.

'No. I'm new in town.'

'Where from?'

'Birmingham,' replied Tracie, saying the first thing that came into her head.

'Too much competition, was there?'

'Yes, that's right. Far too much competition.'

'This place is fine. There's plenty of business, and the punters are generally okay. And they only have to drive you round the corner to the car park, so there's no waste of time. And on top of that, the coppers turn a blind eye . . . provided you treat them every now and then, of course.'

'That's good.'

'How long have you been waiting here tonight?'

'I've only just arrived,' said Tracie. 'You were away when I got here.'

'So you haven't had anyone yet?'

'No. Not yet,' she gulped, suddenly wondering whether she really was in the right place after all.

The other girl turned her head towards the road. 'Well, I think you will now,' she said nodding at a dark blue Sierra that had stopped at the curb. 'I think this one's for you. He looks to be beckoning you over.'

'Oh,' Tracie said weakly, swallowing hard and smoothing down her minuscule skirt.

'No undercutting,' said the girl. 'Twenty pounds for fifteen minutes. Not a penny less.' Wearing her skin-tight micro mini and top, but no knickers or bra, Tracie stepped forward uncertainly. She peered through the half-open passenger window and tried to smile.

'Hello,' said the middle-aged man behind the wheel, sounding pleasant enough.

'Hello,' she managed to respond.

'You are on business, are you?'

'Yes, of course,' she replied quickly, not allowing herself time to change her mind. 'Twenty pounds,' she added. 'I think you'll find that's more or less the going rate.'

'That's fine,' he said cheerfully. 'Hop in and I'll drive round the back of the estate.'

Tracie felt herself starting to relax as she sat back in the comfortable passenger seat, pussy and pubes now on display, due to the extreme shortness of her skirt. 'I like it!'

grinned the man, staring down at her groin. 'All stripped and ready for action.'

'That's right,' she giggled wickedly, pulling her top up and over her head and then wriggling her splendid breasts from side to side for him to admire.

'I can see you believe in giving a man value for money.'

'Of course I do. Then he'll come again.'

'And again and again!' he laughed loudly, turning the vehicle onto the almost deserted car park that served the industrial estate. 'Do you mind if I park over there? I do like a bit of light so I can see what I'm doing?'

'So do I,' laughed Tracie. 'It's never the same in the dark.'

The Sierra came to a stop. 'Here's your money,' the man said at once.

Tracie slipped it into her small handbag, alongside the week's supply of Kleenex she'd had the foresight to pack. 'Do you need any help?' she asked, resting her right hand lightly on the front of his trousers.

'No. I'm as stiff as a board.'

'Yes, I can feel it,' she said happily, squeezing his very promising erection as hard as she dared.

She tugged her almost non-existent skirt the very short distance it had to travel up to her waist. Then she took hold of the man's right hand and used his fingertips to stroke herself between the tops of her thighs. 'I hope you'll find that this is worth all that money,' she said, dipping one fingertip inside the extremely well-lubricated lips.

He pushed a second finger in to join the first. 'I'm sure I will,' he breathed appreciatively.

'Come and see if you're right.'

He clambered out of the driver's seat, fumbling with his zip as he did so. Tracie spread her legs and he knelt between them, his trousers and pants now down to his knees. She took a two-handed grip on the hot pole of flesh that was now veering upwards from below his shirt front, and adjusted her position on the seat by sliding forward towards him. God, was she open and ready for this! It had taken much longer than she'd originally expected. She should have been nestling over Peter's knee by now, in just her stockings and suspenders, looking forward to a really long session in bed. But at least she was about to receive that for which she knew she'd certainly be grateful.

It wasn't Peter's tool, but it was a tool, nevertheless. A tool that would plug her hot little opening and stop it from self-destructing. Oh, Peter, why were you stuck at the office?

He pushed into her fiercely, pleasantly surprised to find how warm and receptive she was. And even more surprised to find that she was starting to come at once, even before he'd impaled her with his first full-length thrust. 'My Christ, you're keen!' he gasped.

'You're right!' she croaked in reply, closing her eyes and moaning with pleasure as she felt the hardness of his member opening her all the way up to the top of her vagina. She wrapped both legs round him and thrust her breasts into his chest. 'Fuck me as fast as you can!' she groaned, wriggling her hips in delicious anticipation.

And very fast it was, too. But, unfortunately for Tracie, not quite in the manner she'd meant. Within thirty seconds it was over, including his climax. It was almost the fastest she'd ever had. 'Oh!' she sighed in disappointment, wriggling her hips underneath him once more. 'That was a little bit quick.'

'It was lovely!' he replied truthfully, already climbing back to the driver's seat and fastening his trousers. 'Just what the doctor ordered!'

'Look,' she said earnestly. 'It hardly seems right to take your money just for that.'

'It was wonderful. Exactly what I needed.'

'Well, why don't you have another go? We've only been gone a couple of minutes. You're entitled to a lot more than that.'

'No, I'm fine, thanks very much. That was all I was after. I was just very wound up and in need of relief. Now I'm feeling great. On top of the world, in fact.'

'I'm sure I could soon get you going again with my mouth. Why don't you let me try?'

'It's okay, love. I told you, I'm fine. That was exactly what I was looking for. There's no need for you to feel you owe me anything more. I'd willingly have paid twice as much for what I've just done.'

Tracie considered offering him his money back in return for a second helping, but decided she'd be guilty of gross undercutting should he agree.

Almost exactly one hour later, Tracie was back on the pavement with the girls again. Back on the pavement for the fourth time, and feeling extremely frustrated. It was ludicrous, she said to herself crossly. Absolutely ludicrous. She'd had four different men in less than an hour and now she was feeling even hornier than before she'd started. How could anyone credit that such a thing was possible? Four times she'd found herself on someone's passenger seat, handsomely hooked. And four times the man in question had spent only a few miserly seconds probing about inside her, before implanting her with the hot, sticky seed of his loins. Why on earth should that be? Was it the very illicitness of the situation that the men found so exciting? Was it the fact that they'd actually gone out and purchased a slice of quim? Did that make them feel so powerful that the thrill of it all shot down to, and straight out of, their groins? Anyway, whatever the cause, the four very fleeting encounters had left her even more desperate than ever. She was sure she'd have felt better if she'd had none at all. It had only served to whet her appetite. And to wet her insides.

Not one of the men had been able to muster more than a dozen strokes. Didn't they know how to treat a sexy young wife who was all husbandless and hot? No sooner had they thrust themselves into her than she'd felt the start of a violent discharge. It had seemed as if they'd simply been using her body to masturbate themselves as fast as they could. Which, when she thought about it further, was very possibly the case.

Two more cars cruised up, stopped momentarily, and then pulled away with a young lady from the pavement inside. Within moments, three other young ladies were safely returned to their pavement positions. Tracie turned to the girl beside her, who was carefully unzipping the side of her hot-pants and jutting a hip in the direction of a crawling car. 'I haven't been doing this very long,' said Tracie.

'It gets easier,' sighed the girl, as the car drove off without stopping. 'Most of the time I just pretend it's my fiancé and that it's his money we'll be using as a deposit on a house, not mine.' She giggled. 'And when we've got the house, I suppose I'll have to pretend that it's his money paying the mortgage, not my immoral earnings.'

'He doesn't know, does he? That you work down here, I mean?'

'Of course not! None of the girls let on about what they do here. None of the husbands or boyfriends has a clue. It's just a bit awkward if you get picked up by someone you know. Last week Jillie found herself getting into a car with her husband's colleague from work.'

'Really?'

'Mind you, the guy was very nice about it. He slipped her an extra tenner for nothing at all. He didn't even want a blow job or anything like that for the extra money. Just gave her thirty pounds for a very quick bang in his car. And told her he'd be sure to ask her for a dance at the firm's do next month.'

'How embarrassing for her!'

'Yes, I know. She's dreading the next time she sees him. He told her that he finds her more interesting than ever – knowing what she does in her spare time.'

'Suppose he tells her husband?'

'Why should he? He's married himself, anyway. So he has to be just as discreet as Jillie. But it'll just be horribly embarrassing for her whenever she had to socialise with him. Which is quite often, apparently. He and her husband are close friends, you see.'

'Blimey! You'd have thought he'd have had the decency to change his mind, once he'd realised who he was picking up.'

'Well, that's the hilarious thing. Apparently he's been trying to get inside her knickers for years, but she'd never really fancied him. So he couldn't believe his luck when he drove past and spotted her on the pavement with all the other girls. He was driving here on business, you see. He wasn't actually looking for a bit of hole.'

'Why on earth didn't she refuse?' Tracie asked, intrigued. 'She could easily have done that.'

'She was worried she'd upset him. Make him turn nasty, I mean. Make him put out the word that she's a part-time highway hooker.'

'So she shut her mouth and opened her legs?'

'That's about the size of it,' agreed the girl.

'Times must be hard in her husband's line of business,' mused Tracie.

'Not necessarily. Most of the girls here are only part-time amateurs, like me. Most have good jobs or are married to someone who works in a bank or building society or suchlike. You'd be surprised how many, in fact. Linzi, over there in the pink hot-pants, will be a barrister by the end of the year. She's working her way through law school in the way she likes the most. Hasn't she got a really sexy wiggle?'

'Very,' Tracie agreed with feeling. 'So what you're saying is that the girls are here for the fun, rather than the money?'

'No, not quite. For both, mainly, I suppose. Some of them love the extra money, and some the extra sex. But there aren't many who do it just for one or the other. Mostly it's a bit of each. The real professionals work in the town centre, where they've got a place to go to. Up here, we're the passenger-seat girls. Just part-timers, with husbands or boyfriends to go home to. I suppose there are a few of us who do it just for fun. But nearly all of us enjoy getting paid for something that's not really work.'

'So it's more the money with you? So you can buy your house?'

'That's right. But sometimes it's a lot of fun. Especially when you get someone young and hunky who isn't just interested in flooding you with spunk as quickly as he can.'

'That's what I was meaning to ask you about.'

'Fire away, then.'

'Do all the men come so quickly? It seems to be all over in a few seconds.'

'Lots of them are like that,' said the girl. 'They're just after some instant relief, I guess. But sometimes you get a really good sorting out that brings you off, too. And you'll often get quite a few laughs, as well.'

'Like Jillie and her husband's business colleague?'

'Yes. And Jennie, for example. She's one of the very few who does it just for kicks. Anyway, a couple of weeks ago it was a very hot night and she was standing just here, wearing only her tiny knickers and bra and showing off her sexy bottom to every passing car. So this car drives up and out gets Sally, all freshly bonked and twenty pounds better off. The driver stares at Jennie as she wriggles her hips at him, and she stares back over her shoulder at him. And guess what?'

'What?'

'The driver is her husband!'

'Oh, my God!' gasped Tracie. 'Whatever did they say to each other when they got home?'

'Lord knows. We haven't seen Jennie any more since then.'

'I'm not surprised,' giggled Tracie.

'We haven't seen her husband either. I mean, he had some explaining to do as well. He'd just paid twenty pounds to shag Sally, after all.'

'Yes, but I bet he didn't look at it that way. I bet he was more concerned with the fact that his wife had been spending her evenings getting herself dicked by anyone who had the cash.'

'I think you're right,' sighed the other girl, stooping forward to stare into a passing car that didn't stop.

'Do you ever bump into any of your customers? At work, or in the town, I mean?'

'Sometimes.'

'Isn't it embarrassing for you?'

'Very. But then again, it's usually even more embarrassing for the man concerned. Usually, but not always. Unfortunately.'

'Tell me,' began Tracie. But she never got to finish her question. A sleek, black, open-topped Porsche pulled up at the pavement beside them. Tracie noted at once that the driver was an attractive, elegantly-groomed blonde girl about four or five years older than she. The girl was expensively dressed in a light grey suit and silk blouse. The skirt was short but extremely smart. Tracie could tell that here was a professional businesswoman who was by no means short of a pound or two.

For several seconds the driver of the black Porsche stared uncertainly at Tracie. 'I don't suppose you go in for pussy?' she asked at last.

'I certainly do!' Tracie cried happily. 'It's one of my great specialities, in fact.'

The Porsche drove away, with Tracie in the passenger seat. 'I'm Susan,' said the blonde girl. 'My husband's away on business and I just fancied doing something a little bit different . . .'

'I know what you mean,' laughed Tracie.

The car turned into the car park and Tracie pointed to a spot on the far side. 'Park over there,' she suggested. 'It's nice and quiet, but there's enough light to see each other.'

Susan stopped the car and turned to look Tracie in the face. 'I'd like you to make love to me,' she said simply. 'You can do whatever you want.'

Tracie leant over and kissed her gently with her tongue. 'You're a very naughty girl,' she cooed, when she'd finished. 'I think I should start off by punishing you for having such wicked desires. I think your ruttish rear end needs to be taught a lesson!'

'Oh, yes please!' breathed Susan, closing her eyes in pleasure at the thought. 'I'd love to have that done to me.'

Tracie opened the passenger door. 'We'd better swap seats then, Susan. I'll need you to be a little more accessible to me.'

Susan settled herself in the passenger seat, looking a trifle unsure. 'You've never done it with a hooker before, have you?' Tracie asked softly.

'No. Never.'

'But you do like it with another girl?'

'Yes. Very much.'

Tracie leant across towards her, placing a hand on Susan's silk-stockinged thighs just below the hem of her skirt. 'I think I'd better put you at ease,' she purred, slowly sliding her hand underneath the skirt. 'Before I'm nasty to you, I mean.'

Almost immediately the palm of Tracie's hand slipped past the stocking tops and glided over the smooth, bare flesh beyond. 'Yes, that would be nice,' whispered Susan, parting her legs to allow the hand to explore further.

Once again Tracie kissed her with her tongue, gently but hotly, and with a passion that the other girl could easily detect. Tracie's fingertips were now resting against the nicely filled crotch of tight silk knickers, and she was savouring the satin-smooth texture of Susan's bare upper thighs, cool in contrast to the heat she could feel through the silk. Slowly she moved her fingers, stroking the lips of the wide-open pussy she could feel inside. Immediately the knickers began to moisten. 'Ohhh!' sighed the female customer, before Tracie kissed her again.

Back and forth worked the fingers, lightly and expertly, arousing the woman more and more with every second that passed. Now the crotch of the silk knickers was soaked, and Tracie could feel the vaginal juices warm and slippery on her fingertips. She wasn't going to bring her off yet. She was just going to give her a little pleasure before it was time for the pain. Just as had so often been done to her.

Susan moaned with desire as she felt one long, slim finger being pushed gently into her sopping-wet channel. Tracie left it there, unmoving, whilst she slid her tongue right into the succulence of the other girl's mouth. At length she drew back her head and smiled sexily into Susan's face. 'You're very fuckable,' she cooed, starting to slide her finger slowly in and out. 'I wish I could do it to you.'

'I don't want to fuck. Not tonight. What you're doing is fine.'

The woman's love-juice was now pouring out of her. Tracie could feel it running down her finger and over the palm and the back of her hand. 'Are you always this wet?' she asked.

'Not always.'

Tracie used a second finger on her. Still very slowly and tenderly making her wriggle her hips in delight. Then she used her thumb to touch the clitoris. 'OH!' gasped Susan, surprised at the sudden shaft of pleasure that shot right up to her breasts. 'Oh, that's good!'

'Try not to come yet,' breathed Tracie. 'It'll be so much stronger and better if you can wait.'

'I'll try,' she croaked in reply, closing her eyes as Tracie kissed her once more, whilst her fingers continued to pamper and please. This was the thing about being made love to by a girl, Susan reflected. Her sympathy and understanding of what you needed was so much greater than that of a man.

At long last Tracie withdrew from the glorious wet warmth of pussy and mouth. 'Are you sure you want me to hurt you?' she asked.

'Oh, yes. Very sure. As much as you like. Provided you'll be nice to me afterwards.'

'Don't worry. I'll be so nice that you'll want to die. I know just what I'm doing.'

Susan was sure that she did.

Tracie's demeanour changed. She half-reclined the passenger seat and unclipped the head rest. 'Kneel on the seat facing the back,' she ordered. 'Then bend forward as far as you can. I want that randy little rump well above the level of your head.'

Susan did exactly as she'd been told. 'Pull your skirt up to your waist,' instructed Tracie, feeling her own internal juices starting to flow even faster at the prospect of what lay ahead. 'And then your knickers halfway down to your knees.' She switched on the interior light and gazed, delightedly, at the nice little bottom that had been bared for her. How mouthwateringly plump it was! And how prettily clad in just those fancy suspenders!

Very stealthily, so as not to give the game away, Tracie unbuckled and then unthreaded the heavy leather belt she wore round the top of her skirt. It was three inches wide and nearly a quarter of an inch thick.

Because of the angle at which Susan was bending, there was ample room for Tracie to lift the belt high above her head. 'I'm sorry,' she said softly, bringing it down with all her force right across the middle of those soft pouting cheeks.

'Arrggghhhh!' Susan howled at the top of her voice, taken by surprise at the severity of that first blow. But she didn't struggle or try to shift position, despite the white-hot pain that was now searing deep into the cheeks of her bottom.

Crack! The belt kissed her once again, with exactly the same response. And *crack!* it did so again, whilst Tracie stared in fascination at the saucy plump cheeks that were bouncing and reddening under her gaze.

'I thought you were going to use your hand,' gasped Susan, tears rolling down her face as she wriggled her hips in pain.

'Is this too much for you?'

'No. I'm all right.'

Crack! The evil leather belt bit home for the fourth time, raising shrieks that were just as loud as before. Tracie squeezed the tops of her thighs together and started a mini-climax that made her wriggle her own bottom from side to side. But she was wriggling with pleasure, not with the distress that was consuming the other girl.

Susan still made no attempt to escape her painful fate, even though the belt rose and fell twice more, making her contort her face in anguish.

Susan had never known anything like it. She was absolutely ablaze. Yet, as she'd always suspected, her pussy was even hotter. It yearned and throbbed with unrequited desire. She could feel her juices simply pouring down her thighs. How much more would her bottom be able to take? A lot, she hoped most sincerely. Even if it meant having to stay on her feet throughout tomorrow's board meeting!

Crack! Crack! Crack! The belt burnt her more deeply than ever.

'Poor little, sore little bottom!' whispered Tracie, bringing the belt down yet again. 'Poor little, sore little bum!'

'Don't stop!' Susan groaned fearfully. 'I can still take some more.'

But at last the instrument of torture was dropped on the floor, and Tracie reached out with one hand. 'I'm so sorry,' she whispered, lightly running her palm across each red hot cheek in turn, trying to soothe the hurt she'd inflicted, and surprised to feel a teardrop running down one side of her face. 'Now I'll make it all up to you.'

'No,' gasped Susan, writhing her hips in discomfort. 'Not yet. I want you to use the buckle on me. Just as hard as before.'

'It'll cut you. I know, because my husband has laid this belt across me.'

'Don't worry. I want to be cut. Use it as hard as you can.'

Now it really was over. Susan sat on the passenger seat, holding her breath as she tried to ignore the agony and concentrate, instead, on the urgent demands of her loins.

Tracie leant over and kissed her tenderly on the side of her face. 'I love you,' she said simply, reaching for the front of Susan's blouse.

'I love you, too,' gulped Susan, wondering if she really was sitting on a bed of red-hot coals.

Tracie's nimble fingers unbuttoned the other girl's blouse and then unfastened her bra. Her breasts were firm and full. 'You have beautiful nipples,' sighed Tracie, taking both of them between forefinger and thumb.

'Thank you,' whispered Susan, snuggling happily back in the seat and allowing herself to savour the manner in which she was being so delicately explored. She loved the way she was now so open and available, both above and below the waist. She loved the feeling of vulnerability. This gorgeous raven-haired girl could do anything she liked to her. Anything at all. She could hurt her or love her as much as she liked . . . Oh, those sweet, gentle hands on her boobs! How expertly she was being pampered and petted! And how wet she was at the junction of her legs! She could feel her juices pouring out of her and down onto the car seat. She could feel the way in which she was being drawn so wide apart that it caused a real, physical pain. Oh, God, this clever young girl was driving her to the very brink!

Tracie lowered her hands and slid the already displaced panties down over Susan's feet. Then she parted the silk-stockinged thighs. 'And now I'm going to show you just how much I love you,' she purred.

She lowered her head and began to lick the lips of the burning-hot quim that was as wet and wide open as could be. Very delicately and deliberately she licked, making Susan groan with ecstasy at the change in the way she was being treated. Slowly Tracie delved deeper and deeper with her tongue and began to chew. Then she lifted her head, her mouth and chin dripping with love-juice. 'Your pussy tastes delicious,' she breathed softly. 'Here, let me share it with you.' She kissed her deeply once more, both girls relishing the salty/sweet flavour Tracie held in her mouth.

Tracie's head was back between silky bare thighs, her lips and tongue devouring the hot, wet flesh there. Devouring it greedily, gobbling, then sucking out the plentiful juice as hard as she could. But however much she sucked and swallowed, there was more than enough to take its place. More and more she gobbled and swallowed, until Susan felt herself wanting to swoon with the strength of the passion aroused in her. She began to gyrate her hips, slowly to start with, pressing her groin into Tracie's face and then moving it up and down over her chin, lips and nose, much to Tracie's delight. Harder and faster worked Susan, gasping in disbelief at the pleasure she gained. Harder and faster she worked, sobbing as she thrust against Tracie's soaking wet face.

But then it was time to finish. Judging that her overwrought companion was as ready as ever she'd be, Tracie held her still, then raised her own head a fraction, before sucking Susan's hard little clitoris into her mouth.

Susan screamed with the intensity of the climax provoked. A shrill, ear-splitting scream of agony and ecstasy that seemed to last forever, whilst Tracie remained head down, sucking as hard as she could.

'Can I drive this back?' asked Tracie, five minutes later, patting the steering wheel of the Porsche.

'Can you handle it, do you think?'

'Yes. I'm quite a good driver. One of my ex-boyfriends had a Ferrari, and I used to drive it a lot.'

'Okay, then. Take it for a spin down the motorway, if you like.'

A few minutes later the needle on the speedometer was registering a hundred and twenty. Susan looked sideways at Tracie as the latter sat bolt upright, concentrating on the road ahead. 'Are you married?' she asked at length.

'Yes!'

'Does your husband know you hang out on that pavement?'

'Not likely!' Tracie replied with a laugh.

'Why does a lovely girl like you have to do it? Do you really need the money so badly?'

'No. Not at all. This is my first time, actually. I went down there tonight because I was desperate for sex.'

'Just like me!' giggled Susan.

'I've had four men in an hour, and I'm still desperate. None of them lasted as long as a minute.'

The car roared down the slip road towards the next exit. 'I'm heading back there now,' said Tracie. 'Sooner or later I'll find someone who'll be able to give me a good time.'

Now the Porsche was hurtling back along the southbound carriage way. 'Aren't you worried about the motorway police?' asked Susan.

'Not at this time of night. Mind you, I did get caught once on a deserted motorway like this. In the Ferrari. Doing about a hundred and twenty.'

'What happened? Didn't you get a ban?'

'No,' laughed Tracie. 'I bought the copper off.'

'How do you mean?'

'Well, I could see he really fancied me as he stood there writing in his notebook. So what do you think I did?'

'You didn't fuck him?'

'No, you're right, I didn't. Not quite.'

'What then?'

'I gave him a blow job. With the driver's window wound right down, he stood there on the hard shoulder, his back to the traffic, while I sucked him off. It didn't take very long. He tasted rather nice, actually. I just reached out for his zip while he was cautioning me, and took out his tool. Without saying a word. Then I started to suck. I think he was rather impressed by my willingness to co-operate with the forces of law and order.'

'I hope your boyfriend wasn't in the car?'

'No. Fortunately, I was on my own. He wasn't the sort who'd have appreciated it.'

They were now only five miles out of town. 'You're really going back to that pavement?' enquired Susan, intrigued.

'Yes. Until I get what I need.'

'God, I admire you! I'd never have the nerve to do that.'

'I've never been short of nerve,' Tracie said truthfully. 'That's the trouble I suppose. If I was different, I'd be too afraid of being caught out to fuck anyone I please.'

'You fuck anyone you fancy, even though your husband might find out?'

'That's just about right. But don't get the idea that I don't respect him. I do, very much. It's just that my pussy rules my life. And unfortunately I have enough daring to let it. I just go out and get what I want. Sometimes I wish I didn't.'

'He doesn't know what you get up to?'

'No. He frets and suspects, but he doesn't know. I wish I could be the wife he wants me to be. But we can't change who we are, can we, Susan?'

'No, I suppose we can't.'

'Provided Peter doesn't actually know, that's the best I can do. Keep him in the dark, I mean. I can't stop him being suspicious, can I? Hell, he'd still be suspicious even if I was the best-behaved wife in the world!'

'Do you love him, Tracie?'

'I guess I probably do. Although I'm not totally certain I know what "love" means.'

'Who does?'

Tracie was back on the beat once again, the delicious flavour of sweet, wet pussy very fresh in her mouth. She was no richer than she had been half an hour earlier, as she'd steadfastly refused to accept any payment for what had been such a labour of love. 'Can we see each other again?' Susan had asked.

'That sounds like a good idea,' she'd replied.

Susan had then slipped a business card into Tracie's handbag. 'Phone me whenever you like,' Susan had urged her. 'The sooner the better.'

Now, back on the pavement, Tracie looked up as a rather beaten-up Ford Granada stopped at the curb right in front of her, four fresh young faces peering eagerly out of the passenger windows. This looked much more the ticket, she said to herself hopefully. Four rather nice-looking young lads. She sauntered over to the car with an exaggeratedly casual air. 'Hello boys,' she drawled sexily. 'What can I do for you?'

'Quite a lot, I should imagine!' breathed the driver, slowly eyeing her up and down. 'I like that skirt you're almost wearing.' With a wide, impish grin, she lifted the front hem a fraction to demonstrate that she was naked underneath. 'Here Pussy, Pussy, Pussy!' she called.

'It's Bob's birthday,' said one of the back-seat passengers, when the laughter had subsided, indicating the fair-haired youth in the front passenger seat. 'We'd like to buy him a present.'

'What did you have in mind?' she asked as innocently as she could.

'We thought you might come up with a few ideas,' replied the driver.

Tracie opened the back door and slid her trim, unknickered rear end inside the car. 'Budge up,' she said to the lad beside her. He was happy to oblige.

'Take the next turn left,' she said to the driver. 'And

then pull into the car park on the right.'

'There aren't any shops on the car park,' he objected jocularly.

'No,' she said slowly, 'there aren't. But at this time of night it is one great big knocking shop. I thought that might fit the bill.'

The Granada cruised onto the well-lit but almost deserted car park. 'Do you give any discount for birthdays?' someone enquired.

'I'm afraid not,' she laughed. 'Not without a birth certificate, at least. Anyone could say it's their birthday, after all.'

'How about for a job lot, then?'

'Eh?'

'How much for all of us? Surely there'd be some sort of reduction for bulk?'

Tracie gave the matter serious consideration. Here was an opportunity not to be lost. 'I must say I'm rather keen on bulk,' she giggled. 'What would you say to four for the price of two? Forty pounds instead of eighty? Does that sound fair to you?'

'Very fair,' they agreed with alacrity, as, at Tracie's direction, the car came to a halt in the partially lit area where she'd earlier entertained Susan.

There followed a short period of slightly uncomfortable silence on the part of the four young men as they sat staring out of the car, uncertain how to proceed. 'What do we do now?' murmured the front-seat passenger, whose birthday it may or may not have been.

'Let me give you a clue,' Tracie said brightly, pressing one buttock warmly against the boy to her right. 'It will be one of these. Either you pay me forty pounds and we sit here for an hour playing eye-spy. Alternatively, you pay me forty pounds and then take it in turn to dick me as hard as you like.'

'I think it had better be the second,' muttered one of the lads, when he was able to find his voice.

'Yeah. You've sold that one to us,' confirmed another. 'Definitely.'

Quickly the money changed hands, Tracie's handbag now bulging more with paper money than paper tissues. 'Now then,' she asked them collectively. 'Who's the randiest of you four lads?'

'Paul is,' replied three of them together, pointing to the boy by her side.

She pulled off her top and then unbuckled and removed her skirt, enjoying the exposure of boobs and pubes to four hungry pairs of eyes. 'That's very handy,' she murmured, turning towards him and giving him a really good look at what was on offer. 'Hi, Paul!' she said sweetly.

He stared hard at the goodies she'd revealed to the sodium light of the car-park lamps. 'Hi,' he croaked hoarsely, catching his breath as she slipped a hand down the front of his jeans. She could feel that he was already semi-erect – and swelling by the second. She used her other hand to free his zip. 'Bingo!' she said, as she drew him out into the open and began to waggle him stiffly back and forth like a wand. 'I hope you're not all so well endowed?'

'I wish I was,' said Bob, the alleged birthday boy.

'So do I,' said someone else.

'Well, that's a relief!' she giggled. 'I do want to be able to sit down again one day!'

She pulled his T-shirt off over his head and tugged his jeans and pants down to his knees. Then, wearing only her high heels, she turned right round to face him, at the same time cocking one leg over his lap. Now she was kneeling on the back seat of the car, straddling his groin, the cheeks of her delectable bottom hovering just above the tip of his penis. She reached out and turned on the car light in order to illuminate the scene even more. As the other three gaped in silence, she began to lower herself down onto Paul, taking her time. There came the squelch of the initial penetration. The reassuring sound of a nicely-oiled vagina accepting the first inch or so of brawn. 'You stay still,' she suggested, 'and I'll do all the work.'

'Sounds fine to me,' he breathed, feeling himself slide right up to the hilt with comparative ease, even though he could tell he was an extremely snug fit.

He really was big, she said to herself, sitting still on his lap and getting used to the way she was being stretched. But not so big that it would be too uncomfortable to ride him as fast as she liked. She'd do that in a while, not yet. For the moment she'd just make sure he was fully acclimatised to her. In that way he might last a little longer than those who'd gone before.

Slowly she began to move up and down, rubbing her swollen clitoris against his magnificent stalk as she did so, enjoying the sensation of filling herself as she sank down upon him. She had to admit that it was fun feeling the other lads watching her closely as she slithered up and down on their well hung friend. Feeling them ogling her bottom as it rose and fell. She was aware that she was a bit of an exhibitionist. She'd never minded being viewed on the job. Much the opposite, in fact. It had always provided that extra bit of spice. She was also aware that she had a body of which she had every right to be proud. That being the case, why shouldn't several men at a time admire the way in which it performed the task for which it had been designed? Perhaps she really should have married Steve? He'd positively gloried in screwing her in front of his mates. And then vice versa, of course. What a difference between him and Peter.

Oh, yes! This young boy was really digging her deep. It was exactly what she'd been needing all evening. Already he'd lasted many times longer than any of the four who'd had her earlier. In fact, he'd lasted longer than all four of them put together. She'd be well and truly poked after this, even if the other three all went off faster than the hare at a dog track.

Squelch! as she sank down on him. *Slurp!* as she lifted her bottom. *Squelch! Slurp! Squelch! Slurp! Squelch! Slurp!* One long, drawn-out sound after another as the watchers goggled with glee – as they watched her bury their friend inside her, then slowly reveal him between her buttocks again. Very gradually she increased the pace until she was bouncing up and down on his lap, boobs and cheeky bare bottom joggling delightfully in time as she went, much to the appreciation of the crowd. Faster and faster she rode, feeling both their climaxes getting nearer as she skewered herself with ever increasing enthusiasm and pressed his face firmly into her breasts.

The three non-participants could sense what was happening. They could see as well as hear the whole length of the thick round penis plunging in and out of her at speed. Thick, round and tall as a mast, it was, and topped with a job that actually seemed to grow bigger as it continued to plunge with all the force her athletic young body could muster.

'Oh, my God!' groaned Paul, suddenly starting to squirt with a velocity he'd never even guessed he might be able to produce.

'Oh, yes, yes, yes!' she gurgled, jerking back her head and bearing down hard on his lap, before wriggling her hips wildly from side to side.

Jesus wept! thought the others, absolutely spellbound at the sight of this lovely young whore writhing in ecstasy at the way she was being shot full of boiling hot sperm.

As Tracie felt Paul starting to contract inside her, she turned her attention to the boy at his side. Showing considerable expertise, she unzipped him one-handed and then peeled back his trousers with a flourish. His penis was already thrusting its way up and out of the top of his briefs – by a considerable margin, she was extremely pleased to note. He lifted his bottom off the seat and she peeled his clothes down to his feet with a single tug of her hand. 'Mmm!' she murmured with approval, wrapping both hands around the proudest part of his person. 'Not too bad, either.'

'So I've been told,' he gulped. 'Not that I've done it very often.'

She lowered her head to his groin and began to run her tongue up and down his erection, coating him with saliva. 'I should hope not,' she replied. 'You're supposed to wait till you're married.' Then she took the bulbous tip in her mouth and sucked gently, making him moan. He was incredibly hot and already quivering slightly, so she decided it might not be a good idea to continue with too much more of her mouth. She didn't want any premature spillage, after all. That was not the object of the night.

She disengaged herself from Paul and moved over the seat until she was squatting over the second lad's lap. then she impaled herself on him, listening to his sigh of contentment as she sank all the way down to his balls. He was an excellent fit, just like his friend had been. Long enough and thick enough to give her all the satisfaction she needed. Slowly she began to ride, loving the sound of her juices squelching rhythmically as she did so. At the end of each downward movement she could feel him poking firmly against the entrance to her womb. She pressed her clitoris hard against his strength and stiffness, and sighed with pleasure. This was what being a girl was all about! This was girl power at its strongest.

Up and down worked her gorgeous bottom, greatly admired by the other three men. Paul couldn't resist it any longer. He reached out and took the nearest bare cheek in his hand. The lad on whom she sat followed suit, squeezing the other cheek equally firmly. Together they held her as she rode up and down, each of them relishing the texture of firm, satin-smooth flesh.

'We can't see her bum!' the driver complained after a while. Reluctantly they let go, and Tracie reacted by doubling the pace. 'That's better,' breathed the birthday boy on the passenger seat, staring at his friend's dripping wet weapon as it raced in and out between bouncing buttocks.

'I like my bottom being held,' panted Tracie. 'But then again, I also like it being watched.'

'You've got a fantastic arse!' enthused the driver. 'It deserves to spend nearly all its life like this, on the job.'

'Then it gets its just desserts,' she said dryly, thrusting down with greater power than before and feeling the second lad starting to jerk with the onset of orgasm. 'That's beautiful!' she sighed happily, relishing the virile young seed gushing powerfully into her womb.

'She really seems to enjoy her work,' the driver whispered

to the front-seat passenger, genuinely surprised.

One after the other, the two remaining young men were done in exactly the same fashion – professionally screwed on the back seat, with Tracie on top, so that everyone could enjoy the show. Then Bob, now wearing the lower half of his birthday suit, was treated to the use of her mouth. It was her free contribution to the birthday celebrations, she explained afterwards, grinning broadly as she wiped her chin.

With an immaculate sense of timing, the last Kleenex was used just as she was returned to the pavement. She tottered forward a couple of steps. 'I'm shagged!' she giggled to the nearest girl. 'I'm going to find my knickers and then go home for a good night's sleep!'

Chapter 5

Flaccid

Tracie turned the red MG midget into her road. She was feeling much better now. Shagging those four young lads on the back seat of that Granada had really done the trick. It had been hard work, of course, but now her pussy was as calm as could be. It was purring happily underneath her recently regained knickers, and not making any demands at all. She could tell that it would be perfectly happy to wait for Peter, even though it was still at least another two hours before he'd be home. At last it was back under control and she was in charge of her own body. That was really rather a relief.

Of course, she wouldn't have had all this trouble if it had been left alone after Pauline had used her mouth on it earlier today. It had been really peaceful and content after that. It hadn't been any trouble at all until she'd helped Kevin lose his virginity in the stockroom. That had started it off, and resulted in her taking advantage of Harry. Then, of course, there'd been Sir Roland, after which the urgent demands from down below had been absolutely unbearable. Still, all was quiet and peaceful again now. Even a tail as wilful as hers had been tamed by her recent excesses. Poor Peter! If only she could find a way of making him come to terms with her raging nymphomania.

Tracie parked in a side street so that Peter would be able to leave his car in the garage. She was really looking forward to him coming home and making love to her. He was superb in bed, she had to admit. He never missed a night, nor a morning. She was always assured of a regular supply of spam and sperm.

Mind you, it was just as well as he was such a lusty lad.

Otherwise, she'd be spending all her spare time looking for a bit on the side. As opposed to about half of it. Christ, it had been fun in that Granada! It had been fun dicking herself silly on one young boy after another. All of them had lasted a good long time, as well. A full fifteen minutes at least. Sixty minutes or more riding one horn after another! It had more than made up for her previous disappointments. Now she could look back on those earlier quick-fire merchants with a degree of pleasure. The four fastest guns in the West. At least they'd penetrated and implanted her.

Good God, she'd never been so busy in such a short space of time! Her handbag full of paper tissues had been emptied in less than two and a half hours. And now it was stuffed with money instead.

And talking about the money, she now had one hundred and twenty pounds in her bag. One hundred and twenty pounds more than when she'd left home. And tax free, too, of course. She'd be able to buy that slinky black dress she'd seen last Saturday. The one that Peter had liked so much. And she'd still have cash to spare, plus the money from Sir Roland that she intended to lavish on Peter. It just went to show what a wonderful world it was. All that lovely sex . . . and a wad of money for doing it! A wad of notes for simply doing what came so naturally.

Tracie walked up the path towards her house, and groaned. Suddenly, the lounge light had burst into life. Peter must have arrived home just before her. Even though it was only a quarter to twelve. Would she be able to avoid him seeing her in this kit? In this tiny skirt and top he'd ordered her never to wear? If she couldn't she might well find herself in trouble. He might well assume she'd been out on the pull. And the last thing she wanted was a row. She just wanted to snuggle up to him in bed and let him introduce his hard, husbandly cock all the way up to the top of her channel.

Stealthily, she opened the front door and slipped inside. The lounge was to her left, the stairs to her right. She tiptoed quietly upstairs and into the master bedroom. Within seconds her clothes were safely back in the wardrobe. Then she whipped her knickers off over her feet. They were noticeably soggy, so she pushed them to the bottom of the dirty laundry basket, grinning mischievously to herself as she did so.

Quickly, she slipped into the short, black negligée that was hanging over the back of a chair on her side of the bed. It was almost totally transparent and only just reached the tops of her thighs. It was about the same length as the mini-skirt she'd just removed. She pulled on the matching knickers. She didn't usually bother with them, but she decided it would be prudent to wear them tonight, bearing in mind she was still leaking seed. Then she pulled back the quilt and rumpled the pillows and sheets. Peter had only just got back, she said to herself. So she'd pretend she'd retired early to bed, in order to rest and await his conjugal services. If he asked why she'd bothered with knickers, she could say that the thought of what he was going to do to her had turned her on even more than usual.

Tracie skipped down the stairs to the hall, bottom and boobs bouncing delightfully under the see-through knickers and top. 'Where's my own personal porker?' she called, as she opened the door to the lounge. 'I've been waiting for hours for my nighttime ration. Why are you still outside my quim?'

She stepped into the room, and screamed. There in front of her was an unfamiliar figure dressed almost entirely in black. He was holding their television set in his arms. 'Don't panic!' he gasped nervously.

'Keep away from me!' she shrieked, diving over to the fireplace and grabbing a heavy iron poker from the hearth. 'Don't come anywhere near me!' she hissed. 'I'm quite capable of splitting your head in two!'

'I'm sure you are,' he muttered, taking a hasty step back. 'But believe me, I won't try to hurt you. I promise I won't hurt you at all.' He put the TV down on the floor in front of him. 'There's no need to scream.'

'Who's screaming?' she asked, sounding dangerous, as she moved to the doorway in order to bar his escape.

'Not you, that's for sure,' he said with a hint of

admiration. 'I think I'm more afraid of you than you are of me.'

'Who the hell are you?' she asked.

He shuffled his feet uncomfortably. 'I'm a burglar,' he murmured apologetically.

She stared hard at the rather fragile-looking young man in front of her. 'You don't look like a burglar,' she said at last.

'How's a burglar supposed to look?'

She eyed him up and down once again. 'Sort of powerful and menacing, I suppose. Sort of evil and nasty.'

'Well, it's not very nice of me to break in here and take your TV set, is it?'

'No. It isn't. I just said that you didn't look much like a burglar to me. I didn't say you weren't being nasty.'

'It's the first time I've done it,' he stammered, staring down at the carpet. 'I'm desperate for money. It was either this, or jump under a bus.'

'Don't be silly. There must be another way.'

'There isn't.'

'Why on earth not?'

'I'm absolutely broke. I don't have more than twenty pence in the world.'

'Surely that can't be true?'

'It is, I swear. I'm completely bombed out. I haven't eaten since yesterday morning. And I shan't be able to buy any food until I get paid on Saturday morning.'

'But why are you so hard up?'

'My wife left me a year ago for another man. My best friend. She took the kids with her. Then she gave him the push and claimed full maintenance from me. I have to pay her nearly all my wages. And I don't even get to see the kids. She won't let me.'

'You should go and see a solicitor,' Tracie said sternly. 'Not steal other people's property.'

'How can I afford to do that?'

'You can apply for legal aid,' she replied at once. 'I know, because I work for a law firm. You'd get free legal aid without any trouble at all. It would cover all of the fees. You wouldn't have to put any money towards them.'

'Are you sure?'

'Of course I'm sure. I told you, I work for a firm of solicitors. My former friend there, George Franks, deals with people like you all the time. With their divorces, I mean. I'll give you his phone number before you go. Then you can ring him in the morning and make an appointment.'

'Aren't you going to call the police?'

She looked at him closely again. Actually, he seemed rather nice. Rather lost and waiflike, and quite good-looking as well. It was a pity his clothes were so shabby. But what could you expect from someone who was so hard up? She could tell that she was definitely starting to feel sorry for him. He was clearly very frightened indeed.

'Don't you think you ought to call them?' he asked again.

'Well, it's not as if you've tried to rape me or anything,' she mused, noting that he was only about her age. And with a very delicate bone structure so far as his face and hands were concerned.

'Of course not!' he protested at once.

'Why "of course not"? Don't you think I'm worth it? Don't you think this nightie is sexy? Doesn't it show you everything I've got?'

'I wouldn't dream of hurting you,' he muttered. 'I wouldn't hurt anyone, in fact. Not even my ex-wife.'

She giggled. 'Lots of burglars do rape their victims, though. I've read it in the papers. And heard about it at work.'

'Not me, though.'

'No, I suppose not,' she said, sounding almost disappointed.

'You're a beautiful girl,' he said softly. 'But I could never do that to you, or anyone else.'

'Most men could if they were really worked up enough.'

He hung his head and looked more miserable than ever. 'I couldn't,' he whispered under his breath.

'Everyone has a violent streak in them somewhere,' she persisted.

'I suppose so. But it's not just that.'

'Exactly what is it, then?'

'I'd rather not say. You'd better call the police if you're going to.'

'Of course I'm not going to!' she snapped, dropping the poker on the floor. 'I feel sorry for you. I don't want you to get into any more trouble than you're in already. I'm just intrigued to know why you wouldn't try to force me even if you were absolutely bursting with lust.'

'I wouldn't do it,' he replied. 'I couldn't.'

'You've said that before. But why?'

'I just wouldn't, that's all. And I couldn't because I couldn't.'

'You wouldn't because you wouldn't, and you couldn't because you couldn't?' she asked, raising an eyebrow.

'I wouldn't because I'm just not that sort of a person . . .'

'And you couldn't?'

'Well, if you must know, I couldn't because I couldn't get it up you, however hard I tried.'

'Are you saying your tackle isn't up to the job?' she asked in surprise.

He sighed despondently, but said nothing.

'I'm sorry,' she said quickly. 'I didn't mean to be so hurtful. I was just taken aback by what you said. It was very thoughtless of me. Very insensitive.'

'That's all right.'

She took a step forward, without thinking. 'How long have you had this problem?' she asked gently.

'It doesn't matter . . .'

'Yes, it does. It must be terrible for you. Why don't you tell me about it? You'd probably feel better if you did.'

'It's embarrassing.'

'You're not going to shock me. You'd be surprised what it takes to do that. Tell me, when did all this start?'

He stood stock-still for ages, staring at his feet. 'After my wife left,' he mumbled eventually. 'I was very upset about losing her. And the kids as well, of course. I haven't been able to do it since then.'

'You have tried, then?'

'Just twice. I simply couldn't get a hard-on. God, it was

awful! I've never felt so bad in my life! Imagine trying to make love to a pretty young girl and not being able to raise the tiniest gallop! Even though she's lying there stark naked and panting for me to perform. I could never make myself go through that sort of thing again. Never.'

'But if you don't try, you'll never solve the problem.'

'I just couldn't put myself through all that again. I'd rather stay celibate.'

'But you can't spend all your life like that!'

'There isn't any alternative.'

'So you won't even have another go?'

'No. I simply couldn't make myself try.'

'No. But I could make you,' she said cunningly, wriggling her boobs under her negligée.

'Pardon?'

'I could make you try again. With me, I mean. Right now.'

'Don't be so daft.'

Tracie felt a familiar warmth welling up inside her. A very familiar warmth indeed. A warmth that she knew would quickly turn into a desire so urgent that it couldn't be denied. She could also feel her juices trickling into the tight little crotch of her knickers at the thought of what she intended to do to the clean-cut young man who was standing directly in front of her. The crotch bit into her even more tightly as her pussy opened like a flower in the sun. It was a delicious sensation that she always loved to savour to the full. 'I could make you have another go,' she repeated, her saliva thickening in her mouth as her knickers became wetter and wetter.

'But why should you?'

'Because I want to help you, of course. I feel sorry for you. And you're quite a shaggable young lad. You make me feel quite randy.'

He stared at her beautiful breasts, the hard pointed nipples clearly discernible through her black nightie. 'Okay. So tell me, how could you make me try?'

'Easy,' she laughed, nimbly stooping to pick up the poker once again. 'By phoning the police if you don't!'

★ ★ ★

He followed her upstairs, his eyes glued to the delightful curves of her buttocks as they wiggled from side to side, right in front of his nose. She looked back at him over her shoulder and grinned as she caught him staring at the seat of her transparent panties. 'I hope I'm giving you ideas?' she asked with a sexy smile.

'Well . . . Yes, sort of . . .'

'You needn't worry about how I'll feel if you can't do it,' she said reassuringly. 'Because I already know what to expect if the worst comes to the worst. It's quite different from the times before, when you were trying to shag some pretty young girl. I'll understand perfectly if you can't get it up.'

'That's true,' he murmured, wondering whether he was right in thinking that he'd just felt a definite twinge inside his briefs. It really was too much to hope for.

She stood in the bedroom doorway and wriggled her bottom at him in an exaggerated manner. 'Anyway, it'll be fun trying,' she breathed.

'I hope so,' he said with a sigh.

'You worry too much. That's part of the problem, of course. The more you worry about getting hard, the more difficult it becomes. As I said, it doesn't matter if you can't do it. We'll enjoy ourselves one way or another. There are loads of ways you can make me come. With your hands or your mouth, for instance. Or I can just lie on top of you and rub my clit into your groin.'

'You're being very kind about all this,' he stammered. 'After I tried to rob you, as well.'

She laid him on his back along one side of the bed. Then she slipped sexily out of her negligée and knickers and hopped up beside him. 'You're overdressed,' she said, pushing his T-shirt up to his neck and then reaching for his jeans. With practised ease they were slid down past his knees, followed by his pants. 'This Action Man kit looks perfectly okay to me,' she murmured. 'Everything seems to be present and correct. It's just a matter of getting it to work.'

'I know.'

Lying on her side, she curled herself into a ball, her face over his genitals and her sweet little bare bottom pointing prettily up at him. He lay back and admired the view. He could easily have reached down to fondle those smooth, shapely cheeks, he said to himself. But for the moment he felt too nervous of the situation.

He was very nicely endowed, thought Tracie. Very generously proportioned in the groinal region. She could tell from the size and shape of his flaccid penis that he'd make quite a sight when fully erect. And she could see that his balls were large and heavy with sperm. All she had to do was press the right buttons and she'd find herself in for yet another treat.

She took his soft round organ in her left hand and cupped the other under his scrotum. She could feel how tightly packed it was. Not surprisingly, she thought to herself. Bearing in mind that he hadn't had his end away for at least a year. Balancing his testicles in her palm, she lowered her head and licked round the tip of his penis. 'Hello there, Timmy the Tonker!' she cooed. 'Is there anyone in there who'd like to come out to play?'

'There certainly is!' he muttered. 'But he seems to be stuck at the moment.'

She licked him again. 'It doesn't matter if you don't get stiff,' she said soothingly. 'I can still make you come with my mouth, even if you stay just like this.'

'But it isn't the same for you.'

'Not the same, but just as nice. Every girl loves getting it in her mouth from time to time. It's just as satisfying. I love the salty taste of the spunk. I love gobbling all of it down as fast as I can.'

'But you'd prefer to have it between your legs?'

'I really don't mind. I told you, I'm just as happy either way.' Slowly she began to massage his genital organs with both hands. 'This is just to relax you,' she purred. 'I'm not trying to make you hard. Just lie back and close your eyes and enjoy it.'

'I am.'

'Just concentrate on the nice feeling it gives you. Don't try to think about anything else. Don't worry about whether or not you'll be able to do it.'

'I just wish I could manage to . . .'

'Stop that!' she giggled, tweaking him playfully. 'Do as I said and relax. You can think about my body, if you like. You can think about the shape of my bum as you followed me upstairs. I know you were staring at it. And I know you liked what you saw.'

She felt a very definite twitch in her left hand. 'Yes, it was very pretty,' he said slowly. 'Very pretty indeed. You have a wonderful figure.'

'And I know how to use it,' she giggled again, continuing the two-handed massage. 'You'd be surprised just how much I know. And what I can do.'

She leant forward and kissed him, pushing her tongue into his mouth and licking lightly. Then she sat up and smiled sexily into his face. 'One way or another I'm going to milk you dry down here,' she breathed, gently squeezing his testicles. 'One way or another I'm going to have every drop you've got.'

'You're very welcome to it,' he sighed with feeling. 'Go ahead and help yourself.'

But Tracie was in no hurry. Slowly and expertly she continued to draw his testicles and plump, but limp, penis back and forth through her hands, kneading and squeezing as she did so. 'Just lie there and enjoy it,' she soothed. 'Just think about how nice it feels. Not about anything else.'

He closed his eyes and followed her orders, relishing the gentle warmth of her hands on his most private parts. Hands that petted and soothed. Soft, patient hands that sought out and caressed every square centimetre and gave no indication that they were attempting to hurry him along. It was very comforting, he thought to himself. Very pleasant and comforting. She'd told him not to worry about getting boned up, and he was following her instructions to the letter. It was good just to be able to lie here and savour the way in which his genitals were being pampered so nicely.

'Your balls are lovely,' she purred, weighing them

appreciatively in one hand. 'Beautifully round and as heavy as anything. And baking hot, as well.'

Once again she started to massage them. A slow, thorough massage that was amazingly peaceful and relaxing. At the same time her other hand continued to work tenderly up and down the remaining half of his wedding tackle, squeezing him and silently reassuring him that it made no difference to her whether he was stiff or slack.

At length she leant over his groin. 'It's time for me to eat,' she giggled, pointing his still slumbering penis up at her face. 'Now I'm going to have all of your lovely thick come, one way or another, like I said.'

She went down on him, sucking the whole of his soft but still sizeable organ into her mouth and petting it with her tongue. It was like an uncooked sausage, she thought. A nice plump little sausage. Instinctively, he slid his right hand down the curve of her buttocks.

She started to suck at him, still massaging his tightly packed scrotum at the same time. In turn, he used the fingers of his right hand between the tops of her legs, lightly stroking the slick, wet lips. He filled her mouth to perfection. The whole of his cock was inside, but there was hardly any space available for the expansion she felt sure she could provoke. Harder and more urgently she sucked, coating him with saliva. Then she began sliding him in and out of her mouth, simulating the effect of sexual intercourse on his unresponsive organ. 'Try to imagine you're fucking me,' she whispered. He closed his eyes and pretended that he was actually slipping in and out of her well-oiled quim. He lay still and concentrated on this thought as hard as he could. In and out of her he slid. In and out of her slick little quim. In and out, in and out, in and out. He ignored everything else except the sensation of his penis moving in and out of her snug little, slick little quim. In and out, in and out, in and out. He visualised it, tall and proud as it slithered in and out of her. In and out, in and out, in and out of her sweetly lubricated little quim. In and out with ease. In and out, in and out, in and out.

He remembered the heart-stopping sight of her bottom

in transparent panties, snaking sexily from side to side as he followed her upstairs. He pictured it underneath him, pressed firmly into the mattress, wriggling and wet with her pussy juices as he glided smoothly and slickly in and out of her sopping wet little quim. In and out, in and out, in and out of her hot little, wet little quim.

As if by magic, he suddenly started to swell. Slowly, to start with. She felt the first movement inside her mouth and smiled to herself. Within a few seconds he was too big to contain entirely. A few seconds after that there were several inches of him protruding from between her lips. Soon only the knob itself was in her mouth and the rest of him was stretched outside, as long, thick and rock-hard as she could have wished.

Slowly she began to fellate him, raising and lowering her head, taking in as much as she could, forcing as much of him down her throat as she was able. And still he continued to grow, his penis aching painfully as it stretched and strained at the leash. 'Oh, my God!' he groaned. 'I'd forgotten what it was like!' At last he was stretched to the full. A great column of hot, hard flesh that quivered with excitement. She lifted her head so that the tip was just between her lips. 'How would you like it?' she whispered, licking him with her tongue. 'In here or down below?'

He thought carefully about the question, but eventually came to a decision. 'Down below, if you don't mind. Your mouth is fantastic but I really do feel the need to be in your quim.'

Chapter 6

Hard

Tracie squatted over him, one knee on each side of his groin. Then, sitting bolt upright, she impaled herself half an inch at a time, loving the way in which she was able to control exactly how much she took and how quickly or otherwise she took it. 'Does this bring back memories, too?' she enquired impishly, when he was fully immersed.

He closed his eyes and gritted his teeth. 'Jesus! Does it just! Oh, God! I think I'm going to come!'

She stopped moving and sat very still on his lower loins, feeling the tip of his handsome erection stretching her to the limit. 'Now's the time to think about something unpleasant,' she said helpfully. 'Now that you've got it up. Think about something you really don't like at all.'

He took her advice and remembered the Divorce Court. Very soon the feeling of uncontrollable excitement passed, and he was left with a deep sense of achievement instead. 'That's better,' he grunted. 'But I don't think I'll last very long. It's been such a hell of a long time.'

Slowly she began to shaft herself on him again, moving up and down, very carefully and deliberately, trying to nurture him as best she could. He cupped his hands round her bottom and kept his eyes shut tight. He could picture himself inside her. He could see his penis moving slowly and smoothly through the channel of her vagina, forcing the willing wet flesh apart as it went. He could see it proudly upright inside her, surrounded by glorious, piping-hot pussy.

Tracie was about to push down on him again when she felt his body stiffen beneath her. She stared down at his face. It was contorted with pleasure and pain. He was obviously on the brink of ejaculation. One more stroke and she knew he'd be there. 'Hold tight, Mr Burglar!' she whispered, thrusting down with her hips and driving him all the way home.

He bucked and groaned, and then suddenly she felt him starting to erupt – like a jet from a high pressure hose. One violent burst followed another. Twelve months or more of frustration were being released into her, jettisoned inside her at speed. And the heat! It was incredible. It made her gasp aloud in surprise. And the torrent seemed endless. Was he ever going to dry up, she wondered. Each powerful spurt seemed to possess just the same volume and velocity as the first. There was no indication that he'd ever subside. She'd never known anyone vent so much for so long. Not even Sir Roland. This was just one long stream after another, coating her womb and gushing back out.

It was quite understandable, she supposed. After all, he had a whole year of pent-up emotion to expel. She was just glad she'd been able to help. And even more glad to be the lucky recipient.

'Oh, mother!' he moaned happily, still expelling vast quantities of the scalding-hot seed. 'Isn't this the very best thing since sliced bread!'

But at last he was done. She rolled off his groin and lay on her side, facing him, his now spent organ cradled stickily in her right hand. 'I'm full!' she giggled naughtily. 'You've flooded every nook and cranny I own. I can feel it pouring out of me in waves. How can anyone come so much?'

Gently he turned her onto her back and got to his knees beside her. 'There's plenty more if you're interested,' he croaked, gesturing down at his rapidly re-stiffening penis, still in her hand.

'Blimey! That was quick! That was more than a little bit previous!'

'I'm trying to make up for lost time.'

She opened her legs and he rolled on top, pushing down with his groin and penetrating her at once. Cream shot out of her as he plunged right up to the root. 'Sorry about the sheets,' he murmured, able to feel what was happening. But she didn't hear him. Her own climax had been triggered by that first fanny-filling thrust. Her head writhed from side to side as she squealed with delight.

This time the coitus was a much more leisurely and laid-back affair. On the burglar's part, that is. He knew he'd be able to keep going for another half hour or more. He knew he was in command. Now it was Tracie who found herself unable to keep control. One orgasm after another rocked through her, making her gasp and groan. She guessed that it was the earlier sex that was responsible. The earlier sex in the car. That was what was making her so incredibly receptive now. It had put her in exactly the right mood for a good, old-fashioned romp in bed. Each thrust seemed to start a new climax, long before the old one had gone – or even before the one before that.

It was one of the best bonkings she could ever recall. Her nipples felt as if they were about to burst. And her insides were now in a state of constant climax. It swept through her in wave after wave.

The minutes ticked delightfully by. 'Ohhh!' she moaned with every stroke. With every long steady push. 'Ohhh! Ohhh! Ohhh! I don't think I can stand much more of this!'

'That's nice to hear,' he muttered, thrusting into her rather more firmly. 'That's very rewarding indeed.'

'Ohhh!' she squealed loudly as her orgasm doubled in strength. 'I think you're killing me off!'

But no mercy was shown. Harder and faster he started to rut, impaling her with every inch at his disposal whilst she twisted and turned on the bed and gasped and groaned at his size. Then she started to pump her own hips up and down against him, in order to get as much as she possibly could. His recently spent seed flew out of her in a spray as each of them humped the other for everything they were worth.

On and on he poled her, her whole body now racked with spasm after painful spasm. 'Oh, Mr Burglar!' she wailed, tears rolling down her cheeks at the intensity of the climax. 'Oh, that really hurts!'

Click-Clack! went the front door latch.

Bang! went the door itself.

'Tracie!' her husband called from the hall below. 'Tracie, are you upstairs?'

'Jesus Christ!' she shrieked in horror, stiffening like a board as she clapped her hands over her mouth. 'I'd completely forgotten the time!'

Tracie shot bolt upright as if she'd been punched in the stomach, causing the burglar to slide down towards the foot of the bed and out of her with an audible 'plop'. 'Quick,' she hissed in alarm. 'Get under the bed! And stay there till I tell you to come out. It's our only chance!' Fortunately, the bed was an old-fashioned springs and mattress affair, so there was room for him to hide.

'Tracie!' came another shout from below.

She glanced down at the floor, observing a pair of boney male buttocks frantically wriggling and worming their way out of sight. 'I'm in the bedroom, Peter,' she called back, rather weakly, hurriedly pulling the quilt cover up to her waist. 'I'm up here in bed.'

'Why's the television in the middle of the floor?' he asked as he walked into the room.

'Oh, er, I was just experimenting with the furniture. With re-arranging it. That's all . . .'

He gazed with evident interest at the lovely firm breasts that were pointing at him so enticingly. The television was forgotten. 'So you've been waiting up here for me?' he mused, starting to unbutton his shirt.

'Yes. I've been thinking about you all night.'

He kicked off his shoes and zoomed his trousers down to his feet. 'Well, I won't keep you waiting much longer,' he promised.

She slid down the bed and lay back, demurely pulling the covers up to her chin. Very carefully she settled her sticky bare bottom over the soaking wet patch on the sheet, praying she could cover enough. She was history if she failed.

Peter kept to his word. Within seconds he was standing beside her, nude and rigidly erect. Every bit as fine a specimen as the burglar who'd gone before. Or rather, gone underneath. Whatever his faults, Peter certainly wasn't lacking in the libido department, Tracie said to herself with a sigh. She reached out and gave him a welcoming squeeze. 'Ready already,' she murmured in admiration. 'You'll find that I am, too.' As she spoke, she mentally crossed her fingers and hoped for the best.

The bedclothes were yanked away without ceremony and Peter was on her and inside her in a flash. He knew full well that foreplay was totally unnecessary. He knew full well that she was always more than game. Why waste time on foreplay? she'd tell him. Why waste time when the real thing could be got underway at once?

'Ohhhhhh!!!' she screamed up at the ceiling, jerking back her head and staring wide-eyed into space. It was the same climax as before. The very same one the burglar had started. The only difference was that now her husband was continuing it for her, whilst the originator cowered fearfully under the bed. One penis had been substituted for another, and her insides had simply carried on as before. One moment the burglar had been porking her into the happy hereafter, less than sixty seconds later it was her husband. And, despite the intervening shock, her orgasm had just lain there inside her in wait. Just lain there in wait until it had, quite literally, been prodded back to life.

'Good God!' whistled Peter, pausing briefly. 'You've made it already!'

'Don't stop, Petie!' she cried, tears running down both cheeks once again. 'Screw me as hard as you can! I need all I can get!'

Peter was more than delighted to oblige, bouncing her up and down on the bed like some sort of life-sized rag doll.

Christ, she was keen, thought Peter. She didn't usually get herself into this sort of state until they'd been at it for a good half hour or more. But tonight he'd managed to bring her off with his very first stab. And she was showing no sign of stopping. In fact, the more he shafted her, the more he was making her howl!

The burglar flattened himself face down on the floor as best he could. But even so, the mattress pounded rhythmically into the small of his back. He was undecided as to whether to stick his fingers into his ears in order to dull her screams of pleasure, or use them to protect his mouth and nose from the prodigious quantities of dust under the bed. He did the latter, deciding he could put up with the sound of a man fucking his own wife into oblivion, even though that wife had so recently been impaled on him. It was better than risking the swirls of dust making him sneeze or cough.

Peter slid both hands underneath the cheeks of his wife's much-loved bottom. 'Hey!' he gasped in surprise. 'Your bum is absolutely soaked!'

The burglar held his breath and prayed. 'It's you,' she managed to croak. 'I've been playing with myself while waiting for you.'

Peter appeared happy with her explanation. The mattress started banging against the burglar once more. It seemed that he was still safe. For the time being, at least. He'd dearly have loved to tug his trousers and pants up from his ankles, but he dared not take the risk. The keys and coins in his pockets might have made a noise. Or the movement under the bed might have been detected. So, for the time being, he was forced to lie there, bare-arsed and not so brave, his hands over his mouth and nose and his genitals pressed stickily into the dusty carpet whilst he listened to the squeals and shrieks of the woman he himself had been dicking just a few moments before.

Tracie could feel him underneath her bottom each time Peter bore down. It definitely added to her enjoyment, knowing that he was there and taking everything in. And probably feeling more than a trifle frustrated, she mused. Did he still have a hard on, she wondered. It was quite possible that he had. Now that was an intriguing thought! One long, stiff dick up here on the bed rogering her rigid, another one throbbing away underneath and wishing it was.

The idea was really quite erotic

On and on went the humping and bumping. The humping of Tracie's much used middle section and the bumping of the burglar's back. Eventually it reached a crescendo. The mattress began to crash down on him at greater speed and with even greater weight than before.

'Oh Peter! Oh Peter! Oh Peter!'

'Yes! Yes! YES!' he bellowed at last.

For no more than a couple of minutes all three persons present lay silent and still, the burglar's seed now significantly diluted with Peter's. Then there came a stirring on top of the bed. 'Second helpings, Mrs Trix!' murmured Peter, squeezing her damper-than-ever rear end.

'Of course,' she giggled softly. 'I'll use my mouth to start with, if you like.'

'Oh, for God's sake!' the burglar groaned to himself in dismay.

One hour later, Tracie leant across the bed and stared closely at the comatose figure of her husband. His breathing was slow and regular and she felt sure he was soundly asleep. 'Peter!' she said in a loud whisper. 'Peter, are you awake?'

There was no response at all. Not a flicker of an eyelid, not a twitch of a muscle. 'Peter!' she said once more, but he didn't reply. Gently she shook him by the shoulder. 'Are you awake, Peter?' she asked yet again. 'Peter, can you hear me? Peter, are you awake? Peter, do you want to fuck me again? Peter, is there anyone there inside your head?'

Satisfied, at last, that all was well, Tracie swung herself off the bed and dropped silently onto all fours. 'Come on, Mr Burglar!' she hissed. 'Follow me . . . and don't make a sound.'

Bare-bottomed and brimming over with fluid, she wiggled her way out of the bedroom and waited on the landing, holding her breath. Thirty seconds later the intruder shuffled after her, his trousers and pants still round his ankles, his face a picture of alarm in the gloom.

'Downstairs!' she whispered, and set off. He pulled up

his clothes and then followed as quietly as he could. Fortunately the hall light was still ablaze, so at least he was able to see where he trod.

She turned to face him at the foot of the stairs, wrapping her arms round him and kissing him lightly on the lips. 'I'm sorry we were so long,' she said in a whisper. 'You must have been very uncomfortable?'

He squeezed her sticky wet bottom with both hands. 'It wasn't too bad. Better than being caught, anyway.'

'I told you I knew how to fuck.'

'You can say that again!' he agreed.

'I could feel you under the bed. I could feel my bum banging against you. It was rather good fun.'

'Yes,' he replied, unconvinced.

'Was it frustrating? Lying there listening to me having it off with Peter?'

'Yes, very. I spent the whole time wishing I was the one between your legs. Your husband's a very lucky man!'

'It made me feel really sexy. Being screwed by Peter and knowing you were there listening, I mean.'

'It just made me feel pissed off!'

She kissed him again and pressed her boobs into his chest. 'Poor Mr Burglar!' she cooed. 'And he didn't even manage to steal any swag!'

He patted her rear end quite firmly. 'But I did get my sexual problems solved. And I got a very nice slice of you in the process. I kept reminding myself of that fact while you were getting yourself dicked by your hubby. I kept telling myself that it was my spunk I could hear churning about inside you.'

She giggled softly. 'There was certainly plenty of that,' she agreed. 'Gallons of the stuff, in fact. Thank heavens Peter never gave it a second thought!'

'What he doesn't know can't hurt him,' the burglar said wisely, if not very originally.

She broke the embrace gently and turned to pick up a pen from the telephone shelf.

'Look,' she said, stooping over the shelf. 'I'm writing down our office address and phone number. Make sure you ring in the morning and ask for an appointment to see George Franks. I'll put his name down here, as well. He'll sort out your matrimonial problems, I'm sure.'

'Okay. Thanks very much.'

'You can always phone me there, if you want to arrange a spot of fun in the future. Just ask for Tracie – I'll write that down too.'

'I certainly will,' he said with feeling, staring down at the delightfully plump little bottom that wriggled slowly from side to side as she wrote. He was fascinated to note that it was liberally smeared with semen. Some of which was undoubtedly his own, he reflected with more than a degree of pride.

She took a bundle of five and ten pound notes from her handbag. It was her immoral earnings from earlier that night. 'And take these, too. Buy yourself some nice food. You look as if you're in need of a bit of nourishment.'

'I couldn't possibly,' he protested.

'Of course you can,' she snapped, pressing the notes into his hand. 'Just make sure you spend it on food, not designer jeans or fancy leather boots.'

'Well, thanks very much indeed.'

He moved towards the front door. 'Where do you think you're going?' she asked, raising an eyebrow.

'Pardon?'

'I thought we had a spot of unfinished business to see to.'

'Surely you don't mean . . . ?'

'Don't you want to carry on from where you left off?'

'But your husband . . . ?'

'He sleeps like a baby. Nothing wakes him once he's asleep. Not even the loudest alarm clock. There's nothing to worry about there. Really there isn't.'

'Christ Almighty! Surely you're joking?'

'I never joke about important matters like sex.'

'Jesus wept!'

'I'm sure you'll be able to manage it.'

'Oh, I can manage it all right. I'm still rock hard from earlier on.'

'Well, then. What are you waiting for? Let's make use of it now. You simply can't waste something as precious as that.'

'But surely?'

Tracie knelt on the floor on elbows and knees. Then she looked back over her shoulder and grinned up at the would-be burglar, wriggling her hips from side to side. 'Don't you fancy a spot of doggie-doggie?' she asked, very matter of fact.

It was a silly question. As she was destined to find out very soon.

Two minutes later, Peter opened his eyes and reached across the bed for his wife, intending to mount her again. She'd been so enthusiastic that the least he could do was to give her a little bit more. It was only proper and fair. And anyway, he was as hard as a brick . . .

But Tracie's side of the bed was empty. Very damp, but totally empty. He switched on the bedside light and glanced across the room. The door was wide open and he could tell that there was a light in the hall downstairs. Tracie must have gone down to the kitchen for a drink or a bite to eat. She sometimes did that if she wasn't able to sleep. Not that he knew her to do it very often, because normally he slept the sleep of the dead himself. Normally she could be anywhere doing anything, once he'd nodded off. It was most unusual for him to wake up in the middle of the night like this. The only possible reason was that he wanted to fuck her again. He'd fucked her twice already, but obviously his libido had decided that a third fuck was called for.

Perhaps he'd give her a surprise. Perhaps he'd creep downstairs, sneak up behind her, and then take her wherever she happened to be. She liked that sort of thing. It showed that he still fancied her something rotten. Even after two years of marriage.

Peter swung out of bed and walked silently through to the landing. There he paused for a moment, listening intently. He was sure he could hear her in the hall. Or at least, he was sure he could hear *something* downstairs in the hall. Something rather unusual. Something rather like heavy breathing, in fact. And a sort of slipping and squelching sound, too. Almost like the sound of . . .

He stepped forward and peered over the top of the stairs. And then he froze to the spot. There was his wife, fifteen feet away from him, stark naked and on elbows and knees. And being shagged, Fido-fashion, by some stranger who was kneeling behind her, his knees straddling hers. Not only was she being serviced, but she was being serviced extremely well. He could see the man's long, wet cock racing back and forth between the twin peaks of her upthrust bottom. And he could hear it, as well. Even over the noise of their puffing and panting, and the smack of groin on bouncing buttocks.

Peter opened his mouth, but was unable to raise so much as a squeak. He just stood there, staring in utter amazement at the sight of his own wife being shafted at the foot of the stairs. Shafted stiffly and with great vigour and enthusiasm on the part of the unknown man. Both of them were far too engrossed in their coupling to be aware of the fact that he was on the landing.

'That's it!' Tracie squawked under her breath, squirming her hips from side to side. 'Keep doing it just like that. Keep giving it to me that way!'

At last Peter was able to move. But just as he was about to charge down the staircase, he suddenly realised that his loins were wracked with intense excitement – with a thrill such as he'd never experienced before. Suddenly he realised that he was thoroughly enjoying the scene below. Enjoying it to the full. Enjoying the spectacle of Tracie being fucked from behind by somebody else. His own dick was longer and harder than he'd ever known. It was positively bursting at the seams. And it seemed to stretch even further every time he saw the stranger thrust lustily into her quim.

Peter stood still, transfixed, staring in fascination and exhilaration as the man piled into her – as the man pillaged and plundered the bounty that was supposed to be his. Why wasn't he angry? he wondered. Why hadn't he raced downstairs and kicked the bugger to pieces? Why was he still up here, watching this glistening, alien penis stuffing his wife for all it was worth?

He gazed down as Tracie started to climax. She was climaxing in exactly the same way that she did for him. She was climaxing with the same mannerisms precisely. The same groaning and moaning and the same thrashing of her head from side to side. And she was using the same terms of endearment, too. Why wasn't he furious about that? Why was his own body wracked with pleasure at the sight?

It was a sort of masochistic pleasure, he supposed. A sort of wounded pride of possession. But it was pleasure, nevertheless. A very great pleasure, nevertheless. Just once before he'd watched another couple, Jillie and Michael, making love. It had been fun, but nothing at all like this. Nothing like watching his very own wife getting it from someone else. Getting it from behind her back, just as he loved to give it to her himself. It was electrifyingly exciting to see this other sod staring down at the cheeks of her exquisitely shaped bare bottom whilst be banged away as hard as he could. It was the most electrifying and exhilarating experience of his life.

A few minutes later, as Peter watched his wife being pumped full of another man's seed, a germ of an idea began to form at the back of his mind. He stole back into the bedroom and lay down, deep in thought. A minute or so later he heard the front door close. Then he heard her walk up the stairs and into the bathroom. He'd have to shag her again when she came back to bed, he decided. He simply couldn't do without it. He'd pretend she'd just woken him up. Yes, he'd fuck her again tonight, and say nothing of what he'd seen. But tomorrow! Oh yes, tomorrow! Tomorrow she'd be in for a really, really big surprise . . . !

Chapter 7

Squash Balls
(Or, Banging It Against The Wall)

The next day, Friday, Tracie had a lunchtime date with Janet – Sir Roland's wife – at an exclusive health and squash club in the centre of town. Janet had rung her at the office during the morning, suggesting a game of squash. 'Are you sure there'll be a spare court?' Tracie had asked.

'Of course,' Janet had replied. 'After all, Rollie owns the place, and I manage it for him. It's just a bit of fun for me. I love squash, you see. Have you played before, Tracie?'

'Yes. Once or twice.'

It had been a bit of an understatement, thought Tracie, as she parked her car and headed for the oak-and-glass swing doors. Last year she'd been runner-up in the county championships. And she'd have won too, if she hadn't been a bit hung over from the party the night before. Normally she'd have beaten Jane Bullinger four times out of five. But that vodka and tonic at Jackie's party had taken its toll on her game. Not to mention its toll on her virtue, Tracie giggled to herself. Fancy her letting that saucy Andrew Waddle have his evil way with her in the downstairs cloakroom!

Janet was waiting for Tracie in the reception area, looking absolutely scrumptious in a silver-blue trouser suit that simply screamed 'expensive!'

'Hi,' said Janet, with a genuine smile of delight.

'Hi to you too,' replied Tracie, flashing her a sexy grin.

'It's nice to see you again so soon.'

'Yes. The feeling is entirely mutual.'

The changing room was plushly carpeted and almost as luxurious as Sir Roland's living quarters at the Royal Hotel. The girls began to strip.

'Did you have a good fuck last night?' giggled Janet. 'With Peter, I mean?'

'Yes. But not quite like I said I would.'

Janet peered intently at Tracie's sexy little bare bottom as she stooped over her squash bag, rummaging for her kit. 'You didn't get him to spank you? In just your stockings and suspenders and high heels?'

'No,' replied Tracie, stepping daintily into a very small pair of smart white shorts. 'He was late getting home from work, so we didn't have time for that.'

'But you gave him a good time, anyway?'

Tracie grinned again. 'I think he was quite satisfied by the time we got to sleep.'

'Do you fuck him every night?'

'Of course. Every night and morning. And whenever else we can. He's really a bit of a stud.'

'You look gorgeous in those shorts!' breathed Janet, staring closely at the tiny pair of sports shorts now stretched so delightfully across Tracie's perfectly moulded cheeks.

Tracie looked at her squash opponent sitting there on the bench seat, unashamedly naked below the waist. 'Not as nice as you look with your hot little fanny smiling up at me.'

'Hot and wet,' Janet admitted at once.

'We'd better get on court. I think you're starting to feel horny.'

'Aren't you?'

'I'm not going to tell you. I got the distinct impression that it's okay for you to do what you like, on condition Sir Roland's there and approves. Am I right?'

'You're too sharp by far, Tracie. Really you are.'

'Does he know we're here together?'

'We're only playing squash.'

'Not yet we're not. Come on, let's get out on court.'

'I'd rather we stayed here.'

'I know. I can tell that much.' Once again she stared down at the pretty pink lips that nestled so openly and moistly between the tops of the other girl's thighs. 'I mean, I can see that much.'

'It was lovely yesterday afternoon,' Janet sighed wistfully. 'In bed with you, I mean. You made me come so often. And so hard . . .'

'Janet!' Tracie hissed in mock anger. 'Get up, get some knickers on, and get on court!'

Janet won the toss and served from the right-hand court. A hard, low serve into the corner. With considerable skill, Tracie returned it to a good length along the backhand wall. Janet dug it out with a boast that was low over the tin. But the boast was returned with a good length lob. Janet replied with a cross-court dive, only to find Tracie in place with a drop shot into the front right-hand corner. This time it was Janet's turn to lob. But it wasn't high enough and Tracie killed it with an overhead smash.

'You *have* played before!' both girls said together, with a genuine smile of admiration.

'But I think you're going to win,' added Janet, collecting the ball and handing it to her opponent. 'Will you kiss me with your tongue if you do?'

'Only if you lose three-love,' grinned Tracie, stepping into the forehand box before unleashing a good smash serve.

'How unfair!' giggled Janet, putting her backhand drive deep into the tin.

'Concentrate!' Tracie advised her firmly, retrieving the ball from the floor. 'Don't talk while you're playing. And stop thinking about sex.'

'It's very difficult. Those shorts are so small and tight. They make me itch to get my hands inside them.'

Tracie looked at her sternly. 'If you don't get on with the game, I'll have to use the handle of this racket across your fat little bum!'

'That would be lovely!' enthused Janet. 'Ouch!' she howled a split second later, as Tracie was entirely true to her word. 'Okay. All right. I'm getting on with it right now.'

Tracie won the first game 9-7. It had been closely fought, but she'd never really felt in fear of losing. Janet was a fine player, but just didn't have the same killer instinct that had always been a part of Tracie's sporting life. They stepped out into the corridor behind the court, towels in hand because they were both flushed and perspiring freely.

'You play really well,' Janet said with feeling. 'I'll be lucky to get a game.'

'You need to be more focused. You can play just as well as I can. Probably better. But I'm not convinced that you really want to win. I think you're quite happy just to play well and come second.'

Janet gazed into her face. 'You look so beautiful when you're all hot and sweaty,' she murmured.

'Do you see what I mean?' laughed Tracie. 'When I'm playing I spend the full forty-five minutes thinking about nothing but the tactics I should use in order to win.'

Two young men stood behind the glass in the upstairs gallery, watching with interest as the girls, clad in their skimpy white sports wear, raced hither and thither with graceful athleticism, firm round boobs and bottoms joggling sweetly back and forth across the court.

'What a magnificent sight!' sighed the one on the left. 'What couldn't I do to either of them!'

'You wouldn't get anywhere with Janet,' said his friend. 'She's far too nervous about her husband finding out. I know. I've tried it on once or twice.'

'What happened?'

'Well, I could tell she'd have loved to step straight out of her panties. But, as I said, she was far too scared of being caught out by that mega-wealthy bugger she married.'

'Do you see the way she keeps looking at that dark-haired piece of totty? You could almost believe she fancies the wench.'

'Perhaps she does. It's not unheard of, you know.'

'Such a waste! Two fuckable women like that!'

'I've shagged the other one, though. Tracie something-or-other, that's her name. She was as keen as mustard. No way is she into women. Except, possibly, as a temporary diversion, I suppose.'

* * *

'He wanted to fuck me so badly,' giggled Janet. 'The blond boy up there, I mean. I felt really sorry for him.'

'You needn't,' said Tracie, walking over to the backhand court, ball in hand. 'Last month I let him have enough of me to keep him going for at least a year!'

'I envy you, Tracie. I simply daren't do that sort of thing. Rollie has eyes and ears everywhere. He'd know about it before I'd even pulled up my knickers. Men gossip so much about who they've had and exactly what they've done to them.'

'So Rollie doesn't mind you having a woman, but doesn't want you to get yourself shagged?'

'Oh, no. He doesn't mind that. I can shag whoever I like. Provided it's at one of our wife-swapping parties, I mean. But not anywhere else.'

'Wife-swapping parties?'

'Yes. Well, group sex parties, really. Just good clean dirty fun. Sex games and that sort of thing. Would you like to come to the next one? It's on Sunday.'

'I'd love to,' she replied. 'But Peter would be the problem. No way would he agree to anything like that. I have to get my oats strictly on the quiet.'

'Are you sure? You'd be a really big hit. And if Peter's the stud you say he is, he'd have a wonderful time too. Are you sure you can't persuade him to come along?'

'Absolutely positive, Janet. I'm really sorry to say.'

Tracie's backhand was working well, both cross-court and straight back along the wall. Janet tried her best to put her lustful thoughts at the back of her mind and concentrate on the game. But she didn't find it easy. She just longed to run her hands all over Tracie's firm, athletic body. She kept remembering the great time they'd had the previous afternoon. Tracie had been such an expert lover, she thought to herself, chasing after a cross-court drive and just managing to reply with a lob. The way she'd loved and licked pussy had simply been out of this world! She'd never been eaten so exquisitely. She'd tried her best to reciprocate, of course. And she could only hope that she'd given Tracie half the pleasure she herself had gained. She supposed she probably had. After all, they'd made each other come time after time.

Oh, those lovely tight white shorts of Tracie's! How beautifully they highlighted the shape of her incredibly cheeky bum! More than half of it was outside them, of course. She'd really love to stop the game and run her lips and tongue over those pert little cheeks. That would really give those lusty young lads in the viewing gallery something to goggle at!

'Why on earth did you play that boast?' asked Tracie, picking up the ball from just in front of the tin. 'You left yourself wide open to the drop shot.'

'I was thinking about your bottom,' admitted Janet.

Tracie dropped her racket, suddenly struck with a fit of the uncontrollable giggles. 'Well, at least you're honest,' she gasped at length.

Tracie won the second game and the girls retired to the corridor to towel themselves down. 'I think you're every bit as randy as I am,' Tracie said with a knowing grin.

'I'm far too randy for my own good,' agreed Janet.

'Do you find that sometimes your pussy's so hot you don't know how you can bear it?'

'Yes. Often.'

'I just have to fuck when I feel like that. Anyone who's available will do. I can't help it. Sometimes I wish I could . . .'

'Don't you find your pussy leaves you alone for a while after you've been with a girl?'

'Yes, I do,' Tracie replied at once. 'Yes, that's perfectly right. I'm much calmer and more at peace with my body after something like that. Do you suppose that's because it's not exactly sex when you do it with a girl? It's more an expression of, well, a sort of sisterly type of affection, I suppose. An expression of the very different sort of love that one girl can feel for another.'

'We must try and find the opportunity to spend the night

together,' whispered Janet. 'To spend a whole night together in bed.'

'That would be nice,' she replied, tenderly running a fingertip down the side of Janet's pretty face.

'I don't know how she does it,' said the blond spectator, nodding at Tracie. 'Gets herself laid so often, I mean. Her husband is incredibly suspicious and possessive. He watches her like a hawk. Yet she's always stepping out of her knickers for other men.'

'I guess he just can't be in two places at once.'

'That's true, of course. When she's safely on her own, she takes whatever opportunity she can to get out of her kit. And brother, what a shag! I thought she was going to wear my prick away!'

'I wish she'd get out of those shorts for me. Just look at the lovely little bum on it! Have you ever seen anything more tasty?'

'I have to admit I haven't. Although Janet's is in the same class.'

'Yes. But she keeps it under wraps.'

'That's true.'

'Oh, look at that! Did you see how your ex-shagee just squeezed Lady Rayke's aristocratic arse?'

'Yes. Nice, wasn't it? I think it means that the match is over.'

As indeed it was. The girls returned to the dressing room, hot and wet, towels and rackets in hand.

'Well played!' Janet said truthfully. 'You really deserved to win.'

'I've told you why,' replied Tracie, dropping her gear on the floor and then lowering the seat of the tiny but exquisitely filled white shorts onto the nearest bench. 'You could beat me if you really wanted to.'

'Really? Could I use a cane? And also a strap?'

Both girls giggled. Then they peeled off their sweat-soaked clothes. Janet glanced tentatively across at Tracie, taking in her nakedness, and then looked her straight in the eye. 'Shall we take a shower together?' she asked.

'I'd be very disappointed if we didn't,' Tracie replied softly, stepping forward and wrapping both arms around Janet's waist, before lowering her hands to the other girl's bottom and starting to explore the silky smooth flesh.

Whilst Tracie was in the shower, kneeling in front of Janet, Peter was in a taxi heading towards Piccadilly Circus. He alighted outside the Regent Palace Hotel and headed north on foot. He was more than pleased with his morning's work. It had taken at least a dozen phone calls, but at last all his arrangements for the evening were now in place. He couldn't wait for the hours to tick by. It would seem an eternity, he knew. God, he could only hope and pray that no new contracts landed on his desk during the course of the afternoon! He'd rather give up his job than miss what lay in store.

'That was very good,' breathed Janet, fifteen minutes later, stepping into her smart blue trousers. 'It's a pity you have to get back to the office. We could go to your house and spend the afternoon in bed.'

'I wish I could, Janet. But I had rather a lot of time off yesterday. As you might remember? I simply have to catch up with my work. I simply have to get back there.'

'I know. It's all right for me. Married to a multi-millionaire, I mean. I know you have a living to earn.'

Tracie kissed her briefly with her tongue, then patted her affectionately between the tops of her legs. 'Peter doesn't need my salary, actually. He's pretty well paid. But I'd hate not to have a job. All those men, if nothing else.'

'You shag them, do you, Tracie?'

'What do you think?'

'I think you're at it whenever you can. Just make sure that Peter never finds out.'

'Don't worry, I've plenty of regard for the health of my hide.'

'I'll see you again, won't I, Tracie?'

'Of course you will,' breathed Tracie, drawing the other

girl towards her and then kissing her passionately once more.

Janet could feel herself lubricating heavily, but decided not to worry about the fact that she wore no knickers under the trousers of her expensive suit. She felt her body melt all the way into Tracie's as the long, lingering kiss continued. She really must find the chance to spend some time with this gorgeous girl. She'd never felt as hot for anyone as she did for Tracie. Perhaps, if she spoke to Rollie, she could persuade him to let them have a proper affair? She and Tracie, she meant. A proper affair, whereby they spent time on their own. Just the two of them. No husbands in the bed as well.

Chapter 8

Surprise

When Peter at last arrived home that Friday evening, his first task was to conceal his recent purchase behind the television set in the lounge. It was a present for Tracie. A surprise present for his wife. Then he strolled through to the kitchen where she was cooking dinner. She was wearing a short T-shirt and white G-string knickers, plus a pair of high heels. She often dressed that way around the house, for Peter's benefit. He felt the normal pang of pleasure that he always experienced whenever he caught a glimpse of her beautifully turned bare bottom. But this time he felt it far more strongly than usual. And, of course, he knew precisely the reason why.

He kissed her softly on the lips and put both arms around her waist. Tracie could feel the heat and urgency of his erection pressing against her stomach, and smiled knowingly to herself. Someone was very pleased to see her. Or rather, some two . . .

Peter ran his hands over her buttocks. 'John's coming round later to watch the snooker,' he murmured, kneading the firm smooth cheeks in both hands as he spoke. 'And also to discuss the final arrangements for Tuesday night's stag party at the cricket club.'

'I'll put some jeans on,' she said at once.

'A skirt will be fine,' he said casually, pouring himself a beer.

Tracie was mildly surprised. He knew that she only had micro mini-skirts in her wardrobe. There was nothing that wasn't short and revealing. She had only those sexy little skirts that he'd not been keen on ever since they'd got engaged. Those skirts he'd loved to letch at to start with,

119

but which had made him jealous after a while. Why were so many men like that, she wondered. Why did they really cream their jeans at the sight of you decked out in your sexiest clothes, before they knew you, yet object like hell once they'd managed to get you out of your knickers a couple of times? Did they really think that they owned you, just because you'd let them get a leg over you once or twice?

Tracie slipped into one of her favourite skirts. It was the blue one that buttoned all the way up the front and covered the crotch of her knickers with no more than half an inch to spare. What a pretty sight she'd make when she bent forward, she giggled to herself. Wearing only her G-string panties, that is. And three-inch high heels, of course, to add even more to the effect. Still, Peter had been quite definite about her wearing a skirt, rather than jeans. But even so, she'd be a little bit careful not to upset him. She'd take care not to flirt too much with his friend. She was always prudent enough not to do that sort of thing when Peter was anywhere at hand. John was hunky and handsome and welcome to get into her knickers whenever he wanted. But, as always, she'd be very careful not to let Peter know she felt that way. Would John ever make a pass at her? she wondered thoughtfully. He'd never done so in the past. He'd always been a complete gentleman towards her. Unfortunately. But then again, she didn't know him all that well. She was sure she could get somewhere with him if she had him all to herself for an hour or so behind safely locked doors. And, according to her friend Jackie, it would be very worth her while to succeed. Jackie had entertained him once or twice when her husband had been out of town, and she'd said that John had by far the biggest cock she'd ever seen. And that was saying quite a lot, bearing in mind how Jackie had played the field. A good ten or eleven inches, Jackie had reckoned, and thicker than his wrist as well. A real pussy-stretcher by the sound of it, Tracie reflected wistfully, as she stepped lightly down the stairs. The sort of weapon that would do her wonders whenever she felt really in need.

And, at the totally opposite end of the scale, there was always the prospect of spending some time with Janet. That would be really nice. She could tell that Janet was as keen on her, or even keener, as she was on Janet. It would be really lovely to have some time alone together.

John watched the well-filled seat of Tracie's blue mini-skirt swish its way sexily across the lounge. This was going to be an interesting evening, he said to himself. Very interesting. And most unusual. But if that was what Peter wanted, then who was he to argue? Who was he to refuse his life-long friend?

'Everything's arranged for Tuesday night,' said John.
'Real ale?' asked Peter. 'And decent grub as well?'
'Yes. Plenty of both. None of the horrible fizzy beer they usually serve at the club house. And we're budgeting four pounds a head on the food.'
'What about the strippers?' asked Tracie. 'Peter wasn't very keen on the ones he booked last year.'
'We've gone to a different agency,' said John. 'This year we should be in for more of a treat.'
'I hope so,' giggled Tracie. 'Last year's girls put Peter off sex for the rest of the night.'
'That was the booze,' laughed Peter.
John caught the very briefest glimpse of pink bare cheeks peeping out at him as Tracie stooped to choose a magazine from the rack beside the fireplace. Pink bare cheeks separated very saucily by a tiny white G-string, he noted. There was a definite twitch inside his Y-fronts as she straightened up and then sat down demurely on a chair to read. Had she realised the nice little flash she'd just given him? Could she see the fairly discernible bulge in the front of his trousers getting bigger by the moment?

Peter reflected on the rather special present he'd bought for Tracie that afternoon and hidden behind the TV. The very thought made his head spin and his penis poke even further up towards his chin. But for the moment he and John would just laze here in their armchairs, sipping beer from a can whilst watching the snooker and wondering exactly how Tracie might react to that other surprise present. The one that John had brought along in the front of his jeans tonight. The one that had won prizes at school for its size. And, in later years, the one that had sent many a young lady home bandy-legged and sore. Peter glanced across at his wife's long, shapely thighs as she sat at the table and read her magazine, blissfully unaware of the fact that she, not the snooker, would soon be the centre of attention. He hoped she wouldn't be too sore for too long.

Tracie came back from the kitchen and placed more cans of beer on the table between the men. 'The snooker is boring,' yawned Peter, reaching out and taking her hands as she stood beside him. He turned towards John. 'Let's do something that's a bit more fun.'

'If you say so,' grinned John, turning off the TV without being asked.

Peter stood up and pulled his wife towards him. For the second time that evening she could feel the bulk of his hard penis pressing firmly against her stomach. 'Not in front of the children!' she giggled, unable to back away because of his hug.

He patted her bottom several times through the seat of the skirt. 'Sounds bare to me,' remarked John, who was sitting directly behind her.

'That's all you know,' she retorted lightly over her shoulder. 'I'm respectable enough underneath.'

'I know bare bum when I hear it,' persisted John. 'You're naughty and knickerless under that skirt.'

'No, I'm not!' she cried with mock indignation. 'That just shows how much you know.'

'I don't believe a word of it. There isn't a stitch of material covering your bum.'

She turned and stuck her tongue out at him. 'You're no expert, Mr Bachelor Man. If you were married, you'd know that you could be wrong.'

'I'm not married and I know that I'm right.'

'Well, see for yourself!' said Peter, suddenly tugging the hem of the skirt right up to her waist and beyond.

'Peter!' she squealed in surprise, still securely held in his arms and unable to resist.

John gazed in admiration at the pretty pink buttocks so prominently on display. Buttocks that were entirely naked apart from the tiny white G-string that hid only her crotch from his view. 'I suppose you could call that being respectable,' he mused. 'But only just.'

Tracie wriggled but was unable to break free or cover her blushing bare bottom. 'Peter!' she protested again, perplexed at the way he was exposing her to his friend. Exposing that cheeky part of her person that he'd always been so keen for her to keep safely under wraps.

But Peter took no notice. 'Isn't that a lovely sight?' he asked conversationally.

'Gorgeous!' John agreed, with a very definite catch in his throat.

Still using one arm to hold her tightly against him, Peter ran his spare hand over the honey-smooth cheeks of her pouting bare bottom. 'Just feel the quality for yourself,' he invited. John was quick to lean forward in his chair and accept the invitation.

'Peter!' she squawked again, as both men began to stroke her. 'What on earth do you think you're doing?'

She was utterly amazed at this turn of events. She'd never expected that Peter would do anything like this. He was always so obsessively jealous and possessive. Now here he was inviting his closest friend to feel and fondle her almost totally bare behind! And still he ignored her objections. 'Smoother than satin,' breathed John, taking a very ample handful of flesh and squeezing it firmly. 'You're an exceptionally lucky man, my friend.'

'And what are friends for but to share?' Peter asked earnestly. 'To share and share alike.'

Tracie couldn't believe her ears. She simply couldn't believe it was real. Peter had never acted this way before. Totally the opposite, in fact. Once he'd even complained bitterly about someone patting her bottom on the dance floor! It was all incredibly weird.

After a while Peter ran a fingertip down the long deep cleft between her cheeks, drawing the G-string all the way down to the tops of her thighs. 'What are you doing?' she whispered, closing her eyes in a mixture of embarrassment and desire. From his seated position behind her, John would now have a clear view of her most private possession. A possession which she knew was already wide open and gushing with love-juice.

By way of response, Peter ran his hand down round her buttocks and started to stroke the lips of her quim. He could tell at once that she was beautifully open and lubricated. 'Why don't you join us?' he said to John.

'Peter!' she gasped again, but to no avail.

Now both of them were fingering her slowly and gently from behind. Both of them were exploring the inside of her hot little hole. Exploring it more and more deeply. Now both of them could feel her juices seeping out of her and running down the palms of their hands. Tracie kept her eyes tightly shut, but allowed herself to begin to enjoy the sensation, to savour the pleasure of having two men poking and probing within. She was still at a loss to know what had happened to Peter, but the point now seemed less important. She wrapped her arms right round him, resting her face on his shoulder and letting her body respond.

Now she could feel a fingertip teasing her bottom, and another tickling her clit. More fingers arrived on the scene. As far as she could tell there were now four deep in her overflowing pussy and two others just inside her bum. She began to move in time with the invading fingers, slowly to begin with, but gradually picking up pace. Then she began to thrust back with her hips, pushing the fingers even deeper, before wriggling as hard as she could.

Back and forth she pushed and wriggled. The harder she forced herself back against the men, the more firmly they replied in kind, their fingers now pushing as far inside as they'd go. Very quickly she became flushed in the face and her breathing started to labour. Frantically she thrust herself back onto the invading fingers, groaning with pleasure each time they filled her. Then she pushed forward once more, jamming her clitoris against the bulk of Peter's erection.

Back and forth she thrust, filling her pussy and bottom with fingers, then crushing her clit. Backwards and forwards, backwards and forwards, crushing her clit against her husband's hardness and then stretching her nice little holes. 'Oh, Peter!' she cried suddenly, hugging him to her with all her strength. 'Oh my God, Peter! You're starting to make me come!'

'Come, then,' Peter said softly. 'Come as much as you like.'

As soon as she'd finished, the men stripped her down to her high heels in a matter of seconds. Then Peter sat back in his armchair and drew her down onto his lap, cupping his hands round her ripe young breasts. She lay with the back of her head on his chest, her lovely long legs stretched out in front of her.

'John's hungry,' murmured Peter, as his old school chum knelt on the floor at her feet. 'I think you should give him something to eat.'

She parted her thighs in delight and allowed John to lean forward and push his tongue as far inside as he could. She bucked wildly and shrieked at the top of her voice. Peter watched in fascination as John proceeded to guzzle with greed. He stared with mounting excitement at the glistening lips and chin of his friend, and at the way he was now spearing her hard with his tongue. He also listened to the sound of John's supper. To the slurp of dripping wet pussy being tongued and then vigorously chewed.

Tracie twisted her head towards Peter and kissed him hard on the lips. A long, sweet kiss of passion and heat. As they kissed, he could feel John's lips and tongue gobbling her insides. He could feel them in the sense that, through the kiss, he could feel her body responding to the intimate attentions of John's mouth. He could feel her body responding through the heat and passion of her kiss. For Peter it was a sensational experience. He was actually feeling his wife being licked off.

A few moments later Tracie was climaxing all over again, even though the last one had only just finished. And the more she climaxed, the more John chomped and chewed – giving her no respite, driving her from one state of abandon to another as he gorged on her piping-hot flesh.

Peter thought that his penis was going to burst. That it was literally going to burst apart at the seams, not simply spew out sperm. It had never felt so swollen with blood. He was sure it must be suffering some sort of damage from the way that it thrust itself violently upwards. And still the feasting continued, causing Tracie to writhe from side to side on his lap as she groaned and thrust forward with her groin.

He could almost taste her himself. Watching and hearing John eating her alive has almost given Peter the taste. The delicately salty flavour of her juices and soft, yielding flesh. And he loved the way she responded. The way she wriggled and squealed for more mouth. The way she gripped John's hair in both hands and tried to force him further inside. Once again Peter thought of the surprise behind the television, and felt his pulse race even faster.

John licked and lapped and chewed. She was unbelievably juicy and succulent, he thought to himself, as he buried his face deep between her thighs. He was swallowing mouthfulls of her delicious elixir, but it was instantly replaced with more of the same.

Her clitoris was huge. Twice as large when he'd first fingered it. It seemed to swell each time he sucked it between his lips. And then, when he returned to his main course, she was hotter and wetter than ever. She was more than ready for shafting. But she'd have to wait for a while. He was relishing his meal far too much to stop yet. It was a shame he had to keep coming up for air. If he had his way, he'd stay inside her forever, gobbling her delightful fare.

Tracie was in seventh heaven. She'd long forgotten to wonder why this was happening. She was just delighted that it was. It was such a thrilling feeling, being cuddled and cossetted on her husband's lap whilst his friend of many years knelt between her legs and scoffed his fill. It was truly unbelievable having Peter assisting in her debauch. Having him watching her every move, and knowing that he was loving all that he saw. It more than doubled the effect on her. It made her want to die of pleasure and lustful desire. She could feel one huge orgasm after another slamming right through her body as John's mouth sucked and devoured. One huge orgasm after another as John's mouth worked away on willing wet pussy whilst her husband kissed and caressed her face, her stomach and boobs.

Peter spread her out on her back on the carpet whilst John stepped casually out of his clothes. She looked up at him and gasped in awe. His penis was truly enormous! It thrust itself upwards almost as far as his breast bone. He was even larger than Sir Roland! No wonder his nickname at school had been 'Long John'! She'd never seen anything like it. And his testicles! They resembled two billiard balls! There must be gallons of the stuff inside them. Gallons of her favourite liquid refreshment . . .

Peter sat on a chair by the table where he could attain a perfect view of the porking to come. It would be one hell of a sight. John was going to stretch her in every direction, and then some more as well. He wanted to be able to see it happening and, at the same time, study the look on her face. It would be interesting to compare it with the way she reacted to him.

As John started to push, she spread her legs wider and wider, fearing there wouldn't be room. For a moment the mighty tip of his weapon was crushed against her vaginal lips and seemed to be going no further. She adjusted her position slightly. 'Try it again!' she whispered. He backed up a fraction and then heaved forward again. 'Gently!' she squawked, as the initial penetration was finally made.

John paused where he was, waiting for her to recover her nerve. Tracie goggled down at her groin. She felt quite full already, even though she could see that there was a massive column of iron-hard flesh waiting outside. At last she relaxed and looked over at Peter. He stared back, holding her gaze while John slowly slithered further inside. He could read the pleasure and the pain in her face. And he could hear the protesting squeak of her internal juices as the incoming penis forced her wide open. Tracie continued to stare into his eyes all the time that John pushed forward, even when he was all the way home. She supposed she was trying to tell him something. She wasn't quite sure what it was. She supposed she felt she ought to involve him for as long as she could. She was his wife, after all. And she had to admit that it was a really sensual and sexy experience, staring into her husband's face whilst crammed full of another man.

Peter could tell that she wanted him to look into her face. He could sense that she wanted him to perceive how much she was enjoying having him there watching John stretch her as tight as a drum. Red in the face, eyes bright with desire, she grimaced and with some difficulty, managed to blow him a kiss. He smiled back at her and did the same. Then John pressed into her even harder, determined to penetrate her as deeply as he could, determined to leave not even the tiniest part of himself outside. 'Ouch!' she mouthed painfully. 'Ouch!' she gasped aloud, as he did it again. But that was his lot. No matter how much he forced and pushed, he was inside her as far as could be. There was nothing left for him to impart. Nothing more for him to embed. 'You're hurting me,' she whispered, still looking at Peter. Then, as John remained massive but stock-still inside her, she felt her body burst into bright, violent orgasm. An orgasm prompted by the pleasure of the pain.

At last he started to shaft her, slowly and steadily, using long even strokes of great force. She held Peter's gaze as long as possible. But in less than a minute she was forced to close her eyes and concentrate on how she was being so mightily extended.

Peter looked down at her groin, fascinated to be able to see the great trunk of penis sliding in and out. Gingerly, she started to gyrate her hips in time with each stroke – just very slightly and carefully, not daring to apply any power to her movements. Peter watched the glistening beads of her juices coating John, as well as trickling out of her. Her face was a picture of agonized concentration as the most terrifying turking she'd ever experienced continued at a smooth, easy pace.

Even in her overwrought state, Tracie could feel Peter's eyes all over her. She could feel them hungrily devouring every detail of how she was being so excruciatingly dicked. The thought made her lubricate even more, which in turn helped to ease her plight. Suddenly she felt her confidence in her vagina return with a surge. 'I'll show the big bastard!' she thought, referring of course to John. She thrust up forcefully with her groin, meeting him halfway and ramming the huge swollen knob of his member hard against the neck of her womb. 'Come on, Mr Bachelor Man!' she muttered bravely. 'Surely you can do better than this.?'

John rose to the challenge at once, sliding his oversized horn of plenty back and forth at speed. Now he was really driving her wild, making her thrash from side to side on the carpet as he skated in and out of her as fast as he could. This was truly unbelievable, she gasped to herself. It felt as it he was pushing all the way up into her head!

She opened her legs as wide as she could. But, even so, he was still stretching her intolerably. She thought about Peter, about how he would be sitting there watching her closely as she writhed about on the end of John's monstrosity. Once again the thought helped her to overcome her problems, and she seemed to lubricate a little more. So she kept Peter firmly in mind as she moved slowly up and down with her hips. Now she could bear John slightly better. Nevertheless, she didn't think she'd taunt him again. That would be decidedly unwise.

Another spasm started to shake her. And this time she was actually enjoying it. 'Oh, Mr Bachelor Man!' she moaned, feeling her insides turn to fire as the climax went on and on. With some difficulty she opened her eyes and looked over at Peter on the armchair, noting at once that his gaze was now glued to her groin. She could see his own erection quite clearly through the front of his trousers. A large lump pressed tightly against the material. Was it her imagination or was he larger than normal? She really needed to see him naked to tell.

Was there any prospect of that happening? Or would he be quite happy just to sit there and watch her being turned inside-out by this tree-trunk of a man?

Ow! Ouch! It was starting to hurt again, despite the fact that she was so well oiled!

'Can you slow down a bit?' she gulped. 'I'm sorry, I was only joking when I asked if you could do better. I won't be cheeky again.'

John immediately complied. 'So I'm the boss, am I?' he asked.

'Yes, of course.'

'And Peter as well?'

'Yes, and Peter as well.'

'Is that any better?'

'Yes. Much better. It's much easier now.'

'I want to have you from behind,' breathed John, several minutes later.

'Of course.'

Slowly John withdrew until he had voided her completely. Once again she was amazed at his length, at the amount of brawn he'd just pulled out of her. How on earth had she managed to cope?

'How do you want it?' she croaked.

'On elbows and knees, I think. That sweet little bum is just too nice to have hidden away underneath you.'

Despite the circumstances, she blushed. 'Like this, you mean?'

'Yes, that's fine.'

John settled heavily on her back, his knees straddling hers and his penis scalding hot as it pressed hard against the cheekiest part of her bottom. He cupped his hands round her breasts. They were full and weighty and he could feel the long pointed nipples boring into his palms as he squeezed. He eased backwards and adjusted his position. Now she could feel the tip of his member poking against the lips of her quim. The wide-open lips of her quim. She waited for him, head down and bottom high, like a supplicant before the Sultan. 'Hold tight, Mrs Trix!' he murmured, at the same time pushing powerfully forward with his groin. She opened her mouth to groan, but found that she had to fight for breath instead. With one forceful push that giant rod of flesh had embedded itself right up to the root inside her. Right up to the root in less time than it takes to tell.

Slowly he started to pole her again, pulling himself almost all the way out and then sliding powerfully back with one long thrust. Another glow of orgasm started to build. Very quickly it overcame her, leaving her shivering and shuddering with the pleasure of his burning-hot penis crammed so tightly inside. Now that she was again getting used to his dimensions, she began wriggling her hips from side to side against each incoming stroke. John stared down at the sweetly dimpled cheeks of her bottom. He gazed in approval as his long, wet stalk worked industriously back and forth between them. It was one of the most satisfying sights he'd ever seen in his life. Gradually he picked up the pace. Slap! Slap! Slap! went groin against soft bouncy buttocks, as he gripped her tightly round the waist and smacked hard into the cheeks of her bouncing rear end. Suddenly she felt him starting to spurt, hotly and profusely, with a power she could scarcely believe. Instantly her own climax was revived. She closed her eyes and groaned loudly as the pangs of orgasm raced through her. Still gushing sperm, John thrust harder and harder into the tightness of her vagina, stoking up her climax and making her squeal and squawk.

A few seconds later she realised that he was still fully erect. As rigid and rampant as ever, even though he'd only just shot his lot. He hadn't slackened in size, or speed, despite the fierce ejaculation. She could feel his hot sticky effusion dripping down the inside of each thigh, mixed and mingled with her own juices. And the more he shafted her, the more he expelled. John, meanwhile, listened with much gratification to the slurping sound of his organ inside her, now more evident than before, because she was even wetter.

Now John was humping as fast as he could, and Tracie was taking it without pain or protest. He concentrated his attention on the silky-smooth buttocks into which he was slamming his groin, and also on the tightness of the sweet little pussy he was stretching as far as it would go. On and on he shafted, determined that she should have as much cock from him as anyone who had given her in the past.

Half an hour later John was on his way out of the house, leaving Tracie curled up on the sofa, semen trickling thickly from the corner of her mouth, as well as down both thighs. It had been the biggest tool she'd ever known, she said to herself in awe. Easily the biggest. She'd never felt so extended in her life. But she'd managed to cope, more or less. Somehow she'd managed to survive. And somehow she'd managed to get the huge round tip right into the back of her throat, and suck. Quite how, she wasn't entirely certain.

Good grief! When she thought about that cock! And how it had swamped her but still stayed hard. How it had remained rock hard and simply carried on as before! A second tidal wave had sluiced into her, and she'd fully expected that would be the end of the matter. But no. Only a minute or so later he'd been hard once again. Hard and filling her mouth, almost dislocating her jaw as she'd yawned wide open to accommodate him. A few minutes later after that, there'd been another vast flood of fluid, filling her mouth and pouring out of both sides. Fluid that had been beautifully thick and creamy, like hot salty porridge. She'd gulped and gobbled as fast as she could, but hadn't been able to swallow it all. She'd noticed the look of excitement on Peter's face as he'd watched her unable to keep up with the outflow.

As the front door banged shut, Tracie looked up at Peter. There was no need for her to voice the question she held in her eyes. 'I saw you last night,' he said softly. 'In the middle of the night. Shagging someone at the foot of the stairs.'

'I'm sorry, Peter,' she whispered, unable to look at him in the eye any longer.

'I couldn't believe what I was seeing. And I certainly couldn't believe how I felt. I was just about to charge downstairs and tear you both apart, when I suddenly realised I was enjoying what I could see. Really enjoying it, I mean. Even more than screwing you myself. It was just so incredibly enthralling. It turned me on more than I've ever been before.'

She looked him in the face once more. '. . . Peter . . .' she stammered, unsure what to say.

'And it was just the same tonight. Even more so, because this time you knew I was watching, and I felt that you were doing it for me just as much as for him.'

'It was wonderful having you there,' she said truthfully. 'I've never known such a thrill. It was like having two men inside me at the same time.'

'From now on you can fuck anyone you like,' Peter said slowly. 'Anyone at all. Provided I'm there to see it, or you tell me all about it. And provided that, sometimes, you accept a little present from me afterwards. The same little present I'm going to give you right now. You wouldn't believe the difficulty I had buying it for you today.'

'Whatever is it?' she asked, intrigued.

'I'll show you,' he replied eagerly, walking over to the TV set and reaching behind it. 'Here. I hope you approve?'

In his right hand Peter was holding a long whippy cane. An evil-looking cane. The sort that was used to chastise errant schoolchildren in years long gone by. Tracie stared at the cruel object in utter astonishment. Then she felt her insides start to churn with a mixture of fear and desire.

'I've never been caned before,' she whispered, after a pause.

'No. But I expect you will be again.'

'Yes, I expect I probably will.'

Peter made her bend over the back of the sofa, her toes touching the carpet and her head resting on the seat beyond.

The sofa was exactly the right height, with the result that her plump little bottom was conveniently raised on high, providing a very soft target indeed for the highly efficient instrument of torture he was gripping purposefully in his hand.

He stared down at the perfect contours of her upthrust buttocks, and was delighted to note a glutinous dollop of semen clinging stickily to the centre of her right cheek. It would add weight to his arm, he decided. As well as another centimetre or so to his erection . . .

Peter recalled the thrill of last night. The thrill of watching the groin of the unknown stranger slapping against these same cheeks. He'd never dreamt that he could feel so aroused. So exhilarated. It had seemed inexplicable at the time: the fact that he was actually enjoying the sight of some sod porking away at his wife. But now he'd come to terms with it all. Now he could see himself and his marriage in a totally different light.

He'd always loved and fancied Tracie. He'd always been intensely proud of her pretty face and beautiful body, and her jet-black hair. And being proud, he'd always felt jealous of her, sometimes to the point of irrationality. But now he could see things quite differently. Now he realised that the only way the rest of the world could truly appreciate his luck in having her, was if he occasionally shared her around. She was still his, of course. But it was only right that other men should know exactly what it was he owned. It was only right that they should understand what a crock of gold he possessed. There was no point in being the proud possessor of something wonderful if no one else knew that you were. Consequently, he now realised how wrong he'd been to be jealous. The only way to enjoy your pride of possession was to let others discover for themselves just how they were missing out.

Peter rested the cane across the high points of her saucy bottom, making her tremble slightly in anticipation of what lay ahead. It had always been his favourite feature, he said to himself. Her pert little bum, he meant. In the past he'd always hated the thought of some other bugger making free with it. He'd tortured himself endlessly with the mental image of unknown others mauling her beautiful buttocks and wallowing in their sheer perfection as she was taken hard from behind. They were supposed to belong to him, after all. He'd married her and she'd vowed to keep them only unto him – not share them around with Tom, Dick or Harry from the office who happened to possess the right tackle and a half-decent line in chat.

But now all that had changed. He could see how wrong he'd been. He could see how much more enjoyment he was going to get by allowing those other so-and-so's to sample the delights of her wifely wares. But, of course, she'd have to understand to whom she really belonged. She'd have to be reminded that he was only parting with her assets on a very temporary lease. She'd have to know that he was still the freeholder and that she was on loan only at his indulgence, only because he so chose. And what better way to remind her of that fact than to lay this long, wicked cane right across her adulterous arse immediately after the loan had been recalled? Immediately after the very short-term lease had expired? What better way than to lay it right across her whilst she was still, as now, throbbing with pleasure and dribbling another man's seed? What in the world could make the point more emphatically than that? What could possibly demonstrate his ownership better than inflicting such an intensity of pain right across her loveliest, and most sensitive, part?

Peter ran the cane lightly over her pouting pink cheeks, watching them twitch in fright. He'd spanked her in the past, of course. He'd spanked her over his knee with his hand on more occasions than one. Sometimes in anger, sometimes in fun. And he'd thoroughly enjoyed what he'd done. The feeling of power and mastery, not to mention the sexual excitement, had been immense. But this was going to be better. This was going to be very much better indeed. This would really make her holler and howl.

This pretty bottom had deceived him. On last night's evidence it was clear that it had deceived him on many more occasions than one. But now it was going to pay the price. A price that would ensure she remained completely aware of the fact that he was the one to whom she owed her allegiance.

As Peter raised the cane above his head, Tracie turned her face and looked helplessly up into his eyes. For several seconds he held her stare, cane raised high above trembling bare cheeks. Then it was time to proceed – to harden his heart and proceed. He switched his gaze to her soft, waiting bottom, and drew a deep breath. She closed her eyes and buried her face in the luxuriously upholstered settee. 'I'm sorry, Tracie,' he whispered, bringing the cane down in a huge hissing arc that homed in with deadly accuracy on the duly appointed target, those soft, shiny, and oh-so-vulnerable twin peaks.

Just as Peter had expected, the intensely satisfying crack of cane across fleshy bare buttocks was almost immediately drowned by the even more satisfying scream of pain. A truly blood-curdling, ear-piercing scream. Tears jetted out of Tracie's eyes as she howled with her mouth open wide.

Peter stared in delight at the thick, vivid red welt that had suddenly materialised, as if by magic, right across the widest part of her bottom. The widest part of her otherwise immaculate cheeks. And the more he stared the more his penis forced its way up towards his rib cage. This was the only way to deal with an undisciplined young wife, he gloated to himself. This was the only way. You bent her over the back of the sofa and made her wait for what must have seemed an eternity. Then, when the waiting was almost intolerable, you laid the cane right across the middle of that plump little bottom with all the power you could muster. And you kept on doing it.

Peter balanced the cane in his hand and waited for the noise to subside. He'd wait until it had become no more than a heavy, choking sob. He'd wait further, until the sobbing was soft and muted. Then, when he gauged the moment to be absolutely right, he'd strike once again, raising a second line right across those impudent cheeks, and making her yell as loudly as ever. Every bit as loudly as she was now.

Peter stared at the cheeky little bottom that now carried the blazing red insignia of his cane right across its fleshiest part. It would take a long while to complete the caning, he thought to himself. Over an hour, he imagined. And it would take much, much longer before his unbelievably stalky young wife would be able to bear even the flimsiest pair of knickers across her sorely wounded parts. And the six straight lines that he intended to paint across her would be with her for several weeks. The six straight lines that he intended to paint right across this unfaithful little bottom . . .

'Ohhh! Ohhh! Ohhh!' Tracie sobbed quietly. 'Oh God, that hurts! You can't believe how much.!'

'Would you like a little more time before the next one?' Peter asked quietly.

'Oh, yes, please!' she gasped with relief.

Stealthily he raised the cane above his head. 'Well, that's not a problem,' he murmured. 'That's not a problem at all.'

Peter measured his aim with great care. If he was going to cane her, then he might as well do the job to the best of his abilities. The very unexpectedness of the next stroke would significantly enhance the effect.

'YOWWW!' she howled at the ceiling, her feet jumping several inches off the carpet as the cane bit savagely across both cheeks.

Peter gazed down at the two wicked-looking stripes that now decorated her sweetly unturned bottom. That was much better, he said to himself. Tracie would be learning, very quickly, just whose wife she was. There was, however, a considerable amount of learning ahead.

For a full two minutes, Tracie continued to squeal at the top of her voice, wriggling her hips from side to side as if she was trying to cool them. Her bottom was in agony, she gasped to herself. She'd never known or even imagined anything like it. She'd been branded with a red-hot poker. She'd never sit down again. And the caning had only just started! There were four more strokes to come! She'd never be able to take it. Her poor bottom was absolutely ablaze. She was burning more and more with every second that passed.

Peter stared with affection at the juicy ripe cheeks he'd always cherished. It was incredibly satisfying to see how well he'd already imposed his authority upon them, with a mere two cuts of the cane. Now they were far from their former selves. Their impertinent perfection was already a thing of the past. Now, as they trembled and shook in fear and agony, each cheek bore the most magnificent hallmark of his mastery right across its plumpest part. And the hallmark was going to grow. It was going to treble in size. Four more lines were going to be added. Four more burning, blistering lines. Four more lines that would emphasise to her the nature and extent of his conjugal rights. The nature and extent of his ownership of those parts he was now putting to the torch.

Peter listened with a strange mixture of pleasure and intense sympathy to the heart-rending howl as the cane rose and fell for the third time across those oh-so-shapely little cheeks. Those soft round cheeks that had been so shiny-smooth and immaculate just a short while before. So shiny-smooth and immaculate, until they'd tasted the weight of the cane right across them. Now they were bouncing wildly under his gaze for the third time that night. He gripped the cane in his right hand and drank deep of the wondrous sight and sound. And there were three more strokes to go before he'd finish scorching this delightful little bottom. This bare, bent-over bottom that had, in the past, been sampled and enjoyed by others who'd had no right.

Peter was more than delighted with his handiwork so far. Three ugly weals had been raised right across the fullest part of each charming dimpled cheek. The second had been raised about three quarters of an inch below the first, whilst the third was a similar distance above. All three red lines were as parallel to each other as he could possibly have hoped. It showed considerable skill on his part, he told himself proudly. Each weal was so suffused that it stood out by at least a quarter of an inch. A tribute not only to the weight of his arm, but also to the quality of the cane. He longed to raise a fourth, but it was much too soon. He must be patient and wait for her to calm down. That was the way in which to maximise retribution. Six strokes with an interval of ten minutes or so between were six times more painful than six strokes one after the other. So he must hold himself back until the screams had turned to whimpers. Then and only then would the cane be allowed to kiss her again.

Some forty minutes later the sixth and final stroke had been laid across her. Laid across her with the same accuracy as the other five. Peter had performed his labour of love exactly as he'd intended. The plumpest part of each perfectly rounded cheek was now decorated by six straight lines spaced evenly apart. Six red-hot ridged welts that positively burst with colour and life. Six welts that would be unable to tolerate the slightest pressure against them. Six blazing welts, the lowest of which ran exactly along the sweet little crease that divided buttocks from thighs. That would cause her maximum discomfort when she moved, Peter thought happily. That would certainly be a worthy part of the reminder he'd just issued to her.

From that lowest cut, the lateral marks of the cane ran upwards and over the peak of each stricken cheek. The first stroke from the cane had raised the contusion that stood up proudly across the very cheekiest part of her bottom. Three more lay below and two above. All of them were parallel to each other and approximately the same distance apart. A glorious array of six scarlet weals painted vividly across the very centre of each oval cheek. It was a sight that would remain with him for the rest of his life. That pert, shapely bottom, which during two years of marriage had frequently tortured and tormented his soul, now bare and writhing before him. Bare and sporting the undeniable evidence of his ownership right across it. For the rest of his life he'd remember how he'd bent it over the sofa and then seared it with his cane. Seared it so thoroughly that when he held the palms of his hands just above her, he could actually feel the heat she was radiating.

Standing directly behind the perfect full moon of her blistered buttocks, Peter at long last reached down for his zip.

PART 2 – TAMED

Chapter 9

Caned and Able

Several hours later, an early dawn was breaking, but the electric light in Tracie's bedroom was still burning. For the third time that night she stood with her back to the full-length mirror, staring over her shoulder at the reflection of her ravaged rear end. God, she looked nice! With those six straight lines right across her! She simply couldn't get over how good she looked! She looked and felt so right. A complete woman. Utterly feminine, and dominated by her man. Fucked from head to toe in his presence, then given her just desserts. She'd never felt so female in her life. So soft and submissive. And how incredibly much she loved Peter! He was her prince and she was his slave. She'd do absolutely anything for him. Absolutely anything at all. If he wanted to give her six more from the cane there and then, she'd happily submit. There was nothing he couldn't do to her. And he was so God-like, she was sure that there was nothing he couldn't do. He could walk on water, if he wanted. He could turn base metal into gold . . .

Very, very gingerly she ran a fingertip over the ridge across the middle of her bottom. The first one that the cane had raised. Jesus, she was in agony! Absolutely agony! And what a delightful sensation it was! Her poor little female bottom roasted alive by her wonderful brute of a man! Her fat little girlie buttocks set absolutely ablaze by her great strong hunk of a husband! Just as they'd so richly deserved. She'd never be disloyal or disrespectful again. She'd simply worship the ground that he walked on. She'd keep him on a pedestal so high that he'd need an oxygen mask to survive.

Oh, the delicious pain! How clever Peter had been! How

cleverly he'd made her understand her situation! Surely there was something she could do for her hero of a husband to show how grateful she was? Surely there was something she could do, over and above the sex in which they'd been indulging for the last six hours or more?

And what incredible sex it had been, too! His cock had been enormous! So incredibly swollen and stretched! Thankfully not quite as colossal as John's, but certainly every bit the size of Sir Roland's. And it had stayed rock hard and upright ever since their first fuck of the night. It had stayed long and stiff and upright, despite the fact that he'd shot five times inside her! An unbelievable *five* times! Each time he'd made it, he'd simply smiled up at her and carried on. Carried on fucking her just as before. He hadn't wilted by so much as a centimetre. Sheer exhaustion had stopped them eventually, but she knew it wouldn't stop them for long. Very shortly she'd slide back on top of him and start to ride him again. No, on second thoughts she wouldn't. She'd take him in her mouth for a change. It was only right and proper, bearing in mind that John had been in there earlier. And that burglar boy last night. After she'd done that to Peter, she'd get on all fours and ask him to come in her bottom. He hadn't been there for weeks. Jesus, how she loved the feel of his white hot fluid sluicing into her there! And how delightful he'd stretch it tonight! She could see his enormous dick right now, stretching and straining up at his chin whilst he lay on his back and dozed. That gorgeous, unbelievable dick that had been in exactly the same condition for hours and hours! How many times would he have to come before it started to slacken? How many loads of lovely thick spunk would he have to plant inside her before then? Oh God! How much she loved him! They just couldn't get enough of each other!

Tracie stood beside the bed, smiling down at her husband, his penis cradled hotly in her right hand. 'I'm going to try to sit down,' she giggled sexily. 'I'm going to have to do it sometime, so I might as well start now.'

'I'm sorry I hurt you so much.'

'It feels incredible, Peter. I really can't describe how it feels.'

She lowered the mutilated cheeks of her bottom onto the mattress, very slowly and tentatively, holding her breath in fearful anticipation. 'Ouch!' she gasped, closing her eyes as teardrops ran down her face. 'Oh, ouch, ouch, ouch! I'll never be able to sit down in comfort again!'

But at last she was reposing on the mattress, her full weight on her sorely wounded nether regions. 'How is it?' Peter asked with concern.

'I could be worse,' she muttered, eyes still tightly shut. 'I think I'm starting to get used to the pain.'

She sat still for a further two or three minutes, then slowly turned sideways towards him, wincing as she did so. 'I'm okay,' she whispered, lowering her mouth towards his rampant groin. 'I want you to come in my mouth, just like John did. I want to be able to taste you, not him. You've already flushed him out of my pussy, now I want his taste out of my mouth.'

Peter lay on his back with Tracie curled up in a ball at his side, fellating him slowly and sweetly. It was a wonderful sight, he though to himself. The sight of his grossly swollen erection moving in and out of her gorgeous mouth, coupled with the view in the mirror of her extensively caned bottom. God, how pretty she looked with the stripes right across her. Right across the same sweet little bottom which, in the past, had tortured him with thoughts of how other men might have plundered and enjoyed it. But that was history now. That was just history, because now he found the idea enthralling. He loved the thought of her sexy little bum rutting and raving with somebody else. It gave him the most intense pleasure imaginable. And it wasn't just the thought. He'd actually watched her being fucked, front and back. That had been utterly fantastic. That had been the most incredible experience of his life. It had made their subsequent love-making totally unbelievable. He'd remained fully erect and as stiff as a board, no matter how many times he'd implanted her. If anything, he'd grown even harder. And he'd never come so often and so copiously in his life!

Peter stared hard at the reflection in the mirror. Well, justice had certainly been done. Her luscious bottom had certainly paid an excruciatingly high price for the times in the past when it had driven him mad with jealousy. How satisfying it had been, laying the cane right across those randy little cheeks and making her howl! He didn't know how many times those cheeks had been unfaithful, and now he didn't care. He positively relished the thought of what they'd been up to. Why shouldn't the men from her office know what a lucky sod he was to have that plump little rump beside him in bed every night? Why shouldn't his friends know the same? Why shouldn't all of them have an occasional taste of the hot little honeypot into which he could dip whenever he chose? It didn't detract from her charms. Much the opposite, in fact. It made her even more interesting, even more precious than ever. Already it had done their marriage a power of good, as witness the incredible sex they'd been having all night – and the glow of adoration in her face every time she looked at him. He could tell that she'd do absolutely anything he wanted. He could tell that he had only to ask and she'd oblige. The combination of cock and cane had worked wonders on her. The fact that he'd fed her full of somebody else's meat, and then demonstrated that she was still his, had produced a miraculous effect.

Peter closed his eyes as he felt himself starting to gush into her mouth. 'I love you!' she gasped out between spurts.

Ten seconds or so later he was spent, but still hard. 'I love you, too,' he wheezed, whilst she licked and lapped the end of his overworked, overstretched organ.

At length Tracie glanced back over her shoulder at the reflection of her candy-striped bottom in the mirror. 'Doesn't it look pretty?' she breathed.

'Very,' he replied with feeling.

She looked at him lovingly. 'I won't do it behind your back again,' she said slowly.

'You can if you have to. Just make sure you tell me about

it afterwards. All about it. All the gory details. That way there won't be any secrets between us.'

'Of course,' she agreed. 'But I don't think it'll be necessary.'

'I want you to keep on fucking other men. I shall find it incredibly exciting to hear about it afterwards.'

'I'll do it for you, if that's what you want. I'll do it for your sake.'

'Do it as often as you like. But just remember who you're doing it for.'

'I'll never forget, Peter. It will be fun . . .'

'Tell me something now,' he asked, intrigued. 'You did shag that bloke at Danny's house last Sunday, didn't you?'

'Yes,' she replied after a pause, blushing as she spoke.

'I knew it! I could just see it in your face. But how did you manage to do it?'

'When you and his wife were helping Janet with the washing up. It was just very quick, Peter. It wasn't really anything at all.'

'And where did you do it?'

'In the tool shed behind the garage.'

'In the so aptly-named tool shed!' he laughed wolfishly. 'Tell me something about it. It's interesting.'

'We did it standing up. He was exactly the right height. And my skirt was so short that I didn't even have to bother to lift it up.'

'I remember the skirt.'

'I just pulled the crotch of my knickers to one side and let him in. It was over in less than a couple of minutes. Then I spent the rest of the afternoon feeling his come gluing the tops of my legs together.'

'Tell me some more,' he asked eagerly.

'Peter, are you sure you want to hear?'

'Yes, of course. It's fascinating.'

'Well, I just wanted him to fuck me. That was all. Just fuck me. I had this weird feeling that I didn't want him to touch me apart from that. Not before or during or after. So the only contact we ever had was his prick inside my pussy. It was nice.'

'Yes, I can imagine. Tomorrow, Saturday, I think we'll get you to do something along the same lines.'

'Pardon?'

'Tomorrow I think we'll see how many times you can get yourself screwed.'

'But by whom?'

'Anyone. It doesn't matter who. Anyone who hasn't had you already.'

'Are you sure?'

'Yes, of course. It'll be fun for me, as well as for you. Tomorrow will be, "Shag A Stranger Day". Preferably in circumstances where I can watch! Do you think you can manage it?'

'Well, yes, I suppose so . . . There's that guy at the video shop in town. He's always making suggestive remarks and leering at me like mad.'

'That sounds promising.'

'But I don't know how I can get to do it with you watching.'

'That's not too important. It will be nearly as much fun hearing about it afterwards. If I can watch as well, that will just be a bonus. The main thing is to get you shagged. As much as possible.'

'You're absolutely sure?'

'How many times do I have to tell you!' he laughed. 'You can do it twenty times a day, if it's for me.'

'I'll be worn away,' she giggled.

'We'll start tomorrow at the video shop, as you suggested.'

Tracie looked thoughtful. 'I could put on a pair of G-string knickers and my tiniest mini-skirt,' she said after a while. 'And hang round in the shop until we're on our own. It's never that busy . . . Are you absolutely, definitely sure that's what you want me to do?'

'Positive. I'll love it. And so will you.'

'When we're alone I can ask him if he wants to see something special. Then I can pull up my skirt and show him the marks of the cane.'

'That should certainly turn him on,' Peter said

enthusiastically. 'You'll be able to slip into the back room and then slip him inside.'

'Without letting him touch me anywhere else. Just as I did it last Sunday. Not that I'd want him getting his hands round my poor little bum!'

'I'll be waiting for you outside in the car. We'll try some other places as well. Just to see how many times you can score.'

'If that's what you want, Peter. I'll do anything you ask. Anything at all, as I said.'

'You'll enjoy it, won't you, Tracie?'

'Yes,' she replied softly. 'It'll be lovely, standing there shagging, and knowing I'll be able to tell you all about it as soon as I've finished. It's going to be great! It'll be even better, of course, if you're able to watch. It was really nice downstairs with John, having you there.'

'It was just as good for me. Probably more so, because I wasn't the one suffering all the discomfort.'

Tracie giggled again. 'He was ever so big.'

'We're going out with Jonathan and Beccie tomorrow night,' said Peter. 'I'm sure you'll be able to find a way of fitting in Jonathan too.'

Tracie blushed once again. 'I've already had it with Jonathan,' she mumbled apologetically.

Peter laughed happily. 'Well, we'll just have to amend the rules a little and allow you to have it again.'

Tracie stared hard at Peter, her eyes bright and feverish with desire. 'You realise you won't get any sleep tonight?' she said sexily, squeezing the thick round root of his penis as hard as she dared. 'I shall want to have this lovely hot horn buried between my legs for the rest of the night.'

'It's morning now, but don't worry. We won't have to get up for hours. And in the meantime, there's no way I won't be getting up you!'

She looked at him even more closely. 'There's something I want to do for you as well,' she whispered.

'You are doing it for me,' he replied at once.

'No, not that. Not getting myself dicked to death tomorrow. There's something I want to fix up for you. A nice little treat. Sometime during the week.'

'What is it?'

'I'll tell you if you like. But I'd rather keep it a secret. That way it will be a surprise. Just like you surprised me tonight.'

'That sounds a good idea.'

'Peter, I'm sorry,' she said suddenly. 'All those dicks!'

'I told you, it's fine. I want to hear about them sometime. I want to hear about them in the same way you told me about that guy in the tool shed last week. Afterwards, you spent hours screwing me when we got home.'

'I know. I'd been feeling so horny all day. And the quickie in the shed just made things worse, not better. I'm sorry, Peter.'

'Don't keep saying that. I love you, Tracie. More than I ever have. Watching you with another man has somehow made you seem even more special. And after tomorrow, God alone knows how much more I'll fancy you!'

She squeezed his penis again. 'And if you get any bigger, God alone knows how I'll be able to cope!'

Suddenly Peter looked at her sharply. 'That guy last night in the hall?' he said.

'Yes?' she asked nervously.

'The one who was shagging you at the foot of the stairs?'

'Yes?'

'He was under the bed!' Peter cried triumphantly. 'It's just come to me.'

'I'm sorry, Peter.'

'If you say that again, you'll get another whack from the cane. I've told you enough times, this is great fun. And I've just figured everything out. All the clues were there and I've suddenly pieced them together. The clues about last night's mysterious stranger, I mean.'

'Go on, then. Tell me what you've worked out.'

'It was like this. When I came home he was shafting you on this bed?'

'I'm . . . *not* sorry at all,' she giggled, turning red, nevertheless.

'He was shafting you for the second time, which was why you were so wet?'

'Yes, Mr Holmes.'

'Telling me it was because you'd been eagerly waiting for me all evening!' he bellowed with mirth.

'I'm . . .'

'So I came back and he was screwing you for the second time,' Peter continued thoughtfully. 'You must have been enjoying yourself because you'd forgotten all about me coming home. And he must have been shagging you for some while, because you were wracked with an orgasm the second I put it in you. The sort of orgasm you get when we've been at it for at least half an hour. Am I right so far?'

'Yes,' she said softly. 'Are you sure you don't mind?'

He ignored the question. 'So there you are, banging away like mad when suddenly you hear me coming in the front door. What can you do? There's only one possibility. He has to hide under the bed. So he dives underneath as I'm coming up the stairs. You pull the bedclothes over you, place your wet little bottom over the wettest part of the bed, and tell me how you've been longing for me to come back and fuck you. I then jump on top of you and roger you as hard as I can. Twice. And all the time your lover is under the bed listening to what we're doing. And probably feeling very fed up. Then, when I'm soundly asleep, you sneak him downstairs and have the audacity to let him finish it off. To let him finish what he'd started a couple of hours before.'

'I feel awful,' she grinned, still very red in the face. 'How could I behave so badly?'

'I'm glad you did,' Peter told her with feeling. 'Very glad that you did. It'll make an incredible difference to our marriage. It already has, in fact. Now then, I want you to tell me all about your past indiscretions. It will make me unbelievably horny.'

'Oh, please!' she giggled. 'Not even bigger!'

'I want you to tell me all about them. I don't mean all tonight. Just bit by bit.'

'It may take a while,' she gulped.

'Tonight you can just tell me about the worst thing you've ever done. The most unfaithful thing.'

'Must I?'

'What do you think? Of course you must!'

'. . . I shagged David, your best man . . . during our wedding reception . . . in my wedding dress . . . on the back seat of his car . . . in the hotel car park . . .'

'You randy little minx! So that was why you weren't wearing any knickers when we went up to bed?'

'I had this lovely little pair of silk and lace panties. White ones. Just for you to slide off me when we got up to the honeymoon suite. Unfortunately, David was so desperate to get into me that he simply tore them in half. I left them stuffed under the back seat of his car. I'm sorry . . .'

Red in the face, despite herself, Tracie rolled over onto her front. 'It's ages since you did it in my bottom, Peter. Would you do it to me now? I want you to put all of it in. Right up to your balls. Not just a couple of inches. There's more than enough spunk to use as lubrication. And don't worry about hurting my sore cheeks. I can stand the pain. It will just be added spice.'

Peter stared hard at the shapely striped bottom she was offering up so invitingly. It had certainly deserved all he'd given it, he thought to himself. And possibly more, as well. So he'd give it a little more now. He'd plug it just as hard as she'd asked. It was such a lovely sight, so saucily plump and inviting, lying there, smiling up at him, decorated so prettily by the cane.

He knelt over her, his knees straddling the tops of her thighs as he stared down at his still erect penis. It *was* longer than usual, he thought to himself. And fatter, too. And all because of the sight of his wife with another man. And the thought of it too, of course. He was finding it fascinating to hear about what she'd got up to in the past. It was almost as exciting as watching her perform. He'd always suspected she'd been getting a fair bit on the side. Now, over the course of the next few days, he'd be able to ascertain exactly how much. He'd be able to learn exactly how much he'd been cuckolded in the two years they'd been married. And great fun it was going to be! It would really turn him on with a vengeance. He'd be stuck in her hot little hole for hour after hour. Her hot little holes, he supposed he ought to say, since she was now waggling that pretty little bottom up at him and waiting for him to shag her in there . . .

Peter moved forward, the tip of his erection now resting comfortably in the cleft between her buttocks. She was already full of semen from the hours that had just passed. As she shivered in anticipation, he dipped a finger into her quim and removed a sizeable dollop of natural lubrication. This he pressed firmly into the tight little hole of her bottom, making her squeal with pleasure. Then, adjusting his stance and position, he pushed forward with his groin. For several seconds nothing happened, despite the steady pressure that he was exerting. Then suddenly she opened, and he entered her where she had wanted. A good three inches, at least. Her bottom felt like a vice around the end of his member. It clenched him just as if she was squeezing him tightly in her fist. She wriggled her lips luxuriously from side to side. 'That's lovely, Petie!' she whispered. 'I can feel you so nicely in there.'

Back and forth he started to frig her, using only the end of his end, but making her moan and groan with delight. 'Hold on to your hat, Mrs Trix!' he growled, thrusting forward again, and this time his full length disappeared right inside.

The pain of his sudden incursion was exquisite. It sent shock waves racing right through her body. She opened her mouth to scream, but found she was too breathless to utter a sound. Peter began to hammer in and out, to hammer hard against her sorely upturned buttocks. Suddenly she felt him start to squirt. She could feel it so precisely in there. She could feel his seed so perfectly. She could feel every globule of every spurt. Indeed, she could almost believe that she could identify each individual sperm as the long, powerful outburst seared and burnt the inside of her bottom, sending her into a swoon.

She writhed her head from side to side as Peter, jammed right up to the hilt, continued to pump out his cream. Never before had he probed her rear end so deeply. Never before had she felt such agonized delight. And never again would she shag anyone he hadn't selected. Never, ever again . . .

Oh, Peter's lovely hot seed in her bottom! His lovely thick come, scalding and burning her bottom! Oh, she just wanted to die!

Chapter 10

Shag a Stranger Day

The man in the video shop gaped in amazement at the six excruciatingly painful red welts that ran right across the plump cheeks of the all-but-bare bottom she'd turned so saucily towards him. 'Jesus wept!' he groaned in disbelief. 'I was watching a tape about something like that last week, but . . .'

'Well, this is the real thing.'

'I can see that.'

'What does it do for you?' Tracie asked over her shoulder with a knowing grin.

'It makes me as hard as hell!'

'Do you want to do something about that?'

'Are you joking?' he gasped.

'Why should I show this to you, if I was only joking?'

'I don't know.'

'Can't we go through to the back before someone comes into the shop?'

'This way then, miss.'

Without pulling her skirt down from around her waist, Tracie followed him through a door behind the counter. It led into a room with a desk and shelves piled high with videos. 'This looks handy,' she murmured, moving over to the desk before easing her G-string knickers down to the tops of her thighs. Then she bent forward, resting her elbows on the top of the desk. 'You can shag me from behind,' she told him. 'But be careful not to press too hard against my poor bum. It's too sore for that.'

'I can see,' breathed the man, still goggling in delight at her beautifully striped buttocks. 'Who did it to you?'

'My husband.'

'Why?'

'For having it off with his best friend, John,' she replied, semi-truthfully.

'So you've decided to get even with him, have you?'

'That's right,' she replied. This time not telling the truth.

'Well, I'll be delighted to help you,' he said thickly, hurriedly stepping out of his trousers and underpants and pulling his T-shirt up to his chest.

She looked round at him. He'd not been lying, she said to herself. He was indeed as hard as she could have wished. His nice thick dick poked proudly up past his navel. Peter would be proud of how she'd managed to get this far so quickly.

She lowered her head onto the desk top and lifted her bottom a fraction higher, thereby enabling him to see the pretty pink lips that glistened moistly in anticipation of what lay ahead. He pressed forward with his groin, pushing his tip gently against them. They opened for him at once, allowing him to slide slickly inside without any effort at all. He could feel the welcoming warm juices all around him, hot and slippery, and yearning to assist in accommodating the rest of his sturdy member. He pushed further forward until he was halfway home. Then he stopped and looked down, enjoying the moment. Enjoying the spectacle of his penis wedged solidly between hot, cruelly caned cheeks.

'Don't worry,' he murmured as she wriggled her hips against his rigidity. 'There's plenty more to come. I'm just admiring the view.'

He pushed forward once more. 'Ouch!' muttered Tracie, as his groin brushed lightly against her upturned buttocks.

'Sorry,' he said at once, pulling back a fraction of an inch. 'I'll be more careful in future.'

Slowly and deliberately he started to move back and forth inside her, glorying in the warmth of her slippery, snug little channel, coupled with the sight of the severely stricken cheeks between which he was working.

Peter looked at his watch. The shop was empty apart from Tracie, and she'd been gone long enough to suggest that she'd met with a degree of success. He decided to take a risk rather than wait for her return. Locking the car, he slipped down the narrow alleyway at the side of the shop. There was a gate to his right, which led into a small back yard. He stepped inside and moved stealthily up to the window that looked out of the back of the building. Gingerly he inched his head forward and peered inside. Then he gasped. There, just a couple of feet away, was the lovely full moon of his wife's bare bottom, bent over a desk and pointing three quarters towards him. And there, in between each vividly striped cheek worked a stiff male organ, the large fat tip of which he could see exiting and entering her with oily ease. Peter's own tackle stretched rapidly, until within seconds it throbbed and ached with painful desire. But there was nothing he could do, except stand there and watch.

The man was reasonably well hung, Peter noted. Certainly he was long enough to stretch her, rather than get lost inside. And he could see for himself that the bulbous end of the penis was opening her far enough to provide the sort of satisfaction she needed. The root was even thicker, but of course it was hidden from view as it sank inside her. As was most of her scrumptious rear end. It was only when the man drew back that Peter was afforded the delightful spectacle of her bottom and wide-open pussy, wherein several inches of penis were still housed. The guy was taking his time, Peter thought to himself. He was clearly in control. He was clearly in no hurry at all. He was just gliding his weapon back and forth at moderate speed. All the way back until the tip was right out in the open, and then all the way home. And he was staring down at her upthrust buttocks as he wended his way in and out. It looked as if he was going to be perfectly happy to carry on like this until such time as he had to erupt. Perfectly happy to keep feeding her one leisurely length after another, until he was unable to hold back any longer.

And indeed that was the case. Patiently the stranger continued to feed himself to her, admiring the cheeks of her beautifully formed bottom as he did so. Admiring, also, the way in which they'd been so savagely dealt with by Peter's cane.

Suddenly she felt him begin to stiffen and jerk. She knew what was about to happen, but still he maintained the same even pace. He must have a great deal of self control, she said to herself, just before the first jet of seed began to scald her insides.

At last the video shop owner was spent. He tottered back a couple of paces and instinctively reached down to his feet for his clothes. 'I don't suppose you fancy some more?' he wheezed, gulping in quantities of air.

'Surely you're not ready again already?' asked Tracie, still leaning right over the desk and enjoying the warmth of his fluid inside her.

'No. But I know my pal in the pet shop next door would love to have a go.'

'That sounds fine to me,' she giggled. 'I'll just wait here for him like this.'

Feverishly, he grabbed the telephone beside her and punched in a number. 'Jack!' he cried down the line a few seconds later. 'It's Bill. Get round here at once, if you've got any sense at all. I'm in the office at the back. You're never going to believe this!'

Jack stood in the doorway, gazing in astonishment at the scene beyond. 'What the hell's going on here?' he eventually managed to croak.

Tracie had remained in the same pose, bottoms up over the desk. She twisted her head and looked back at him. 'Hi,' she said brightly, wriggling her hips in his general direction by way of welcome. 'Would you care for a slice of the action as well?'

'What's going on?' Jack enquired once again, blinking his eyes as though he thought he might be dreaming.

The video man spoke up. 'This young lady is getting her own back on her husband. For whacking her bum with a cane. She's after as much dick as she can get, by way of revenge.'

'This isn't some sort of set-up?' asked the pet shop man, sounding rather doubtful about the whole affair. 'Some sort of a joke?'

'Of course not!' cried Bill. 'I've just dunked her myself . . . and thought you might like a turn. Look, you can see how thoroughly she's been caned.'

Indeed Jack could. He could also see the tell-tale signs that his friend had just finished himself off inside her. The pretty pink lips were wide apart, and flecked with white. 'Christ Almighty!' he whistled, reaching down to unbuckle his belt.

'That's more like it,' Tracie said encouragingly, still looking round behind her. 'Come over here and help me to get even more of my own back.'

Peter stared in delight as the newcomer moved up behind her, trousers round his knees and testicles swinging weightily below his short but incredibly thick erection. Suddenly the great fat end stabbed forward and vanished inside her. Then it began to frig in and out at speed, an inch or two at a time. Then two or three or four. And then the whole weapon itself. Peter was intrigued to see that it was already streaked with the first man's sticky effusion. His own member ached more than ever. He'd simply have to get inside her as soon as she'd finished. There was no way he could wait till they got home.

'Ouch!' shrieked Tracie, on the far side of the window, the man's groin began slapping hard into her bottom. 'Hey! You're not supposed to do that! It hurts like hell!'

Jack gripped her tightly round the waist and continued to hump. 'I can't help it,' he panted. 'You'll just have to do what they do in Hastings.'

'What's that?' she asked hopefully.

'Put up with it.'

Smack! 'Ouch!' *Smack!* 'Ouch!' *Smack!* 'Ouch!' Tracie closed her eyes as the searing hot pain of each slap, coupled with the stretching of her insides, rushed her into a series of powerful climaxes. Had she known Peter was watching, she'd have climaxed even more powerfully.

'Come round here,' she gasped to the video shop keeper, indicating the side of the table that was directly in front of her face. Perceiving her intentions, he was there in a flash, unzipping his trousers once again. Hungrily she took him into her mouth. He was sticky and still very limp, but started to stiffen the moment she started to gobble. Within a very short space of time he was fully erect and she began to give him head. Peter noticed that a wall mirror was positioned at just the right angle to give him a perfect view of the fellatio. He watched enthralled, as one penis plugged pussy, whilst the other slithered briskly in and out of his wife's mouth. He knew he was in danger of being spotted, either in the mirror or by the video man, but he decided to take that chance. Watching his wife being doubly dicked in this way was easily worth the risk. In and out of her raced both of the men, their thick round erections glistening wetly in the overhead light. Peter could see her bottom getting redder as the porking continued at pace. Then, to his delight, Tracie suddenly pulled back her head and opened her mouth to receive spurt after spurt from the penis she was holding a few inches in front of her lips. Some of the come splattered and splashed into her face, but most of it shot through her wide-open jaws and down her throat. As she licked her lips greedily, the man standing behind her began to spout. He continued to work in and out of her, pulling all the way out and then ploughing all the way in, thereby treating Peter to the exhilarating sight of yet more seed jetting fiercely into his wife. Jetting, this time, into the lips of her vagina as opposed to those of her mouth. In and out slid the ejaculating penis, treating Peter to even more of the same. Some of the outpour failed to find its target and clung thickly to her vaginal lips and pubes. And one particularly misdirected stream shot stickily across her left cheek.

Tracie stood up slowly, the hot, sticky juices trickling from pussy and mouth. Gingerly she edged her G-string panties up over her bottom and into place. Almost immediately the flimsy little crotch was soaked through.

'Well, thank you, gentlemen,' she muttered breathlessly, pulling her skirt down from her waist and then wiping her chin with the back of her hand. Within seconds she could feel their fluid pouring out of her knickers and running warmly down the inside of each leg. 'Thank you very much for your help. I feel a lot better already. A lot better disposed towards my dear husband, as well.'

'Our pleasure,' the video shop keeper chortled happily. 'Anytime he does it again, you know where to come for more help.' He turned and looked at his friend as she swished her hips out of the room. 'Fucking hell!' he mouthed slowly and silently.

As he spotted Tracie hurrying down the pavement towards him, Peter was suddenly struck with a brilliant idea. 'Quick!' he said, shooting an arm round her waist and guiding her across the road towards the back entrance of an old-fashioned department store. 'In here!'

'You're going to buy me a present!' she exclaimed.

'No. I'm going to fuck you as hard as I can!'

'This is so unexpected,' she giggled, as he hustled her in through the side door and bundled her along a passage. 'But you'll have to let me clean up first. I'm soaked.'

'I can't wait for that,' he muttered, pulling her by the wrist into the menswear department. It was massive and all but deserted.

'But I'm really brim-full.'

'I know. I was watching through the back window while they shagged you one after the other.'

'Peter! How clever! Was it fun?'

'What do you think?' he growled, pressing her hand hard against the lump in the front of his trousers.

'But where are we going to do it?'

He rushed her along between two vast rows of expensive morning suits. 'Standing up here,' he said urgently. 'There's hardly anyone in this part of the store. And no one's going to come over here looking for this sort of a suit. No one buys them these days.'

She giggled and pulled up her skirt. He slid his hand

between her dripping wet thighs and cupped it round the even wetter crotch of her knickers. 'Christ! You are soaked, for sure!'

'You really don't mind?'

He pulled out his penis, by way of answer, and thrust it urgently into her hand. 'Get me inside you as fast as you can!' he ordered.

She tugged the gusset of her G-string to one side and fisted him in. She was hot and unbelievably wet. He thrust violently three or four times, and then began to ejaculate forcefully. 'Peter!' she gasped in amazement, whilst he continued to thrust.

He finished gushing but, as she'd expected, he stayed hard and huge inside her and frantically continued to thrust. Less than a minute later he climaxed fiercely again. And again a minute or so after that. She peered over the top of the row of clothes and looked anxiously around the store. No one was near enough to suspect what they were doing.

The stream of surplus fluid had almost reached her knees. Peter could feel it pouring out of her as he gritted his teeth and strove to implant her for the fourth time in about as many minutes. Feverishly he fucked her, wanting to rattle her teeth in her gums and her brain in her skull, wanting to pump her so full that it shot out of her ears. The sight of her being had by two men, coupled with the presence of their juices inside her, had driven him to heights of desire he'd never dreamt he'd be able to attain. His one burning ambition now was to replace the other men's seed with his own. It wasn't that the thought of theirs inside her bothered him, it merely spurred him on to greater efforts.

Tracie squawked with pleasure as her husband's penis whipped in and out at lightning speed, almost toppling her backwards with the power behind each thrust. She reached out and steadied herself by taking hold of the nearby clothes rail, her other hand still holding the G-string to one side. Without even thinking, Peter clamped his hands tightly round her bottom. She opened her mouth to scream, but found that the intense pain made her come instead, just as it had in the back of the video shop a few minutes earlier. The strength of her spasms excited him further, and with a muted cry he threw back his head and shot deep inside her again. 'Oh, Peter!' she sighed in admiration. 'You make me love you so much!'

At long last Peter started to shrink. 'See that assistant over there?' he breathed, carefully trucking himself away and zipping up. 'Go and bring him over here on some pretext, and then fuck him. I can watch from behind that rack of clothes.'

'You've got to let me go to the Ladies',' she panted. 'My legs are sticking together all the way down down to my knees.'

'Don't be too long,' he replied. 'You've got five minutes to get yourself full of more cock!'

The rather too dignified Deputy Assistant Manager (Menswear) followed Tracie over to the far side of the shop floor, his eyes nevertheless admiring the lateral swing of her buttocks under the short blue skirt. 'These trousers, Madam?' he enquired politely, as she led him along a row of expensive grey slacks.

'Yes, that's right. I want to buy a pair for my husband.'

'And how can I be of assistance?'

'Well, you're exactly his size. I wonder if you'd mind trying them on? So I can be sure that they'll fit him.'

'Me, Madam?' he asked in surprise.

'Yes, if you're not too busy. It's always trousers that seem to cause problems, don't you find?'

'Well, I suppose I could, Madam.'

Tracie lifted a pair of slacks from the rack and handed them to him. 'Thank you very much,' she said with a dazzling smile. 'I always think it's important for a man to be seen in trousers that fit properly, don't you? Particularly around the buttocks and crotch.'

The man coloured slightly. 'I suppose so, Madam,' he said.

'Baggy trousers are such a turn-off,' Tracie continued. 'If a man has something to be proud of, then I think it should be nicely displayed.'

The Deputy Assistant Manager coughed, but said nothing. 'I'm sure your wife feels the same,' added Tracie. 'Men who're in really good shape should take trouble to make sure that we girls can appreciate the fact. Don't you agree?'

'Oh, er, yes, I suppose so,' he stammered.

'Be a sweetie and slip into them for me,' she urged.

He moved towards the nearby changing room. 'Do you need a hand?' she asked pleasantly, as he stepped inside. He stared at her in confusion, and then quickly shot the curtain across. Tracie looked over to where Peter was crouching behind a row of sports jackets and caught his eye. She gave him a wicked little wink and waited for the shop assistant to reappear.

Somewhat red in the face, the slightly overstarched young man eventually drew back the curtain and stepped out of the cubicle. 'They seem to fit rather well, Madam,' he said stiffly.

Tracie stared thoughtfully down at the trouser front. 'Could you take off your jacket?' she asked. 'I'd like to see how they are across the hips.' He had no alternative but to oblige. 'Not too bad,' she murmured, walking round behind him and running her hand lightly across his buttocks. 'Not too bad at all. You're very slim and lithe across the bottom. Just like my husband. I always appreciate that in a man. I think most women do.'

To his consternation, she sank to her knees right in front of him. 'Are they tight enough here?' she asked, staring at his crotch.

'Er, I think so,' he mumbled unhappily.

'Not too tight, I hope? After all, a man needs room to expand, doesn't he? You know what I mean?'

'. . . I, er, um . . .'

'Let me just run a few tests,' she murmured, reaching out with both hands.

'Pardon?' he gasped nervously, taking a step back as he spoke.

She moved up to him, still on her knees. 'There's no need to be shy. Don't forget, I'm a married woman. You're married too, I assume?'

'Yes,' he gurgled, as she placed one hand under his testicles and used the other to search for his penis through the trousers. She located it without difficulty, and started to rub. 'Oh, my God!' was all he could croak.

'Just relax,' she purred soothingly. 'I only want to be sure of the fit.'

Slowly but surely she felt him come to attention. 'That's much better,' she cooed, squeezing him gently. 'How does that feel? The trouser fit, I mean of course.'

He opened his mouth, but couldn't find the words he wanted. She continued to rub slowly up and down his full length. 'You seem to be about the same size as my husband. Cockwise, I mean. But would you mind if I made absolutely sure?'

She took his silence to mean assent, unclipping the trousers and then running the zip all the way down. His penis was standing up rigidly, poking out of the top of his briefs. She allowed the trousers to fall to his knees and peeled the briefs down after them. Then she unbuttoned the lower half of his shirt. The man stared down at the top of her head in disbelief.

'You look good enough to eat!' she giggled, slowly licking the stem up and down and then sucking the knob right into her mouth. 'Just like my husband, in fact.' He closed his eyes and let himself enjoy the blow job. From six feet away, Peter groaned with pleasure as he stared at the man's dick inside her pretty mouth. Up and down she worked her head, sliding him backwards and forwards with practised ease, and coating him with her saliva.

He was already hard and large, but she could feel him stretching even further as a result of the use of her mouth. After a while she lifted her head and rose to her feet, holding him firmly in both hands. She looked him straight in the eye. 'I wonder if you can fuck as well as my husband?'

'I can certainly give it a try,' he replied immediately, all signs of his previous disquiet having vanished into thin air.

★ ★ ★

Rather suspecting what Peter might have in mind, Tracie slipped her knickers off over her feet, instead of simply pulling the crotch aside. As the Deputy Assistant Manager glanced quickly around the nearly empty store, she eased his penis inside her. 'You're beautifully lubricated!' he murmured appreciatively, starting to thrust.

'Thank you,' she replied, smiling inwardly. 'And you're a very snug fit.'

Peter crawled forward on his stomach, passing under one rack of clothing before he found himself staring at the backs of his wife's high heels, just inches in front of his nose. Beside them lay the sopping-wet G-string knickers she'd discarded a few moments earlier. He breathed a sigh of relief. Tracie had been clever enough to guess what he'd meant to do. Stealthily he looked up, and almost climaxed on the spot. From his position on the floor between her feet he was granted a perfect view of her little pink pussy stretching to accommodate the man's suitably thick cock. A perfect worm's-eye view of everything that was going on between the tops of her legs. Unlike the scene in the video shop, or last night with John, there was virtually no restriction on what he could see. Because of his position, she was fully open and watchable even when the man was buried in her up to the hilt. He was able to watch every inch of penis sliding in and out of her milky-wet little opening. Suddenly the milkiness doubled in volume, indicating that the shop assistant had climaxed inside her. Peter stared in fascination as the sticky white substance began to seep down the inside of each thigh.

He backed up several inches as Tracie dropped to her knees and wrapped her lips round the other man's sad, shrinking member, sucking it in and out of her mouth as fast as she could. 'Come on, Mr Shopkeeper Person!' she mumbled indistinctly. 'I want a lot more dick than that!'

It took a couple of minutes, but then he was as hard as before. Tracie stood up and turned her back to him. 'Do it again!' she ordered, pulling her skirt up to her waist.

'Christ! Your bum!' he cried in surprise.

'That should put even more lead in your pencil,' she said over her shoulder.

'It does indeed!' he breathed, inspecting the damage at close hand. 'You must have been a very naughty girl.'

'I was. And I still am.'

Saucily, she tipped her buttocks up at him and he hooked her with a single thrust. She straightened up, enjoying the feel of his hardness lodged right up the full length of her channel. Very gingerly, she eased her bottom back even further against him, savouring the flash of fire it produced. He could feel the heat from the caning. He could feel the wicked ridged welts scraping the skin of his stomach and groin. In her high heels she was the tallest, so once again he was able to shaft her quite comfortably whilst she stood upright in front of him, legs slightly apart. 'That's nice,' she murmured softly. 'But don't press too hard against my poor little cheeks!'

Peter wriggled forward once more, taking in the view from the opposite angle. Now her plump little clitoris could be seen moving almost imperceptibly in time with the slithering penis. Tracie could just see his head poking out from under the clothes rack. The excitement of seeing him there watching made her start to come gently. She reached down and stroked herself, sharply increasing the strength of her spasms. Who would have thought this possible, she asked herself happily. Less than twenty-four hours ago, who could possibly have thought that this might happen? Thank God for that burglar! Thank God she'd overlooked the passage of time! And thank God Peter had woken up in the middle of the night and seen her getting it, doggy style, at the foot of the stairs . . . !

The shop assistant pulled almost all the way out of her, still long and as hard as a rock. 'Bend forward a bit,' he said, slightly breathlessly. Suspecting what he might want, she was more than happy to obey. He slid the head of his penis out of her and then upwards until it was pressing lightly against the hole of her bottom. She shivered with delicious anticipation. She was still very sore after last night. After Peter had been in there. After Peter had been all the way in there! But she'd simply love to be made even sorer.

He pushed forward, forcing himself a good three inches into her eagerly waiting bottom. Immediately he started to spurt, the extreme tightness of the opening having brought him off in a rush. She squawked and squealed with delight as she felt his semen burning its way inside. All the way inside. She could feel it so nicely in there. So very precisely. The scalding of her ultra-tight little passage brought her back to the boil once again. On and on he pumped, filling her full of fresh sperm. But there was no room to contain it all. Already it was starting to ooze out of her – even before he'd finished. Now she was leaking profusely from both of her lower orifices.

Tracie hauled the tiny G-string panties up into position. They were already saturated, so wouldn't provide her with anything more than purely cosmetic cover, she thought to herself. They weren't going to retain any of the lovely hot juices she could feel gushing out of her. And anyway, she rather suspected that Peter would have them off her again before she was a great deal older.

'I've got to go and find my husband,' she said to the half-naked man at her side, playfully tugging the end of his now flaccid member. 'Wrap the trousers and he'll call for them later. I assume there'll be a generous discount?'

Half an hour later, Tracie bustled out of the bank and clambered into the car, lowering herself very tentatively onto the passenger seat. 'Success?' Peter asked anxiously, as he pulled away from the curb.

'Of course,' she replied with a smirk. 'Bankers aren't all wankers, I've discovered. At least that one certainly isn't. Judging by the amount he was able to shoot.'

'Tell me about it,' he urged. 'From the beginning.'

'I said I wanted to see someone about our overdraft, but I didn't have an appointment. I flashed my boobs at this nice young lad and smiled a lot and he said he'd see what he could do. A few minutes later he came back and said Mr Appleton would see me there and then.'

'Who's he?'

'One of the managers. A bit long in the tooth, but he was definitely able to do the business.'

'Go on, then.'

'He was very polite and proper. He stood up and shook my hand and said, "How do you do". All that sort of thing. He said it was nice to put a face to what had always been just a name on a file. Then he asked me to sit down. "I'm afraid I can't," I replied. "Pardon?" he said. "My husband caned my bottom last night," I said. "Six of the best right across my poor bare bottom, whilst I bent over the back of the sofa. Because I'd been unfaithful to him, you see. So I simply can't sit down at all. It's too painful."'

'What on earth did he say to that?'

'Nothing,' giggled Tracie. 'Nothing at all. But you should have seen the look on his face! He was a picture! He just gaped at me, with his mouth hanging wide open in astonishment. Then he collapsed back on his chair, his mouth flapping open and shut like a fish. I think he felt he ought to say something, but didn't know what it could be.'

'I'm not surprised,' laughed Peter.

'So I told him we were wanting to increase our overdraft facility. I told him you were wanting to buy me an expensive present to make up for caning me so severely. "Oh?" was all he could mutter, rather lamely. "You can see how much he owes me," I said, turning my back on him and lifting my skirt up to my waist. Just briefly. Just for a second or so.'

'Then what happened?'

'I told him that if he increased our limit by a further five hundred pounds he could lie on his back on the floor and get the best fuck he'd had all year.'

'So he did?'

'That's right,' she giggled naughtily. 'All three things. What shall we spend it on, Peter? I could do with some new knickers, for start.'

'I think I can just about afford that. But let's go home. I can fix us some lunch and you can have a bath.'

'And then we can drive to the railway station!' she cried with sudden excitement. 'It's the first day of the football season. I've just had a brilliant idea. Here, let me explain.'

The football special was packed, including the corridor. Despite the heat of the August afternoon, red-and-white scarves were everywhere. Peter sat with seven other men in the six- to eight-seater compartment. The door slid open and Tracie poked her head inside. 'Oh, I see,' she said very correctly, in her best convent-school voice. 'I was just checking whether there were any spare seats.' Eight pairs of eyes turned towards her, taking in the details of her tight T-shirt top and the short, bouncy skirt that reached no more than an inch below the join of her legs.

'You can have my seat,' Peter offered at once.

'How kind!' she exclaimed. 'But I wouldn't dream of taking it from you. Not in these days of sexual equality.'

'Are you sure?' asked Peter.

'But perhaps I could just sit on your knee?' So saying, she lowered her bottom, very gracefully, onto his lap. Not his knee, his lap. She could feel his groin pressing against the plumpest part of her buttocks. Already he was starting to stiffen.

'It was rather embarrassing having to stand out there in the corridor, actually,' Tracie announced to the compartment as a whole, treating everyone to a sweet smile of total innocence.

'Why's that?' asked the man sitting directly opposite.

'Oh, because I'm not wearing any knickers, you see,' she said brightly. 'And this skirt is so short that it doesn't really protect me as it should. Not from the view of people such as yourselves sitting down on these seats, I mean.'

'Why aren't you wearing any knickers?' asked a rather cheeky young lad in the corner.

'It feels so much nicer without them,' she replied candidly. 'If you can understand what I mean? So much more free and unrestricted . . . And, well, I suppose I ought to tell the whole truth. They're not all that comfortable for me at the moment. My husband caned me last night, you see. Six of the best across my poor little bott. So it's much nicer and easier for me to be bare.'

'You're joking!' gasped one of the men opposite.

'No, it's perfectly true. Look, you can see for yourself.' She got to her feet and flipped up the seat of her skirt, treating the four passengers on that side to a split second glimpse of very bare, very striped bottom. Then she returned daintily to Peter's lap, wincing slightly as she sat down. 'I never tell fibs,' she said, very demurely. 'I don't think it's right, do you?'

'Jesus!' muttered several men.

'Well at least you're a United supporter,' one added. 'If you see what I'm getting at?'

'Oh, I do indeed follow your drift. Red-and-white striped scarves, red-and-white striped bum.'

'Why did he do that to you?' asked Peter, pleased with the progress to date.

'Oh, it was my fault entirely. I'd been very naughty, you know. With one of his close friends. So he bent me over the settee and gave me six of the best with this long, whippy cane. Six of the very best. I thoroughly deserved it, of course.'

'Doesn't it hurt?' asked the man on Peter's right, when he'd recovered his wits.

'Yes. It's agony. But it's really nice now I've got used to it. It makes me feel incredibly sexy. I suppose I really ought to be wearing knickers, because I'm wet all the time.' She smiled round at Peter and gently wriggled her hips. 'But you needn't worry, Mr Gentleman Jim. I'm keeping the tops of my legs tightly together. I promise I won't wet your jeans.'

The men exchanged looks of astonishment.

Tracie wiggled her bottom. 'Oh, dear!' she said to Peter, but also to the compartment at large. 'I'm ever so sorry. I seem to be giving you a hard on!'

'It's all right,' breathed Peter. 'It's my fault really.'

She wriggled some more. 'Your prick is incredibly hot!' she announced, the words belying the primness of her well-modulated voice. 'I'm so very sorry.'

Now the men really couldn't believe their ears. 'You're not to blame,' said Peter.

'Perhaps I ought to find another knee to sit on?'

Seven hands shot high in the air. 'Over here!' the other passengers chorused as one.

She chose the man sitting opposite Peter and settled herself prettily on his lap, squirming her hips until she was completely comfortable. 'I'm Tracie,' she said politely, shaking his hand.

'I'm George,' he breathed.

'I used to know a George once. But he wasn't a very nice man at all. He kept fucking me when I was trying to get on with my typing. I'm sure you're not like that?'

George opened his mouth, but simply couldn't formulate the words. Tracie looked over at Peter. 'Oh dear!' she tutted again, looking down at the very prominent bulge in the front of his trousers. 'Just look at the condition I've left you in! Your cock is almost pushing itself out of the top of your jeans. I do apologise most sincerely. Really I do.' She squirmed her bottom again, feeling George's half-hard penis against her. 'And you're not much better, George,' she added with a hint of a girlish giggle. 'I wonder why I always seem to have this effect on men?'

'I can't imagine,' grunted the cheeky-looking lad in the corner.

'I shall just have to put matters right,' she said, still very primly, standing up as she spoke. 'I hope you don't mind?'

The men gaped in amazement as she bent forward and undid Peter's trousers, then eased his penis out with both hands. 'My, you are in a state! And it's all because of me. I was silly enough to refuse your very kind offer to give up your seat. The least I can do is make full amends now, I think.' Without further ado she bent right forward from the waist, straight-legged, and swallowed him all the way down to the root.

George and the other three passengers goggled in awe at the perfect round bottom revealed by the way her skirt had ridden almost up to her waist. They goggled in awe at the perfect round bottom and at the six angry red lines that ran right across the fleshiest part.

Slowly and expertly she gave head to her husband, knowing how the men behind her would be gazing at the spectacle she made. The passengers on Peter's side of the compartment were torn between the reflection of her bottom in the glass door, and the sight of the long smooth dick slithering in and out of her lovely mouth. Peter himself simply closed his eyes and allowed her to bring him quickly to climax. 'Goodness me!' she gasped in mock surprise, as he began to squirt powerfully into her face and mouth. 'That was jolly fast, I must say!'

Having packed Peter away, she sat down on the groin of the man beside him. 'Oh, sorry!' she said, but making no attempt to move. 'Wrong knee. How silly I am!'

'It's okay, love.'

'Good Heavens. You're rock-hard already! Well, at least this time it's got nothing whatever to do with me.'

'But this has!' said George, sitting almost opposite. 'Aren't you going to do something to help me out with this beast?'

'I'm not at all sure that I should,' she said very properly, licking the last of Peter's sperm from the side of her mouth. 'I am a married woman, after all.'

He pointed at Peter. 'But you just sucked him off!' he protested.

'So I did. I'd almost forgotten. Okay, then. Undo your belt and unzip your flies.'

Once again she bent forward from the waist and began to fellate the hot, hard organ that had been exposed to the light of that Saturday afternoon. The man beside Peter, on whose lap she'd just been sitting, could stand it no longer. He got to his feet and placed the palms of his hands, very lightly, on the burning hot cheeks of her bottom. She lifted her head at once, holding George's erection in both hands, and looked back at him over her shoulder. 'Can I help you?' she enquired politely.

'You certainly could!'

'I suppose you want to fuck me? Your name isn't George as well, by any chance? Very well, then. But please, would you mind getting a move on? My pussy is even hotter than the fat little arse you have in your hands!'

Whilst the man gripped her tightly round the waist and shagged her from behind as hard as he could, Tracie continued to gobble George in expert fashion. Both men ejaculated fiercely together. 'Next!' she said, taking a step to her right and then reaching for the zip of the passenger now direct in front of her. Then she twisted her head to look back over her shoulder. 'Come on!' she urged the man beside the man who'd just fucked her. 'We haven't got all day, you know. There are two more to go after you. And those gentlemen out in the corridor are looking quite interested, too.'

When the train disgorged its passengers, Peter and Tracie headed for the West End of London, instead of the match. 'A porno cinema,' said Peter. 'That's what we need before we catch the train home. A porno cinema in Soho.'

'Excellent!' enthused Tracie. 'But first I think I urgently need to buy a packet of Kleenex. Those football fans were a lusty lot.'

'You were fantastic!' Peter said with genuine admiration. 'Those guys on the train just didn't know where you were coming from!'

'It's the benefit of a convent education. All the girls there were the same. Talk posh and act dirty. It confuses the boys no end.'

They were outside the Regent Palace Hotel. 'I'll just nip in here and clean up,' said Tracie. 'Without knickers, there's nothing to stop the stuff spilling all the way down my legs.'

'I can see.'

'Have I done enough to earn the next caning?'

'No, not nearly enough. It will be months before you can have the next little treat.'

'You're so mean!' she exclaimed, sticking her tongue out at him. 'How can you expect me to last that long?'

'I'll wait for you inside,' said Peter, following her into the hotel.

A few minutes later, Tracie stood in the hotel foyer, gazing round for Peter. Where on earth had he got to? Suddenly she caught the eye of a youngish man waiting at the counter nearby. He blushed, but didn't look away. Then he raised his eyebrows in a very evident gesture of enquiry. Tracie, quick-witted as she was, decided there was nothing to be lost by giving him a smile and a saucy wink. There might even be something to be gained, she mused.

He walked over to her, still red-faced and looking somewhat embarrassed. 'Are you, er, by any chance, er, Sylvia from the, er, agency?' he asked uncomfortably, dropping his gaze to the floor as he spoke.

Again Tracie thought fast. 'Sylvia from the escort agency?' she enquired.

'Er, yes . . .'

'Yes, I am indeed. And you are?'

'Robert.'

'Nice to meet you, Robert. Sorry if I'm a bit late. Do you have a room here?'

'Yes. Room 206.'

'Let's go and have a look at it, shall we?' she suggested with a knowing smile. 'Show me the way.'

As she followed him towards the stairs, she spotted Peter and grinned back at him over her shoulder. He followed at a discreet distance, watching as they disappeared into room 206. The door of the adjoining room, 204, was wedged open with a bucket and mop. A pile of sheets lay in the corridor outside, plus a vacuum cleaner. Clearly the room was in the process of being cleaned. He put his head round the door. The room was unoccupied, so he slipped inside. Picking up a glass tumbler from the handbasin, he held the rim against the dividing wall and applied his ear to the other end of the glass. He could hear the conversation next door quite clearly.

'The agency told you about the, er, special requirements, did they?'

'Yes, of course,' she replied at once.

'That's why I asked not only for a pretty girl, but for one with a particularly shapely bottom,' he said, blushing again.

'And I can see you fit the bill. I can see how nice your bottom is, despite your skirt.'

Tracie realised what he was after. She turned her back on him. 'Have a closer inspection,' she giggled. 'I'd like you to be quite sure I'm up to specification.'

He lifted the seat of her skirt and gasped. 'You've been caned!'

'Yes. Last night. By my husband.'

'It looks terribly sore and painful.'

'It is. But I can stand it. It should add to your enjoyment, I'd think?'

'It certainly will!' he breathed with feeling, gazing at the vividly striped bare buttocks. 'It most certainly will!'

'Touch it, if you like. Just gently.'

Slowly he ran his palm over the stricken cheeks. 'You're burning hot,' he murmured.

'That's hardly surprising, Robert. Six of the best I got. Six of the very, very best.'

'What a lovely little bottom!' he enthused, both hands now stroking very lightly. 'So plump and shapely! So saucy! And so soundly caned! What more could any man ask.'

'The caning is free, by the way,' she said light-heartedly. 'There's no extra charge for that. It's on the house, so to speak.'

'Which reminds me,' said the man, peeling notes from his wallet. 'Three hundred pounds. That's right, isn't it?'

'It certainly is,' she replied, dropping the money into her handbag. 'Are you sure you want to spend so much? It's an awful lot of money.'

'Of course I'm sure. I've spent years dreaming of doing it this way.'

'You've never done it before? You've never taken a girl in her bottom?'

'No, never. This will be a very special treat. Especially a bottom like yours!'

'Do you have some lubrication?'

'Yes. I've got a jar of quite expensive cream. Here it is. Will that be okay?'

'Yes, it'll be fine.'

She turned to face him, her arms round his neck, his hands still caressing the cheeks of her red hot bottom. She wriggled her hips. 'I like getting it in there,' she said softly, before they kissed.

They undressed in front of each other without embarrassment. 'You're a beautiful girl!' he sighed, when she was bare before him.

'Thank you,' she smiled.

He was fully erect already. And Tracie was relieved to note that although adequate of penis, he was by no means over-endowed. Her bottom was still suffering from the way Peter had shafted it so deeply the night before.

She reached out and gently squeezed his erection. 'How have you fantasised about doing it?' she asked. 'Do you want me to lie on my front? Or do you want me on all fours? Or elbows and knees?'

'On elbows and knees,' he gulped. 'That's how I've always imagined doing it. On elbows and knees on the bed.'

The headboard of the large double bed was almost against the wall that divided rooms 206 and 204. Peter could even hear the springs of the mattress starting to creak as they clambered on top of it. If only there was a spy hole, he sighed wistfully.

Tracie peered back at Robert over her shoulder as she knelt on the bed. 'Put a dollop of that cream on the end of your dick,' she told him. 'And then press an even bigger dollop into me.'

'Oow!' she giggled naughtily, the coldness of the cream making her squirm. 'Do that again, it's quite nice.'

He moved forward against her, his knees on either side of hers. 'Let me guide you in,' she whispered, reaching behind. With her help he slid smoothly into her, right down to the root. 'Oh, yes!' he gasped in delight, gripping her round the waist. 'You're so tight!'

After less than a minute of frantic activity, he began to ejaculate powerfully. His seed was even hotter than Peter's, she sighed happily. Presumably he'd been so pent-up and anxious after waiting years to do it this way.

Tracie felt her own climax start to shake her. One that was orientated solely towards her anal passage, not her quim. She wriggled her hips and groaned with pleasure as his white hot fluid soon filled her to the brim and beyond.

'Leave it inside me,' she said, when he'd fully ceased. 'Don't pull it out yet. If you leave it where it is, you'll get hard again in a couple of minutes. Then you can do it all over again. After all, you deserve a bit more than that for your money. You deserve a bit more than you've had so far, for three hundred pounds!'

Peter listened to the creaking of the mattress. This was a much less frenzied affair than the first one. It had already lasted a good ten minutes. If only he could watch! But at least he was close by and listening. He could hear her squeals as she came again. But the creaking hadn't altered. So presumably the man was still rampant and onboard and not yet ready to swamp her? He had to admit that she was doing much better than he'd ever expected. She'd sucked and fucked on the train . . . and now, here she was, getting it for the second time today in her sweet little bum!

They stood outside the porno cinema, gazing at the poster for 'Jack, Jill and the Giant's Beanstalk'.

'Look at the supporting features!' giggled Tracie. '"Bo Peep Meets Little Boy Blue," and "Snow White and the Seven Dwarves – Her True Story!"'

'I'll go in first,' said Peter. 'Give me five minutes.'

'Okay.'

'How much?' Peter asked the man at the window.

'Twenty pounds,' he replied, holding up a spool of twenty-pound tickets.

But Peter knew the ropes. 'Sorry. That's too much. I'll leave it, thank you.'

'Okay,' the man said at once, picking up a spool of ten-pound tickets. 'Ten pounds, then.'

'Is there any membership charge when I get inside?'

'Nope,' said the man, looking Peter straight in the eye.

Peter paid the money and walked down the darkened stairs. 'Membership card?' said the burly man at the foot.

'I was told there was no membership charge,' sighed Peter, knowing it was hopeless.

'There isn't if you're a member.'

'How much?'

'Twenty pounds.'

Peter turned back towards the stairs. 'Forget it. I'll go and buy a dirty magazine instead.'

'Five pounds, then.'

'Here you are. I don't suppose I get a membership card?'

'Run right out of them, squire. Come back tomorrow and I'll give you one. Do you want a drink?'

'A can of de-alcoholised lager for forty pounds?'

'Yep.'

'No, thanks.'

Soho, thought Peter. The rip-off capital of Europe. But at least there didn't appear to be any hostesses who charged you two hundred pounds for passing within twenty metres of them.

The cinema was small and about a third full. Peter took a seat in the second row from the front and lit a cigarette. The screen was almost completely filled with a shapely female bottom being caned.

'Do you allow women inside?' asked Tracie, flashing a sexy smile at the man behind the window.

'Of course! Free entry for women today. And here's a membership card, too.'

'How kind! Are there any other girls inside?'

'Er, not yet. But we're expecting some shortly.'

'Oh, that's all right then.'

'Here's my phone number, miss. Ring me anytime.'

Tracie selected a seat on the front row, directly in front of Peter and with an empty seat on either side. She looked up at the screen where a couple were having sex in the back of a Rolls-Royce. Quite cleverly done, she thought. Boobs, bums and muff fluff were on prominent display, but not a dick or pussy could be seen. She rather suspected that they might actually be doing it, judging by the reactions of the girl.

No sooner had Tracie sat down, than the bearded man to her right moved to the seat beside her. The man to her left immediately followed suit. She crossed her legs and tugged down her skirt, very demurely.

Without a moment's hesitation, the bearded man's left hand snaked out and settled warmly on her thigh, several inches above the knee. As she uncrossed her legs, the other man's hand alighted on the other thigh. Then both hands began to creep higher, sliding slowly over satin-smooth flesh. Tracie parted her legs just enough to allow them access all the way to the top. A few seconds later, as Tracie's eyes remained resolutely glued to the screen, two pairs of fingers were gently probing just inside the warm wet lips that had drawn right back to welcome them. Together the fingertips slid a little deeper, and then a little deeper still. Then they began to move, slowly and easily, gliding back and forth inside slippery, slickly-oiled pussy, exploring it gently but very thoroughly.

Still staring up at the film, Tracie unfolded her arms and then lowered a hand onto each male groin, her arms now crossing the men's. Both of them were hard already. In time with the movement of the fingers, she began to rub with her fingers and palms. By leaning slightly to one side, Peter was able to observe what was happening. And so were the three other men who sat in his row. The screen was forgotten as they watched the real thing unfolding in front of their eyes. The hem of Tracie's skirt was now revealing just the faintest hint of pussy and pubes, and the men behind could see that her hands were now inside both trouser fronts, moving in synchronisation with the hands of the men. Two men from the seats behind Peter slid forward to his row in order to monitor the progress more closely. Throughout all this, Tracie and the men at her side never allowed their gaze to stray from the silver screen.

At last the bearded man leant towards her to whisper in her ear. The man on her left leant sideways as well, in order to hear. 'The gents' toilet,' the bearded man murmured, nodding to one side of the auditorium. 'Follow me.' He stood up, and so did Tracie and the other man. They trooped down the short flight of stairs in single file, Tracie in the centre, and through the door marked 'Gentlemen'. Peter felt the zip of his jeans threatening to burst open. The others in his row were in much the same state.

'Give them a couple of minutes,' said the man next to Peter. 'Then we'll take a wander and see what's going on.'

'Why not?' replied Peter. 'After all, we've paid good money to watch sex.'

A few minutes later the door of the toilet pushed slowly open and six men squeezed into the doorway to view. They had to take a step inside, because several others had followed them down. What a sight met their eyes! There was Tracie, tall and proudly naked apart from her three-inch high heels, standing with her back against the far wall, eyes tightly closed, and moaning softly with pleasure. The bearded man was using his mouth and fingertips to attend to her firm round breasts and pointed nipples. The other was on bended knees in front of her, his tongue delving deep between the junction of her legs. Peter and the original voyeurs were obliged to take a further step inside as yet more men joined the viewing gallery. Tracie and her two lovers were aware of the watchers, but took not the slightest notice. They were far too concerned with the delightful task in hand. Tracie just stood there, leaning back against the wall, eyes shut and hands by her side, letting the men pamper and pet her however they pleased, savouring the luxury of their mouths and fingers as they worked on her with considerable expertise. And also, very secretly, enjoying the feel of the seed that was still trickling slowly out of her bottom.

The man with his face between her thighs stood up and tore down his trousers and pants. Whilst the bearded gent continued to tease and please her beautiful breasts, she lifted her right leg and hooked it round the other man's left hip, sighing sweetly as he pushed his full length right up to the top of her dripping wet passage. The bearded man stepped to one side to allow the other full reign. For several minutes he fucked her with long even strokes, pulling almost all the way out before sliding all the way back – and kissing her with his tongue so that she could share the exquisite taste of her own juices. Then it was the turn of his colleague. As if by mutual agreement, the first man withdrew completely and took a couple of steps back, gesturing down at his groin. As Tracie moved forward and then bent to take him in her mouth, the bearded man whipped open his jeans and entered her smoothly from behind. Each time she raised her head, the bearded man pulled back. Each time she lowered it and swallowed cock, he slithered all the way inside. Up with her head, and back drew the man behind her. Down with her head, and he was all the way inside again. Head up, and out slid two men; down, and back inside they slithered. Up, and out they slid, all the way to the tip. Down, and back they slithered, all the way to the hilt. Up and out, down and back. Up and out, down and back – pleasing and probing as they went.

Then it was time for a change of tactics. Tracie stood upright between them, sandwiched between them, the bearded men still buried inside her from behind, her clitoris now rubbing firmly against the hardness of the man in front. Then the man behind pulled out and pressed his very upright weapon into the delightfully deep cleft of her cheeky little bottom. The other man lost no time in replacing the bearded one. He sank into wet willing pussy and started to thrust. Two minutes later the man behind was in there again, and her clit was jammed against the penis in front. Then that penis was back inside her, and the other was working up and down in her cleft. Then that one was shagging her, and clit was rubbing against cock once more. Turn and turn about, they took. First one and then the other, deep in her quim. Back she pushed, rubbing her anal opening against the man in her cleft. Then forward she thrust with her clit as soon as they'd swapped over. One dick deep inside her, the other stimulating clitoris or bottom. Every minute or so the men changed over, making her gasp and groan as she was penetrated anew.

The bearded man was the first to implant her, spurred on by the sight of her well-caned bottom and the heat of it against his stomach and groin. She groaned loudly as she felt him starting to spurt powerfully and profusely.

No sooner was he spent than the man in front thrust fiercely back inside her and instantly came to the boil. Tracie threw back her head and fought for breath at the thrill of being flooded by two men, one immediately after the other.

'Oh, brother!' she groaned, when the second man was finally through.

'Yes indeed,' agreed the man with the beard. Peter silently concurred, as well.

She looked over to the tightly-packed doorway. 'You're missing the film,' she said simply, before stooping to retrieve her clothes from the floor.

Tracie was in need of a rest. So tea and buns at the Savoy was followed by a well-earned taxi home. It would cost eighty pounds, but she had the three hundred pounds in her handbag from the escort agency client who'd had her twice in her bottom.

They sat close together on the high back seat of the cab as it worked its way out of Greater London and headed for the coast. 'You were fantastic!' breathed Peter, his hand resting lightly on bare wet quim.

'I did it for you, Peter.'

'Didn't you enjoy it?'

She squeezed his groin affectionately. 'Apart from last night, it was the best day of my life. But I need you, now. I've had enough dick from other men to last me a lifetime. Well, to last me until we go out with Jonathan and Beccie tonight. It's yours I want now. Your loving, husbandly dick.'

'As soon as we get home, you'll have it.'

'I can't wait that long.'

She leant forward and tapped on the glass partition. 'Excuse me, Mr Taxi Driver,' she called sweetly.

'Yes, love?'

'Excuse me, but I'm feeling terribly randy back here.

Would you mind awfully if I shagged my husband here on the seat?'

'Not at all, love,' the cockney cab driver drawled evenly. 'Provided you're the one on top. I don't want the image of his hairy male arse in my mirror!'

'Will you keep your eyes on the road if I'm jiving up and down on top of him?'

'Probably. Some of the time.'

Twenty minutes later Peter tapped on the glass. 'Would you like me to drive?' he asked.

'You don't have a licence to drive my cab.'

'No. But, on the other hand, neither do you have a licence to fuck my wife.'

'That's true, squire,' muttered the driver, swerving into a lay-by and applying the brakes.

'I wish I'd brought a pair of knickers!' sighed Tracie.

Late that night Tracie stood on the pavement outside the now-closed discotheque. She was wearing a most fetching pair of hot-pants with crossover shoulder straps. Hot-pants so cleverly tailored that they only just covered that part of her bottom which had received the lowest cut from Peter's cane. She squeezed her thighs together and was pleased to feel that she was still suitably damp. Earlier, she'd pulled Jonathan off the dance floor and dragged him into the men's toilets, where she'd entertained him in one of the cubicles, much to his surprise and delight. And much to the surprise of the five other men who'd been using the urinals at the time. A few minutes later she'd been back in the same cubicle with Peter, her hot-pants once again round her feet, and six different occupants of the toilet listening intently outside the door. In addition to the unmistakable sound of a man energetically screwing a woman, they'd been astonished to hear the woman describing how she'd just been had by somebody else.

'You can go back for a drink with them if you like,' Beccie said to Jonathan. 'I just fancy going home to sleep.'

Tracie and Peter looked at each other. This was an

unexpected bonus. Tracie had already done the business with Jonathan, but here, possibly, was a chance for her to perform once more.

'Are you sure?' asked Jonathan.

'Of course. You can always phone for a taxi back.'

And so it was, twenty minutes later, that the three of them were in Tracie's lounge, already well plastered, and each now with a large tumbler of brandy in hand. As the men flopped down into armchairs, Tracie pressed a button on the hi-fi and began to move to the slow, sexy strains of the CD. Jonathan stared at the beautifully filled seat of her hot-pants as they gyrated right in front of his face. He'd been there, he said to himself. He'd been there less than a couple of hours before. He'd been jammed right up inside her, for the second time in his life. He'd been wedged tightly inside her and shagged her until both of them had come off with a bang. Twice now he'd had a slice of that shapely, saucy little bum . . .

Tracie turned to face him, so that her back was now directly towards Peter. She winked, and was delighted to see him blush. He shot a quick glance at Peter and was relieved to note that he appeared fully occupied in studying his wife's tightly clad rear end. She was being a bit blatant about all this, thought Jonathan, as Tracie grinned sexily and then blew him a kiss.

'What do you think of these hot-pants?' she asked him, still swishing her hips slowly from side to side in time with the music.

'They're very sexy,' he replied truthfully, once again darting an anxious look at her husband.

'They are, aren't they?' Peter remarked casually.

'But not as sexy as what's underneath,' giggled Tracie, flipping the straps off her shoulders so that they dangled down to her knees.

'Christ!' muttered Jonathan, downing a huge gulp of brandy.

'Do you want to see what I mean?' she asked sweetly.

Jonathan emptied his glass with one swallow.

'Don't worry about me,' said Peter. 'I don't mind her

showing herself off. I know she enjoys it.'

Apart from her high-heeled, knee-length boots, Tracie was only wearing two other items of clothing. Slowly she began to unbutton the cuffs of her blouse, still facing Jonathan and still swaying to the music. Then she undid the front, starting at the top. Thirty seconds later she was naked above the waist, her firm, pert breasts pointing prettily in Jonathan's direction. 'Jesus Christ!' was all that he could say.

Before he could recover his composure, come-soaked hot-pants were round her ankles and the tight little opening he'd plundered earlier was exactly level with his eyes, the curled-back lips smiling at him sweetly.

Tracie stepped out of the fallen hot-pants and stooped to retrieve them, demurely bending her knees to do so. 'She'd like you to fuck her again,' Peter said pleasantly, his eyes now fixed on Jonathan's.

Jonathan coloured. The significance of the final word had not been lost on him. 'Jesus!' he gasped once more.

Tracie spoke up. 'Do you remember me telling you to keep your hands off my bottom?' she asked. 'When we were shagging each other in the loo?'

He nodded without speaking. 'This is why,' she informed him, turning round and showing him her savagely caned cheeks. 'What do you think about that?'

'God, you look nice!' he breathed, hardly daring to trust his eyes.

'Peter did it,' she said over her shoulder. 'So that I can fuck anyone I want. Provided I tell him all about it. Or let him watch me on the job. He likes watching me enjoy myself. It's the best thing that ever happened to us.'

Tracie knew exactly what Peter wanted. Kneeling on the armchair, with her legs straddling a half-naked Jonathan, she lifted her bottom high in the air until the whole of his fiercely erect tackle was in her husband's view. Then she sank down slowly, taking him inside an inch at a time, enabling Peter to watch his friend vanishing into her by degrees. Up and down she began to move her hips, easing him back and forth at a gentle pace, and allowing Peter to see exactly how she was spiking herself on him. As the beautifully striped bottom rose and fell, Peter sat back in his comfortable armchair and savoured the sight. His own weapon was in the same condition it had been for most of the preceding twenty-four hours: longer and harder than it had ever been before. So rigid that it positively hurt.

Tracie twisted her head and looked back at him. 'Don't you want to get into me too?' she whispered, as she sank all the way down on Jonathan. 'Wouldn't you like to be where you finished off last night?'

Peter stood up and reached for a jar of face cream that Tracie had left on a shelf by the fire. It was hideously expensive, but he fancied his wife so much that he'd willingly have stuffed hundreds of pounds worth into her bottom whenever she wanted him in there.

For the next ten minutes Tracie knelt on the chair, stock-still and sobbing with pleasure as she let the men shaft her as hard as they could. Suddenly they erupted together and she screamed with delight, their piping-hot fluid burning the inside of her bottom and womb.

As soon as they'd finished, she slid off Jonathan and stood up. 'Carry me upstairs, Peter!' she sighed, turning and wrapping her arms right round him. 'You know what we're going to do for the rest of the night?'

'I'll let myself out,' murmured Jonathan, collecting his trousers and underpants from the carpet as he watched Peter pick her up in a fireman's lift and then turn towards the stairs.

Chapter 11

Sunday Morning, Go for a Ride

The following morning Tracie sat up in bed beside Peter, bare breasts pointing straight out in front of her, telephone in hand. 'Hello, Janet,' she said, having dialled the number she'd been given on Friday. 'It's Tracie. How are you?'

'Tracie!' cried the voice at the other end of the line. 'How lovely to hear from you! Oh dear! My pussy's starting to gush with juice just at the sound of your voice!'

'You're incorrigible!' laughed Tracie, snuggling up against Peter.

'I don't know about that. But I'm certainly in love with you.'

'I thought you said you were in love with your husband,' teased Tracie.

'I am, of course. But it's a totally different sort of love, isn't it? You don't spend all your time wanting to ream me out with some grossly oversized prick, do you?'

'If I had one, I would,' giggled Tracie. 'Believe me. There's nothing I'd like better.'

'That would be nice,' Janet sighed dreamily.

'Anyway, Janet, that's not what I rang to tell you.'

'Oh? That's disappointing.'

'I wondered if I could take you up on your offer?'

'Which one? To spend the night together?'

'No. Your invitation to the party tonight.'

'Really? You want to come to our sex romp? I thought you said there was no way that Peter would agree?'

'I did.'

'So he's away from home, is he? You'd like to come on your own?'

'No. He's sitting right here beside me in bed.'

'But you told me . . .'

'I know what I said. But everything's changed since then. It's a long story, but I'll tell you all about it later. The upshot is that we'd *both* like to accept your invitation. If it's still standing, of course.'

'Of course it's still standing! So Peter's right there listening, is he?'

'Yes.'

'Say hello to him for me.'

'Hello from Janet,' Tracie said to her husband.

'Hello back to her,' he replied with a grin.

'I heard that,' said Janet. 'He's got a really sexy voice, hasn't he?'

'And the rest of him more than lives up to it,' Tracie assured her. 'As I hope you'll find out tonight.'

'I can't wait to meet him. Look, come over to lunch and then stay the rest of the day. We're at Rollie's house in the country, Rayke Hall. Come over as soon as you like. And stay the night, of course.'

'Are you sure?'

'Well, we've got over thirty spare bedrooms, so it isn't much of a problem. All our party guests will be staying overnight. But I'd like to see you before then. Do you want to come for lunch?'

Peter nodded at Tracie. 'Yes, we'd love to,' she said happily. 'What sort of time?'

'Oh, as soon as you like. Are you doing anything for the rest of the morning?'

'Yes. We're shagging each other's brains out.'

'That's good. Drive over as soon as you've finished. But if I were you, I'd keep something back for tonight!'

'I think Janet has designs on me,' Tracie said lightly, as Peter drove them through the sun-drenched countryside.

'I thought you'd already had each other twice.'

'We have. But I think she wants us to start an affair. How would you feel about that, Peter?'

'Excited.'

'I think she wants us to sleep together occasionally. Just

the two of us, I mean. No husbands in the bed as well.'

'That's not a problem with me. I know I can trust you to tell me how you spent your night of lesbian lust.'

'Of course you can. I won't ever do anything that I'll keep quiet about, Peter.'

'But what about Sir Roland? What will he think about the idea?'

'I don't know. I don't think Janet knows either. If he says "no", then that will be that. She won't risk him finding out she's been at it behind his back, I'm sure.'

'Very sensible, since the old buffer's so stinking rich.'

'Perhaps I should remind you how the "old buffer" – as you call him – spent over three hours last Thursday dicking me till I was fit to drop.'

'Let's hope he does the same to you tonight.'

'Let's hope you do the same to Janet.'

'Yes, let's both of us hope both of those things.'

A light lunch was served on the lawn nearest the house, in the shade of a huge copper beech. All four of them were getting on famously – the men shared a common interest in almost every conceivable type of sporting activity, and Tracie could see at once that Janet, in her mind, was already rutting away with Peter. Sir Roland, being the son of one of the *nouveau riche*, was as down to earth as anyone could have wished. And Janet, being a lovely, sexy young girl of aristocratic breeding, with a good sense of humour, would have been welcome in any right-minded gathering.

'It was really funny,' giggled Janet, sipping her iced mineral water. 'Somehow this rather nice young chartered accountant hadn't realised what sort of party it was. I cornered him alone in the billiard room before dinner, and sat him down on the edge of the snooker table so I could tug down his knickers. Then Rollie walks in just as I've sat on his cock! You should have seen the look on his face! I thought the poor man was going to have a heart attack! But Rollie put him at ease, didn't you, pet? Rollie just picks up this silver salver and asks him if he'd like some canapés while he's on the job.'

'I hope he declined,' said Tracie. 'I mean, it would have spoilt his appetite for dinner.'

'He didn't have time to answer,' chuckled Sir Roland. 'At that very moment one of our other male guests walked into the room carrying the accountant's wife over his shoulder, her evening dress up round her waist and her knickers dangling round her left ankle.'

'Well, that must have helped to settle his conscience, didn't it?' mused Peter.

'Actually, he was more than a bit put out,' said Janet. 'You see, his wife hadn't realised what was going on, either. She'd just thought she was letting some handsome young blade have a very quick dip on the side.'

'We must be a bit more careful with the guest list in future,' Sir Roland said thoughtfully. 'Irate husbands do not make ideal material for a wife-swapping party.'

A game of tennis was suggested, so the girls peeled off to one changing room, whilst the men headed for another.

'I understand my wife's fallen in love with yours,' Sir Roland said conversationally.

'Apparently so,' confirmed Peter.

'Can't say I blame her. Tracie's a beautiful girl. You're very lucky.'

'Thank you. I agree.'

'What are your views, Peter? Should we let them have an affair?'

'I can't see why not. It will be fun for them. And probably for us, as well. Personally, I relish the thought of Tracie romping around in bed with another girl. I find it quite a turn on. And it won't mean she'll love me any the less.'

'I think I'll let myself view it the same way,' Sir Roland said slowly. 'It will make Janet happy. And let's face it, she never objects to anything I do. Much the opposite, in fact. It would be different if she wanted to start a love affair with a man.'

'Why's that?'

'I'm not exactly sure. She shags plenty of them, that's for certain. But at least I'm around and able to keep an eye on things. I don't think I'd be very keen on her getting close to one of them, that's all.'

'Not even if she was totally frank with you about what they'd been doing together? And how she felt about him?'

'I'm not really sure.'

'I think I know what you mean, Roland. Getting herself fucked is one thing. Getting fond of the mother-fucker concerned is another.'

'Aptly put.'

Very briefly, Tracie gave Janet an outline of what had happened between her and Peter on Friday night, and also on how they'd spent their Saturday together.

'That's wonderful for you!' enthused Janet, watching closely as Tracie stepped out of her clothes. 'But oh, your poor bottom! Your poor, poor bottom! Just look at it! It must be absolute agony.'

'It is. And I love it!'

Janet ran a fingertip very lightly down one blistered buttock after the other. 'You look lovely, though!' she breathed thickly. 'Really, really lovely! And you're so hot! You're almost burning me when I touch you. That's the only trouble with Rollie. He'd never do that to me, however much I begged him. He's far too softhearted, you see.'

'He seems very nice,' Tracie said with feeling. 'Will I get to fuck him again tonight?'

'Yes, of course. He's the host, after all. The bossman. He makes the rules.'

'That only seems right.'

'Kiss me, Tracie!' Janet pleaded suddenly. 'Just a little one before we start the tennis.'

The girls looked gorgeous in their short, virgin-white tennis skirts and tiny matching knickers. 'I've been talking to Peter,' Sir Roland said with a gentle smile, opening the gate that led to the six immaculate, emerald-green courts.

'What about?' Janet asked anxiously.

'About you and Tracie, of course.'

'And?'

'And I think it's quite right that you should do whatever you both want to do.'

Janet threw her arms round her husband. 'Oh, Rollie! I love you to pieces.'

Tracie smiled at Peter and winked.

'Are you sure, Rollie? Really, positively sure?'

'Yes. Of course.'

'Can we go to bed this afternoon? After the tennis, I mean?'

'If that's what you want, then of course you can. Peter and I can have a hack round the golf course.'

Janet turned to face Tracie, an imploring look on her face.

'That would be nice,' Tracie said simply, tennis knickers damp with desire.

Six hours later the girls lay exhausted in each other's arms, happy and completely at peace. No sperm had been spilt, no balls had been banged against bottoms, no pricks has ploughed through pussy at speed. Instead, tongues, lips and fingertips had petted and probed gently but deeply, boobs and bottoms had been tenderly fondled, and long, sweet female kisses had been exchanged and exchanged again. And one slow, soft, lingering orgasm after another had smoothed its way delightfully through gently writhing frames. In between, female thoughts and ideas had been spoken – confidentially, one girl to another.

'You're so beautiful!' sighed Janet, kissing the side of the other girl's neck.

'And you're so fuckable!' breathed Tracie, squeezing soft round buttocks in her right hand. 'You deserve a really stiff one.'

'That's going to happen very soon,' murmured Janet, looking at her watch. 'To both of us.'

'I'm really looking forward to it. Aren't you?'

'Yes. Very much.'

'What's the time, Janet?'

'Half past eight. Everyone will be downstairs, sipping champagne.'

'Won't they wonder where their hostess has got to?'

'No. Rollie will have told them that we're up here together in bed.'

Tracie wrapped a second arm around her new lover. 'Don't be embarrassed,' she whispered.

'I won't,' Janet replied at once. 'I'll be proud.'

'Lick me off just one more time. It'll only take a moment. Then we'll go down and feast on the men!'

Chapter 12

Half & Half

'How was it?' Peter asked quietly, as the assembled gathering made its way towards the huge mahogany dining table. The party consisted of twelve couples in all, plus the hosts. Twelve elegantly and expensively groomed young couples from the teeming middle classes of Southern England. The men were in dinner suits, the wives in full-length, figure-hugging evening gowns. Jewellery and cleavage abounded, as did high heels and make-up that had taken hours to apply (amongst the wives, that is).

'I'm in love,' Tracie said with a happy smile. 'She'll be really good for me.'

'I know. I'm very pleased for you, Tracie.'

'You're so wonderful I could eat you!'

'You'll get the chance later, I'm sure.'

'Janet and I are going to Rollie's chateau in France. This Thursday and Friday, when you're at the Torquay conference.'

'You'll have a great time, I know.'

'I wish I could fuck her, Peter!'

'I'll do it for you tonight, if you like.'

'Oh, yes please! That would be lovely. Give her yards and yards – just for me.'

'Just for you.'

'You're an angel, Peter. You know I've always loved you, despite the other men.'

'Yes. I know it now, at least.'

'You're not jealous of Janet, are you, Peter? There's no need to be, you know. Loving her is nothing like loving you. It's just the same word to describe two totally different feelings.'

'I know that,' he grinned handsomely, smacking her bottom rather firmly and making her shriek.

'Stop that!' Sir Roland raised his voice. 'That's your own wife you're manhandling so familiarly. How dare you! Do you have so little respect for this gathering of like-minded men?'

'Sorry, Roland!' Peter said with a look of mock contrition.

Peter sat down and stared in surprise at the menu: 'Pussie de foid gras, followed by Cock au very Vin.'

'Rollie can't resist his little joke,' said Janet, who sat prettily beside him. 'Actually it's a seafood night. Scallops with bacon and caviar, giant prawns in garlic, oysters and lobster balls, and sole in a champagne and fresh truffle sauce.'

'Sounds very ordinary,' snorted Peter, nodding politely to the servant to indicate that he'd like his glass filled to the brim. 'Why not cod and chips?'

Janet pushed a fork into a huge ball of succulent white lobster, then transferred it to her plate. 'I've fallen in love with your wife,' she whispered to Peter, placing a warm hand on the top of his thigh.

'I know. And she loves you too. She just wishes she was able to fuck you, as I'm sure she's made you aware. So I've promised I'll do the job for her. I hope that's okay with you?'

She squeezed his leg with sudden passion. 'You're making me terribly wet!' she replied. 'Loving Tracie makes me keener on men than ever. And that really *is* saying something!'

Now the vintage wines were really in flow. Janet leant forward across the table to speak to Tracie, who was sitting directly opposite Peter. 'I'm going to enjoy watching you shag,' she said quietly. 'I'm going to enjoy it just as much as Peter does.'

'I'm going to enjoy watching Peter shag you,' countered Tracie, with a smile of affection for each of them.

'I'm going to enjoy both!' enthused Peter, gulping down the rest of his wine.

* * *

'Sue and I are new to this,' said the pleasant-looking man sitting to Tracie's right. 'This is our first party at Rayke Hall.'

'Same here,' replied Tracie, delicately forking a delicious portion of filleted sole into her mouth.

'Have you ever been to anything similar?'

'Er, no. Not really. Peter's quite a late convert to this sort of thing. Only a few days ago he'd never have dreamt of it.'

'What changed his attitude? If it's not a rude question?'

'No, it's not rude at all. He suddenly discovered how much he liked watching me perform. He caught me out red-handed, you see. But instead of separating my head from the rest of my body, he got his best friend to do it to me the next night, while he watched. Then he gave me a very sound caning and told me I could fuck whoever I liked in the future, provided he knew all about it. How come you two are here?'

The young man looked a trifle confused. 'I'm not all that certain. Sue got to know Sir Roland, somewhere . . .'

'But you're quite happy with what's about to happen?'

'Yes, I think so.'

'But you don't know for certain? I mean, you've never done any swapping before?'

'No. Never.'

'Will you enjoy watching her, do you think?'

'I hope so.'

'You're not an accountant, by any chance?'

'How on earth did you know that?' he cried.

'Oh, er, I didn't. It was just something Janet was telling me about this afternoon that made me ask.'

Peter leant sideways towards Janet. 'How long have you been holding these parties?' he asked, surreptitiously reaching down and squeezing the top of one thigh through her expensive silk dress.

'Oh, Rollie's been at it for years. He's so incredibly randy.

That's what broke up his first marriage. The parties and the women. But I'm different. I can handle it. I get more than my fair share of fun from this sort of thing.'

'I bet you do!'

'I got gang-banged a couple of months ago. On the chaise longue in the living room, in front of everyone. Eight men, one after the other, in less than twenty minutes. Rollie thought it just happened – but I'd set it up in advance.' She giggled wickedly and pressed her leg against his.

'I wish I'd been one of the eight!'

She placed a hand over his. 'You'll get your turn tonight. I'm going to make sure that you're the first to have me. If that's what you'd like.'

'What do you think?' he asked, glancing, not very discreetly, down the front of her creamy-smooth cleavage.

'I think you'll be just as good a lover as your wife,' she replied.

'How long have you been married, Janet?'

'Five years. Since I was nineteen. Daddy was furious. He's the Earl of Hunstanton, you know. So he considers Rollie an upstart. Rollie's father was the first one to have the title, whereas Daddy's is over seven hundred years old.'

'But you didn't take any notice of Daddy?'

'No. None at all. I knew he was jealous of Rollie – because Rollie's about a hundred times richer. He's the only Englishman to own a casino in Las Vegas.'

'So you're a genuine, blue-blooded aristocrat?'

'Yes. I was Lady Janet for nineteen years, before I became just plain Lady Rayke.'

'I think you and Rollie are fantastic. I've never known anyone like you. No airs and graces, despite the title and all that fabulous wealth.'

'What do you do for a living, Peter?'

'I trade bonds.'

'Bonds?'

'Yes, bonds. You know, securities. I work for a merchant bank. I buy them when they're cheap and sell them when they're expensive. Well, that's the theory, at least.'

'It's the other way round with women. We're so cheap

when you first bed us. But much, much the opposite when you cut us free.'

'Do you think you'll stay with Rollie?'

'Oh, yes. Well, I hope so, at least. It's not really the money. I do love him, you know. And with Tracie helping to keep my hot little pussy happy, it should all work out just fine. That's what I really need to make my marriage work out. Someone like Tracie. I'm not being nasty, but cock is ten a penny. Someone like Tracie would do my marriage a power of good.'

'I think you and she together as a couple will be good for me, as well as for you and Rollie.'

Janet looked at him thoughtfully. 'You're going to make a really lovely fuck!' she said at length.

At last the coffee and liqueurs were more or less finished and Sir Roland rose to his feet, amid an expectant hush. The dinner party was hanging on his every word. There were two couples new to their little gathering, announced Sir Roland, introducing Tracie and Peter and the couple sitting opposite and alongside: Sue and the chartered accountant. So, before the usual free-for-all began, Sir Roland continued, there would be a special half and half party in order to initiate the newcomers into the flock.

'What's a half and half party?' Tracie asked in surprise.

Sir Roland explained explicitly.

'You're joking!' gasped Sue, the vivacious young wife who was sitting on Peter's left, her thigh touching his. 'You mean that Tracie and I have got to do *that* . . . !'

'Yes indeed,' Sir Roland replied smoothly. 'Yes indeed, exactly that.'

The party then adjourned to the enormous living room at the rear of the house, drinks in hand.

Sue, a sexy dark-haired girl of about twenty-six, was told that she was to start the ball rolling. Her various options were explained to her by Sir Roland in great detail, making her blush and giggle, whilst her husband simply looked unsure. 'I think that last one,' she said after a pause, blushing even more. 'It does sound rather fun . . .'

Her husband, Bill, looked at her nervously, as if wishing they could skip the half and half party and move straight on to the orgy.

Sue, having chosen 'The Mysterious Stranger' as her method of being halved, lay on her front in the middle of the ultra-plush carpet, a cushion tucked underneath her groin, her nicely turned hips enticingly displayed through the lightweight material of her full-length evening gown. Bill lay on his back so that they were at right angles to each other, but face to face. Sue eased herself up on her elbows and began to smooch him enthusiastically, unbuttoning his shirt and caressing his torso as she did so. Slowly she reached down to his groin, her tongue still inside his mouth, and started to massage him through his trousers, lightly and gently, displaying an expert touch that soon made him hard. Then she unzipped him and slipped a hand inside. 'Someone's been expecting me!' she mumbled, squeezing firmly, her weight on her other elbow.

Lots had been drawn and Richard, a tall young man with well-kempt shoulder-length hair, was to be the lucky man of mystery. He remained seated for several more minutes, watching with interest as Sue's kiss became deeper and more passionate, whilst her hand continued to work away inside her husband's trousers. Slowly and steadily it worked, rubbing and squeezing, and then delving even deeper to pamper and pet.

Tracie could sense the excitement building up in everyone present. She pressed her thighs together and all but climaxed. She was aware that it was her turn next, and longed for it to start. She knew that the longer she was kept waiting, the hotter she'd become. Perhaps she should have chosen the same method as Sue, she wondered.

Richard knew exactly what he was doing. He knew exactly the right time to make his move. He would do nothing, he decided, until the couple on the floor were fully engrossed in each other. Already Bill had unzipped his wife's dress and peeled it down to her waist. Now he was removing her bra and fondling her breasts with relish.

Firm, pointed breasts that he held, one in each hand, whilst she kissed him and played with him below the waist.

Bill was fully enjoying his half of his wife. He was savouring the succulence of her mouth and the texture and weight of her beautiful boobs, as well as the way that her long, cool fingers were working on him inside his boxer shorts. And Sue was evidently enjoying herself too. The others watched as she wriggled luxuriously and ground her groin rhythmically into the cushion. 'Mmmm!' she murmured appreciatively.

Slowly she withdrew from the kiss and ran the tip of her tongue down his chest as far as his navel. Then she began to lick. After about a minute she slid her mouth up to his nipples and attended to each in turn, sucking hard and then nibbling gently. Then she returned to his mouth, still resting on one elbow, still rubbing his rock-hard penis with her spare hand. And still pressing her clitoris back and forth into the cushion with one long, graceful rotation of her lightly clad hips. 'Mmm!' she purred once again.

Cometh the hour, cometh the man, thought Richard, the mysterious stranger. He stood up from his armchair and knelt on the floor beside the slowly gyrating rear end. Sue's evening dress was slit at the back, exposing the backs of her silk-stockinged knees and then three or four inches of thigh. Without further ado, Richard slid his right hand inside the slit and between her legs. Pushing slowly but inexorably upwards, his hand crept stealthily past her stocking tops and then over the smooth, naked flesh beyond. 'Oh!' she gasped suddenly, so interested in snogging her husband that she hadn't even noticed the stranger until his fingers had found the already wet crotch of her knickers and begun to explore.

'No looking behind you,' warned one of the wives with a giggle. Quite unnecessarily, because Sue had already been made well aware of the rules of the game. Slowly and gently two fingertips continued to stroke the plumply-filled knicker crotch, causing it to become even wetter. She wriggled against the fingers and her breathing became noticeably deeper.

Whilst still kissing and fondling her husband, she felt a pair of strong, thick fingers pluck her knicker elastic to one side and enter her from the rear. 'Oh!' she gasped again, but this time not through any element of surprise. Again she wriggled against them, savouring the really forceful way in which they had already commenced their task. Quickly a rhythm was found. Quickly there was synchronisation between the way she was petting her husband and the good stiff finger job she was receiving from behind her back. She felt her first mini-climax rushing to meet her and had to lift her mouth from Bill's until it was past.

'That was quick!' murmured Bill, continuing to massage hot, hard nipples between fingers and thumbs.

'Sorry,' she said, blushing slightly.

Satisfied, Richard withdrew from the boiling-hot little quim that was now running with juices. He removed his hand from inside her dress and reached for the zip, which had already been lowered as far as the base of her spine. Having tugged it as far as it would go, he began to ease the dress down over her hips, exposing first the top of the cleft between her buttocks, and then a tiny pair of white satin bikini knickers two or three inches below. Down and down he slid the dress, snagging it momentarily across the dramatic swell of her satin-clad hips. Then it was free and drawn easily over her feet and away, leaving her lying there in knickers and matching suspenders, stockings and Gucci high heels.

All eyes in the room, including those of the girls, were rivetted to the tiny white knickers and the sexy little bottom they highlighted so well. After a short pause for everyone's benefit, Richard returned to work once again. Slowly but surely the knickers followed the same course as the dress, revealing two pouting pink cheeks to the assembled view. Smooth and dimpled they were, and quivering slightly in anticipation. Cheeks which for the past five years had been her husband's pride and joy. And very understandably, too. Cheeks which had never before seen the light of day on an occasion such as this. They had, once or twice during those years of marriage, been bared for someone other than Bill

– when Bill had been many miles away. When he'd been safely out of town and blissfully ignorant as to their fate. Not that Sue had ever actively sought these encounters, of course. But, as she'd said to herself quite frequently, sometimes that sort of thing simply couldn't be helped. Accidents would occasionally happen, particularly to a pair of buttocks as extensively hunted as hers. But bared and briefly shared though they'd been, they'd never found themselves exposed in this manner before.

Richard ran the palm of his hand lightly over each saucy plump orb of delight, savouring the creamy-smooth texture as the pressure on his zip increased.

Now the mysterious stranger had his half of Bill's wife fully prepared and oven-ready. Purposefully he got to his feet. His own shirt, trousers and pants hit the floor in rapid succession, leaving it obvious to everyone why he was known as 'Big Dick'. Carefully he lowered himself onto her back, his legs on either side of hers, his erection pressing hotly into the fine firm flesh of her bottom. He took his weight on his hands, so that Bill's half would not be imposed upon unduly. Then he arched his back and thrust. So open and ready was she, that he found her immediately, making her squeal in surprise. Then he proceeded to shaft her, using quick, urgent strokes from the very beginning, much to the entertainment of those seated around.

It was pork of the highest quality. Nothing was spared. No mercy was shown, no quarter asked or given. Richard pulled himself back as far as he could, then immediately drove himself home. Then out of her as quickly and far as he could, then brutally home with a splat, his stomach muscles noisily splattering the cheeks of her bottom, his long powerful tool lancing her insides.

Gasping and closing her eyes, Sue adjusted her position underneath him, turning her shoulders and twisting her head down to her husband's groin in order to transfer him from hand to mouth. Bill sighed happily and cupped his hands under his head. Now he was watching his own member slithering back and forth in her mouth, as well as Richard's pumping wildly in and out between the much-loved cheeks of her upturned bottom. He found the spectacle fascinating. Poignantly fascinating. The sight and sound of some hairy young gorilla taking his wife from behind should have been the worst in the world. Instead, it was the most erotic thing he and she had ever done. The combination of jealousy and desire was irresistible. Each slap of groin against buttock, each squelch of plundering penis, each groan of pleasure from Sue, seemed to make his own erection expand.

Incredibly, the trespassing stranger was somehow able to increase the pace even further. Bill goggled in awe as the long, wet cock ripped back and forth. One second it was withdrawn and fully visible in all its rampant male splendour, then it was gone, rammed forcefully into his wife. Buried deep inside his own wife as far as it would go. Which was indeed a considerable way. Further than he himself could penetrate her, Bill was fully aware. And he could tell that she was thoroughly appreciating the extra measure. He knew that much from her reactions. He knew from the way she wriggled and squawked.

As the bitter-sweet excitement intensified, Bill knew other things as well. He knew that the second Richard started to implant her, he'd find himself jetting powerfully into her mouth. And he also knew that he and Sue would spend tonight, and every night for the next few months, fucking each other until they were blue. He'd spend hours lying on top of those fat little buttocks, shagging her for all he was worth. Shagging her and recalling exactly how this oversized young stud was shagging her right now. And no doubt Sue would spend those hours in the matrimonial bed wriggling and writhing her pretty little bottom underneath him in repeated waves of ecstasy as she recalled the same thing.

Ten minutes later, and very red in the face, Sue rose to her feet rather unsteadily. She covered herself with her hands as best she could. 'Has anyone seen my knickers?' she mumbled sheepishly, suddenly finding herself more than a trifle embarrassed now that everything was over and done.

'Over there, by the fireplace,' said Tracie. 'Under your dress.'

Sue stooped to retrieve her clothes, bending demurely from the knees. Twenty-five pairs of eyes followed the contours of her still very bare bottom as it snaked its way towards the door. It, too, seemed be blushing, but probably only as a result of the way it had been mistreated by Richard's iron-hard loins.

'Don't be too long,' one of the men called after her. 'We don't want to wait too long before the next performance.'

Sir Roland stood up. 'Don't worry,' he said kindly to Sue, patting her playfully, but quite loudly, across her oh-so-temptingly naked nether regions. 'We'll all have a drink while you visit the bathroom. There isn't any rush.'

'Thank you,' she stammered over her shoulder, her face and buttocks seeming to redden even more.

Was he the one who'd just had her, she wondered to herself. If not, it was rather familiar of him to smack her bottom like that. In front of her husband, as well.

Fifteen minutes later, Sue slipped quietly back into the room, studiously avoiding anyone's gaze but Bill's. 'Hi,' she said softly, starting to blush all over again.

The two wives who'd been talking to Bill had the decency to drift away and leave the couple to themselves. 'Are you all right, darling?' Bill asked with mild concern.

'Yes, of course.'

'You were a long while, that's all.'

'I was just plucking up courage to face everyone.'

'There's no need for you to feel embarrassed. It was fun.'

'I know. But I can't help it. I'll feel happier once Tracie has had her turn.'

'Of course.'

'And, Bill. Please don't tell me who it was. I think I'd rather not know.'

'Okay, darling.'

'Has anyone been talking about me?'

'No,' he lied. 'Not a word, I promise.'

'You don't think too badly of me, do you, Bill?'
'Don't be silly! Why should I?'
'Well, you could see how much I was enjoying it. You could tell how much it was making me come.'

Lots were not drawn for Tracie, as the host, Sir Roland, selected himself to attend to her needs below the waist. No mysterious stranger was to be involved this time. As with all incidents of halving, her top half was the preserve of her husband, her lower half that of the guest. In this way, Peter was to be the host while the host would temporarily become the guest. This is to say, Peter would be hosting his wife, while the dinner-party host would be making a guest appearance below the belt. Below the suspender belt, to be perfectly accurate. This was an invariable rule which governs all such half and half parties, and cannot be altered even with the consent of everyone concerned. The husband always takes care of the top half, the visitor makes free with the rest. And no encroachment is allowed. Overlapping is strictly forbidden. The visitor can poke and probe the other man's wife to his heart's content, but he is not allowed the indecency of straying above her navel – except internally, of course, should he be fortunate enough to possess the wherewithal.

Now Tracie's time had come. She was sitting on Peter's lap, wriggling her bottom sexily into his groin, her eyes shining into his. 'Can you unzip me, Peter?' she asked sweetly. He was more than happy to oblige. She eased herself up from his knee and moved a step forward. After a short pause for dramatic effect, she stepped gracefully out of her dress, revealing a matching set of bra, G-string knickers, suspenders and stocking tops. Slowly she turned full circle, smiling at the murmur of surprise and approval instantly provoked by the six fiery red marks of the cane. 'You look beautiful!' one young wife murmured truthfully, staring at the near-naked bottom so prominently on display. 'Did Peter do that to you?'

'Yes,' Tracie said proudly, over her shoulder. 'Doesn't it look nice?'

Bill opened his mouth to speak, but was unable to formulate the words. 'What an exquisite sight!' he said to himself instead.

'That's the prettiest thing we've ever seen at one of these parties,' Sir Roland announced happily.

'It's the sexiest thing that's ever been done to me,' replied Tracie, loving the attention. She caught Janet's eye, and smiled tenderly and lovingly. Janet smiled back, the intensity of her feelings quite apparent.

'I just love those knickers, too!' chuckled Richard, referring to the lacy pink G-string panties that hid nothing but pussy from view. And a mouthwateringly plump little pussy it was, too. Everyone could clearly see that. Her bra, suspenders and stocking tops were made from the same frothy pink material, and the stockings themselves were the palest shade of pink. Earlier that evening Janet had been lying on the bed ogling her as she'd slipped into her delightful undies, knowing that she'd be seeing them again quite soon. Now Janet felt a sharp pang of pleasure and pride. Particularly pride. No one could deny what a heart-stopping picture her sweet young lover made, standing there in next to nothing at all, and showing not a hint of embarrassment or shame. Everyone knew that the two of them had spent the afternoon and early evening together in bed. And everyone knew that her husband was now about to pleasure the same lovely young body.

Peter was on his feet. He wrapped his arms round her and kissed her, long and lovingly, feeling himself become powerfully erect. He was not aware of the fact that behind her back Sir Roland, their host and her guest, had reached out from his chair and taken a gentle two-handed hold on the red hot, but silky smooth, bare bottom that was pouting at him so provocatively from just a couple of feet away. Strictly speaking, this was against the rules. But since he was the host (of the dinner party), no one felt they could complain. And Tracie was enjoying the sensation. With each squeeze from Sir Roland, she pushed forward against Peter's groin.

Sir Roland stood up behind her, maintaining his hold

on the cheekiest part of her bottom. Tracie sighed inwardly. Being attended to by two men always made you feel extra special. It always made you feel you were being given a treat. But when one of them was your lawfully wedded husband! That was really something else! That really added an extra edge. She'd had a few threesomes in the past, but it was even more fun having your own husband helping you to get yourself screwed. It made you see him in quite a different light. It made you feel so warm and tender towards him, even though he'd only just realised that Sir Roland's hands were roaming all over your bottom . . . and well beyond . . .

Tracie broke off the kiss and looked up at Peter, with a light in her eyes so soft and adoring that it made him catch his breath. 'I love you, Peter,' she whispered into his ear, too quietly for anyone to hear. Then she pressed forward, grinding her clitoris against his bulging erection as Sir Roland fingered her from behind, and as everyone else in the room began to realise that they were feeling as randy as hell.

She slipped out of her bra without any bidding, and cast it away. Then she unbuttoned Peter's shirt and pressed her fine young breasts into his chest. Her nipples were scalding hot against his skin. The fingering from behind continued, but she forced herself to concentrate on her husband. She told herself that she was making love to him. That Sir Roland's very robust attentions were just something that would accentuate that love-making. Peter was the object of her attentions, she reminded herself. As her G-string knickers were slowly peeled down to her ankles, she told herself to persevere with that idea. She told herself to make love to her husband, even though it would be someone else inside her. It was the least she could do for Peter.

Tracie had chosen the good old-fashioned armchair method of halving. She lay back in the comfortably reclined chair, wearing only her pink suspenders and stockings. Peter was kneeling to her right, leaning over to kiss her and stroke her breasts. Sir Roland knelt between her outstretched legs, his erection in her hands. He moved forward against her and she slightly readjusted her hold so that, when he pushed, he entered her with ease. With one single movement he slid all the way up to the top of her soaking-wet channel. Tracie closed her eyes and allowed herself to savour the sensation of having her husband's tongue deep in her mouth, but another man's bone-hard flesh plugged tightly into her lower opening.

Peter didn't need to look down to know that Sir Roland was now fully inside her. He could tell it from her reactions. In fact, he could feel it from them. As he continued to kiss and caress, he could feel the other man's penis crammed deep inside her body. And when Sir Roland started to move, he could feel that too. He could feel the swollen head of the penis pushing back and forth inside her. He could feel it pulling all the way back, pausing, and then filling and stretching her once again. It was a most peculiar sensation. He wasn't just watching or listening to someone else fucking her, he was actually feeling it for himself, almost as if she were now part of him. And he could feel her enjoyment, too. He could feel how her insides reacted to each separate poke and prod. He could feel it through the kiss and the caress that they still shared, and through the way she breathed and moved. He could feel that the intruding organ was already bringing her close to climax. It was an incredible experience. They were actually sharing her fuck! And he was certain she felt the same way. He was certain that she knew he was sharing it with her.

Tracie wriggled and groaned as she felt her insides turn to fire. God, this was truly unbelievable – being kissed and fondled by Peter whilst at the same time another man's oversized dick was scouring her out! There was something unbelievably erotic about the situation. It would have been sexy enough if both the men had been strangers. But to have her own husband wrapped round the top half of her body, whilst a roomful of people watched her being porked by somebody else!

And she could tell that Peter was enjoying himself too. She could tell that he was fully aroused. And not only because her hand was now jammed down his trousers. She could just sense the excitement building up inside him as Sir Roland continued to thrust.

Suddenly Tracie felt her orgasm bursting upon her. 'Oh, Peter!' she squealed loudly, pulling her head away from him and then burying his face in her boobs. Instantly he started to suck. 'Oh, Peter!' she shrieked again. 'I've never come so hard!'

A split second later she could feel Sir Roland starting to gush. 'I love you, Peter!' she gasped, wriggling her hips as fiercely as she could in order to milk Sir Roland of every last drop. Just as with the fucking, Peter could actually feel her being implanted. He could feel the other man's seed pumping into her. And he could feel the way in which it was intensifying her own climax.

At last the free-for-all was announced. Each of the partygoers clutched the nearest member of the opposite sex and started to pull off his or her clothes. Tracie stood up from the armchair, enjoying the feel of the freshly shot fluid inside her. 'Come here, Peterkins!' she giggled. 'Let me get you ready for all those lucky young wives!' As she started to undress him, she noticed two men set upon Janet with determination. Seconds later she was stripped down to her high heels, stockings and suspenders, and two pairs of hands were all over her.

Within less than a minute the disrobing was complete. Bare boobs, bottoms and stocking tops were everywhere, dicks in various stages of erection abounded, and pubes and pussies were on show. Wherever you looked, hands were groping and mauling and mouths were pressed against mouths. Then, very quickly, several mouths were lowered to below the waist. Sue was already being taken from behind, under the watchful gaze of her husband. Tracie tried to interpret his expression, but couldn't decide whether or not it was one of lust. Then she was obliged to divert her attention to the young man who was urgently trying to enter her. 'Here, let me,' she said, slipping him comfortably inside.

'Oh God, you're far too lovely!' gasped the man, starting to pump her as hard as he could. 'You're going to bring me off with a hell of a bang!' Tracie glanced over his shoulder and was relieved to see that Sue's husband was now happily embedded in one of the other wives. He was, however, still casting the occasional glance at his own wife in order to monitor her progress.

Janet had made a beeline for Peter as soon as she'd managed to extricate herself from the two pairs of hands that had stripped her. 'Not yet,' she'd said firmly to the eager young men, both of whom had been desperately trying to impale her at the same time and in the same place. 'I have a promise to keep.'

Now, whilst Peter lay back on the settee, his mouth glued to hers, Janet was astride him, her gorgeous bare bottom rising and falling with aristocratic grace as she rode him, her breasts pressing hotly into his chest as she did so. Temporarily she broke the kiss – one of her former pursuers had climbed onto her back and started to push himself into her invitingly upturned rear end. 'I thought I told you to wait,' she said over her shoulder, through a faceful of hair.

'I can't!' he pleaded. 'I've been watching you all night. It won't take a second.'

'All right,' she sighed patiently, bearing down on Peter whilst her other suitor began to hammer in and out. 'But be as quick as you can. Peter and I are wanting to do something a little bit special.'

'I told you I wouldn't be long!' he croaked a few seconds later, starting to swamp her with seed. 'My friend will be just as quick.'

'Oh, no!' gasped Janet, realising that the other young buck was queued up behind him.

'I can wait,' Peter grinned.

'That's the trouble with these parties,' said Janet, as her plump bottom was skewered again. 'It's not always possible to avoid outside interference.'

* * *

And so it proved. The penises just wouldn't leave her alone. 'Let's go upstairs,' she suggested eventually, licking her lips and wiping her chin with her hand. Peter followed, his eyes on the deliciously lascivious curves of her fabulous bottom, his cock hard and upright and wet with her juices. 'We'll use a spare bedroom,' she told him. 'This is where Tracie and I spent the afternoon.'

They crashed onto the four-poster bed and Peter rolled on top of her, entering her fiercely and starting to bounce her up and down with the weight of each thrust.

'Your dick feels as big as Rollie's!' she panted, closing her eyes as another mini-climax began.

'It seems to have grown since Friday night.'

'I wish Rollie would cane me!' she sighed. 'But perhaps that would make him too big to fit inside!'

Peter began to pump sperm deep into her womb. But he could tell that he wasn't going to shrink when he'd finished. He could tell he was going to stay stiff. 'How do you do that?' she gasped, when she realised he was still as erect as ever, despite having implanted her profusely.

'I don't know,' he replied, shafting her just as sharply as before. 'Sometimes it just happens. When I'm really worked up, I mean.'

Janet writhed her hips in pleasure. 'It's a glorious feeling,' she breathing. 'Tracie's such a lucky girl!'

The evening had started with great promise, Janet said to herself, as Peter continued to bounce her up and down with abandon. To start with, two men had emptied themselves into her bottom and two more in her mouth, all of them whilst she and Peter had been powerfully coupled on the settee downstairs. And now she was getting this really wonderful treatment from Tracie's handsome young hunk of a husband. She was finding that being in love with Tracie made her fancy Peter as much as she'd ever fancied anyone. She just revelled in the idea that she was sharing him with her . . . Oh, how lovely! Peter was flooding her again!

And still the bonking continued at pace. Still he remained

stiff as a board inside her, poking hard against the neck of her womb with every push. Another orgasm began to build inside her, much stronger than any of the previous. 'Ohhhhh!' she groaned in delight, wriggling her bottom from side to side and pressing her sharply pointed nipples even harder into his hairy male chest. 'Oh, Peter! How clever you are! Oh my God! You're making me come all over again!'

The climax hammered right through her, bright flashing pangs of pleasure shooting back and forth between nipples and overwrought groin. 'Oh!' she squealed loudly. 'Oh Peter! Ohh! Ohh! Ohh! Ohhhh!'

Peter turned her over onto her front and remounted – his legs straddling hers, his hands underneath the plumply rounded breasts, and his groin slapping hard into the cheeks of her bottom as he parted soaking-wet pussy with gusto. He stared down at those bouncing pink cheeks, glorying in the way his penis was racing back and forth between them. It seemed to him, in this position, that he was an even tighter fit than before. Harder and faster he piled into her, her bottom bouncing more wildly than ever as he increased the pace of the coupling. A third stream of his boiling-hot essence jetted into her, bringing her off once again. Yet still the marathon fuck continued, Janet now shrieking at the top of her voice as she squirmed and writhed. *Slap! Slap! Slap!* went his groin against her buttocks. *Squelch! Squelch! Squelch!* went his iron-hard penis, as it flew back and forth through copious quantities of cream. And 'Ohhhhh! Ohhhhh! Ohhhhh!' howled Janet, quite unable to believe how comprehensively she was being taken from above and behind.

Now he was driving into her as hard as he could, arching his back and pulling himself all the way out, then slamming back inside with all the force he could muster. Again and again and again. Tears rolled slowly down her face as she gasped and moaned and groaned, and wriggled her buttocks for all she was worth. But still he wouldn't give up. Still he rammed one mighty stroke after another inside her, stretching her to capacity and spanking her bottom with his stomach and groin.

On and on went Peter, plunging and pillaging with ever-increasing joy, his overstretched erection flying in and out between those delightfully dimpled cheeks. On and on he shafted, glorying in the strength and power of his penis as it parted her and probed her all the way up to the top of her sweet little passage. On and on and on, one long, brutal thrust after another filling her and stretching her to the limit. On and on and on, without relent, making her squawk and squeal ever more loudly, making her writhe her head as well as her bottom as he plunged with all his might.

This was the mother and father of all fuckings, he told himself. No doubt the sweet Lady Janet had been poked pretty fiercely before. But he rather suspected that this was as good as ever she'd had. Three times he'd swamped her already, without slackening by so much as a centimetre. And who was to say that he wouldn't be able to continue after the fourth?

'You'll wear me away!' she only just managed to gurgle, the fat little cheeks of her bottom still bouncing happily under the weight of the assault. 'There'll be nothing left for the rest of the guests!'

But, fortunately, she was wrong. When they eventually staggered downstairs, some thirty minutes later, Janet was pleased to discover, almost at once, that she still had plenty to share. And before he knew it, Peter was accosted by Sue, her pretty mouth closing round his wilted member as she began the process of penile resuscitation. He looked up from the armchair in which he was sprawled and noticed Tracie on the far side of the room, doing her utmost to accommodate the two young blades who'd earlier insisted on getting inside Janet's bottom. They were then joined by a third, and Peter watched with delight as Tracie seemed to disappear amidst a flurry of arms, legs and rigidly upthrust tools – these latter then vanishing into her at varying angles and points.

'That's more like it,' enthused Sue, removing him from

her mouth and then slowly lowering her oh-so-shapely bottom onto his groin. 'Oh, that's nice! I can feel you all the way up to my tonsils!'

And so the party continued well into the early hours of Monday morning. Couples would disappear and reappear later. Others would copulate openly wherever and with whoever they could. Men and women took well-earned breaks to gulp down liquid refreshment, before throwing themselves back into the fray.

But at long last most of the gathering was finally spent. Tracie came over to Peter, grinning broadly and leaking like a sieve as she took him affectionately by the hand. 'Come upstairs,' she urged him. 'I need a bath . . . and then a good solid husbandly bonk. I need a cock that loves me, not one that just loves to fuck me.'

'I'll try,' he wheezed as he came to his feet.

She looked down at his drooping equipment. 'Don't worry,' she said confidently. 'I'll soon have that up and running. There's no way you're going to be able to hide him away from me!'

Chapter 13

Of Masks and Men

Next morning, at Rayke Hall, Tracie awoke early in the huge four-poster bed that she and Peter had shared during what had remained of the night. She was delighted to find that Peter was already lying on top of her, unmoving, his penis wedged tightly and deeply inside. Very tightly and deeply inside. 'Good morning, Mr Trix,' she murmured drowsily, pushing up with her groin in order to force him in as far as he'd go. Despite the rigours of Sir Roland's party, they'd made love three times during the course of the night. 'You feel gigantic!' she breathed, wriggling her bottom appreciatively. 'Even bigger than ever!'

'I fancy you so much,' he whispered. 'I just can't get enough of you.'

'I feel exactly the same about you, Peter.'

'I keep thinking about all that cock I saw you take last night. I felt so proud of you. So proud of the way all those men were enjoying my wife. It makes me want to shag you till the spunk flies out of your ears!'

'That's a lovely thought!' she giggled. 'But you've spent all night trying to do it, and still haven't succeeded.'

'There's no reason why I can't try again, is there?'

Tracie pulled his face down to her superbly upthrust breasts. 'Absolutely not! Give it your best shot. It's just a shame it's Monday morning and we've got to go to work.'

Peter started to slide powerfully back and forth. 'I used to worry about what you got up to at the office.'

'I know you did. But you needn't anymore. I'll never do it behind your back again.'

Peter felt as if his penis was ready to burst. 'I've told you before, I don't want to stop you shagging. Shag whoever you like – just tell me about it afterwards, so there'll be no secrets between us. The more you shag other men the more I'm going to treasure you.'

Tracie sighed happily. 'And the more you say that, the more it'll make me love you. But I only want to fuck for you. I don't want it if it isn't for you.'

'Do it for me, then. Whenever you like.'

'When are you going to cane me again?'

'Not until your poor little bottom is completely recovered, at least. Probably not for quite a while after that. I want to keep it special. Something we do only very occasionally.'

'You're a spoilsport! You know how much I enjoyed it. Or rather, you know how wonderful I felt once it was done.'

'How does it feel now?' he asked with genuine concern. 'Is it as painful?'

'Not quite. It still hurts like hell, but I think it's a little bit better. Plus I'm getting used to it too, of course. It still makes me feel great, though, Peter. It still makes me worship you like some sort of God. Mind you, that won't change, not even when I can sit down without holding my breath.'

Very carefully and tenderly, he slid his hands underneath her, once again savouring the heat of the angry ridged weals. 'I want to watch you shagging again,' he whispered into her ear. 'I want to watch you doing the sort of thing you did last night. I want to see you getting yourself shagged stupid by several men. I want to watch all those dicks hammering into you, once after the other. It made me feel so proud!'

'You will. We're going to Rollie's next party, after all.'

'I can't wait that long, Tracie. I can't wait four more weeks. I want to see you getting yourself well and truly gangbanged long before then.'

'In that case, I'll see what I can arrange. You know I'll do whatever you want. You know I'll do anything for you.'

He began to thrust into her more firmly. 'You're the perfect wife,' he said, his erection seeming to swell even more.

She smiled sexily into his eyes. 'Peter-Peter, Pussy-

Beater,' she murmured, before opening her mouth to accept his tongue. He felt absolutely enormous inside her, she gasped to herself. He felt half as big again as normal. He was stretching her so delightfully. And she just loved the pain from the way he was now grinding her poor, sorely striped bottom into the mattress!

That evening Tracie was curled up on Peter's lap in front of the television, wearing nothing but the marks of the cane. 'I've phoned cousin Jean,' she teased him, kissing the side of his face.

'What for?'

'For some help. I'll need it.'

'What on earth are you talking about?'

'The gangbang you wanted to watch me take part in.'

'Oh?' he asked with sudden interest.

'Jean works for an escort agency in her spare time. When David's away from home, I mean.'

'Really? I'd never have guessed. Surely she doesn't need the money?'

'Of course not. She just needs the sex.'

'Jesus! The wife of our local Tory councillor is on the game!'

'Great, isn't it?' laughed Tracie. 'I wonder how that would go down with the voters.'

'How long has she been doing it?'

'Oh, since about two years before they got married.'

'You're kidding me!'

'No, it's true. She's spent the last seven years providing "escort facilities" for anyone who can afford the price.'

'So what have you asked her to do for you?'

'Help out at the gangbang, of course. I can't handle all those men on my own.'

'What gangbang? What men do you mean?'

Tracie giggled wickedly and squeezed the bulge in the front of his trousers. 'Listen carefully, Peter, and I'll tell you exactly what I've arranged. I think you'll be pleased.'

She slid off his lap and knelt on the carpet between his legs. 'I'll tell you all about it,' she said, reaching for his zip.

'But I want some company while I'm doing it. I can talk to you in between sucks.'

Ten minutes later she raised her head, once again removing his long, wet penis from her mouth and holding it against the side of her face. 'So that's it, really, Peter. That's what I suggest we should do.'

'Fantastic!' he breathed as, once again, she swallowed him all the way down to the root. 'What a truly mind-blowing idea! I'm sure we can work out the details. It will just take a bit of planning, that's all. And I love the thought of the masks. It will really add that extra touch.'

Temporarily she disgorged him again. 'You're sure you're quite happy to run the risk of me being recognised by some of your friends?'

'Yes, of course. They can't actually recognise you, can they? They can only wonder whether it might be you. And that will be part of the fun. Whenever they see you afterwards, they'll never quite know whether or not you were actually one of the girls. They'll never know for certain whether they've had you or not. They'll stare at the nicely filled seat of your mini-skirt and wonder whether or not they've really been there.'

'Yes,' she said slowly and thoughtfully. 'That will be rather good fun. I'll enjoy the thought that they might be suspecting they've fucked me, but that they can't be sure. Your dick tastes lovely, by the way. And it's so incredibly hot!'

The following evening, Tuesday, was the annual stag night at Kirkley Cricket Club. The tiny club house was teeming with young men, all of whom had eaten well at the buffet and drunk even better at the bar. And the beer was still flowing like a river in flood. Spirits were high in anticipation of the female entertainment that Peter and his close friend, Long John Rowley, had arranged. Or rather, rearranged at the last moment.

'John says this year's strippers will be something else,' the reserve wicket keeper said to the club captain standing beside him.

'They couldn't be worse than last year's. I've never seen so much flesh. When that brassy blonde bird suddenly whipped off her bra, the guys at the front actually ducked!'

'I know what you mean, Jim. They were rank. Everyone kept shouting, "Put 'em on!" But this year will be different – according to John.'

'I only hope he's right.'

'Do you know what he reckons?' the wicket keeper muttered conspiratorially. 'He says they're going to do us a turn.'

'Yeah? I've heard all that garbage before. It just means they collect a boatload of extra cash from us, then do some sort of half-hearted lezzie act. That's all.'

'Not according to John. He says that he and Peter have booked the real business.'

'The real business?'

'Yes. He says they're going to fuck!'

'Pull the other one!' scoffed the club captain.

'Well, I asked Peter about it, and he said it was true. He said they were from a special agency and that they'll fuck anyone who can get it up.'

'Well, after all the beer, that rules out everyone here.'

'Speak for yourself, matey.'

'Can you imagine shagging some stripper in front of all these drunken buggers?'

'Er, well, possibly you have a point there. It would depend on the girl, I suppose.'

The opening bowler was at the bar with the tricky leg spinner who was in and out of the first team. Both of them were downing pints as if they would soon go out of fashion. 'I hear the entertainment is going to be a bit special,' said the fast bowler.

'So do I,' replied his much slower team-mate. 'Mind you, I don't believe a word of it. I've lost count of the number of stag parties where I've heard the same rumour. All that happens is that the girls pick on some poor sod, strip him off and then cover him in baby oil, or suchlike. After they've been paid a king's ransom by way of inducement.'

'You're a cynic.'

'No. Just a realist. Do you really think we're going to see a couple of girls come out here and actually fuck us?'

'I'm an optimist, so I'll say, "Yes".'

'I'm in possession of all my faculties, so I'll say, "No".'

Peter sidled over to John. 'You did phone the agency and cancel the strippers?' he asked quietly.

'Yes, of course. This afternoon.'

'What did they say?'

'They were happy with half the agreed fee. I expect they knew they could find another booking.'

'It's almost time for the show,' murmured Peter, glancing quickly at his watch.

John looked at him, semi-perplexed. 'What the hell's got into you, Peter? On Friday you get me to pork your missus. Now you've arranged for her and her cousin to come here and fuck as many blokes as can make it. You used to be so possessive of Tracie.'

'I've changed, John.'

'You can say that again! Christ, I can remember the time when you had a blazing row with her after you'd seen some guy patting her bum on the dance floor!'

This year, as always, John was in charge of the entertainment. At his direction, the tables and chairs were moved back to the walls for the cricketers to sit on. One table was left in the middle for use by the entertainers. This was all standard stuff. The assembled gathering had seen it time after time. Despite the scepticism, there was a buzz of happy anticipation. Of course the girls weren't really going to fuck. But it was a nice thought, and one that would add to the general enjoyment of whatever act they were going to perform. You'd be able to watch them prancing around in their birthday suits and try to visualise what it would be like if they ever did happen to live up to the rumours that had preceded them . . .

John stood in front of the door that led to the kitchen, the girls on the far side. He held up a hand and shouted for silence. 'Fill up your glasses and sit down quickly,' he bawled. 'We mustn't keep the ladies waiting.'

There was a rush for the bar, but with the help of the two medium-paced seamers the pint mugs were soon refilled, and the audience retreated to the peripheries to await proceedings. John pressed a button on the tape deck and the music began. 'Gentlemen!' he called above the sounds of Oasis. 'Let's have a big hand for our lovely young entertainers, that delightful, dick-jerking duo, the Sisters Salacious! Otherwise known as the Cousins Cunnilingus!'

The door swung open and out skipped the cousins, to be greeted by a loud roar of approval. Both girls were six feet tall in their high-heeled, knee-length boots. Their only other wearing apparel consisted of a pair of skin-tight white hot-pants, a tiny matching top, and a close-fitting mask of sheer black silk. The masks covered their heads completely, with large oval slits for the eyes and mouths. The men were immediately reminded of a female version of an executioner's mask. Jean's blonde shoulder-length hair was partially visible, but Tracie's much shorter hair was covered completely. The girls moved gracefully to the centre of the room, gyrating to the music, accompanied by raucous applause and gratuitous advice. Face to face, they began to dance slowly and sexily, arms round each other's waists. To another howl of delight they began to kiss, hands now exploring tightly clad bottoms as they swayed gracefully back and forth. Soon the hot-pants were loosened at the sides and the hands were delving inside them, stroking and caressing honey-smooth cheeks as the girls danced on. 'Ouch!' Tracie giggled under her breath. 'Don't squeeze too hard. You know the state of my poor little bum.'

'Sorry,' Jean whispered in her ear. 'I got carried away. You feel so nice.'

Soon the girls were topless, each having stripped the other down to the waist. Again they kissed, firm bare breasts pressing warmly into each other as they continued to move to the music. A short while later Jean was naked, apart from her white leather boots, Tracie having removed her hot-pants, slowly and sexily. Now it was time for Jean to return the compliment. Carefully she unbuttoned Tracie.

Then, holding the hot-pants in place with one hand, she gestured to the men to gather round behind her half-stripped colleague, so that all could stare freely at the posterior she was about to unveil.

Slowly and very, very deliberately, she lowered the tiny white hot-pants. There came a collective gasp of astonishment as the men goggled in awe and disbelief at the beautiful bare bottom, so pert and proud and pouting, yet decorated so vividly by the six straight lines from the cane. Six straight lines that were still very red and visible. Six straight lines that they could see still throbbed with painful heat. Six straight lines that contrasted starkly with the smooth pale flesh across which they'd been so cruelly laid.

'Jesus Christ!' groaned the club captain. 'What a sight for sore eyes! What a poor little, sore little bum!'

The men returned to their seats and the girls kissed again, more passionately than ever, swaying to the strains of the music as they did so. Now their hands were deep down round each other's buttocks, fingertips dipping lightly into nicely oiled quims. Then the fingertips dipped more deeply, and then more deeply still. Now both girls were firmly fingering each other from behind, nipple to nipple, groin to groin, wriggling with pleasure as they danced and kissed as well. The men could see exactly what they were doing and fell silent as their interest soared. All eyes were glued to the sight of slim female fingers delving deeply but delicately into soaking-wet pussy.

Tracie stopped temporarily, and withdrew from the juicy heat of the other girl's snug little opening. The reserve team all-rounder was sitting nearby, so she held out her hand and motioned to him to suck her dripping wet fingers. This he did with relish. Then the dancing, kissing and fingering resumed. Over the course of the next few minutes several more members of the audience were treated to the taste of sticky fingers – both Jean's and Tracie's. A treat that they accepted with obvious enthusiasm and appetite. 'Over here!' came the cries of those who'd been unlucky enough to miss out. 'That tastes beautiful!' groaned one of the chosen few, sucking the last remaining drops of Tracie's juices from Jean's middle fingers.

'I told you these girls were different,' the reserve wicket keeper said to the club captain, gazing in fascination as two more of his team-mates licked hungrily at outstretched hands.

And still the fingering and the feeding of the hungry continued. Showing considerable talent for short-term memory, the girls worked their way round the floor until everyone had enjoyed a taste of either Jean or Tracie, or, just occasionally, of both.

'Who did that to you?' asked one of the men, reaching out and tapping Tracie's bottom very lightly. 'And why?'

But the girls maintained their silence. They would speak only to each other, and then only in whispered tones that were inaudible to their audience.

'I'm sure that's Peter's wife,' Poke Anything Paul murmured to the opening bowler who sat beside him.

'Don't be daft! You know what Peter's like.'

'Yes, I know. But I'm sure it is. I spent the whole night with her a couple of months ago when Peter was away. I had every inch of her gorgeous body. And that is definitely hers.'

'Fuck off, dickhead!'

'Say what you like, but I'm sure it's Tracie. It's the way she moves, as well as everything else. Can't you see that for yourself?'

'There's some sort of similarity. But that's all. Do you think Peter wouldn't recognise his own wife, if you can?'

The men had now been fed, so the girls moved slowly over to the empty table that was strategically placed in the middle of the room. Then they signalled to the men to gather round. No further bidding was needed. Tracie lay on her back on the table, her feet just touching the floor, her legs wide apart and Jean standing between them. Slowly Jean stooped forward until her face was between silky-smooth thighs. The men stared in delight at the pink, wet pussy so prominently on display, as wide open and inviting as anyone could have wished. Jean also gazed lustfully at all that was on offer, before pushing her head forward a little further and starting to lick.

Tracie was brought to a shuddering climax in less than a minute. The excitement of having an audience had sped her on her way. The girls then swapped positions and roles, and Jean climaxed almost as quickly and violently. The men were left in no doubt as to the authenticity of the orgasms. They could tell that neither girl was faking, even though their faces were masked.

Tracie straightened up, leaving Jean on her back, legs apart, now even wetter and more open than ever. She moved over to Peter, who was standing to her right, and sank to her knees in front of him. Seconds later she'd opened his zip and he was in her mouth, hardening rapidly as she sucked. The men stared in amazement as she proceeded to give him head.

After a while, she disgorged him and stood up. Then, with her hand wrapped tightly round his bulging erection, she led him to the table where Jean was still spread out on her back. With a wink and a knowing squeeze, she pointed to the hot little quim that waited for him on the table top. 'Why don't you help yourself?' were the only words Tracie spoke to any of the men that night.

Whilst Peter followed his wife's good advice with alacrity, Tracie turned to the club captain, who was standing directly behind her. She was down on her knees and he was in her mouth in no time at all. As soon as he was stiff she got to her feet and led him, by the dick, to the table, exactly as she'd led Peter. Then she bent forward, placing her head and forearms on the table and pointing her extensively caned bottom high in the air by way of invitation. Jim needed no further bidding – he was deep inside her in a flash, pumping away just as hard as Peter was pumping Jean by his side. Together they porked glorious wet pussy, whilst the rest of the male audience stood there, watching in fascination. Together the two men porked and poked, one girl on her back on the table, the other bend forward across it.

'Do you believe me now?' asked the reserve team wicket

keeper, directing his question to his club captain as the latter flew in and out of Tracie at speed. The captain saw no call to reply.

Peter glanced sideways, admiring the cheeks of his wife's shapely, uptilted bottom, and the way that the other man's glistening wet tool was working away between them. It felt to Peter that he was having sex twice over. Much as he was enjoying cousin Jean's sweet little passage, he was gaining equal, if not greater, pleasure from watching his own wife having hers stretched and probed at the same time.

John took control of the entertainment. Both girls had now been creamily implanted, so it was time for the proceedings to get underway in earnest. Or rather, in Tracie and Jean. John was a systems analyst with a degree in pure mathematics, so he was ideally qualified to take charge. His job was to ensure that everyone present had their fair share of the girls. Quite a daunting task, bearing in mind the number of men desperately anxious to take their turn.

The girls, still in their white knee-length boots, were now spread right across the table top – bottoms up, but facing in opposite directions. There they lay, side by side, legs dangling down at right angles, toes only just touching the floor. There they lay waiting, Tracie's pretty, candy-striped cheeks beside Jean's head, Jean's equally plump little bottom nestling nicely beside the head of her cousin. An epic topping 'n tailing party was about to begin.

'That looks so much like Peter's wife,' muttered one of the cricketers.

'It does, doesn't it?' agreed the middle-order batsman at his side.

'But of course it can't be?'

'No. I suppose it can't.'

'Unless . . .'

'It's a nice thought.'

At John's command the men rushed to form queues on either side of the table, jostling good-naturedly, if roughly, for prime positions. Eventually four semi-orderly queues were formed, two behind upturned bottoms and two in front of pretty young mouths. Further instructions were given. Once the fucking had started, the persons at the front would move clockwise every two minutes – from mouth to pussy and so on. Or, more accurately, from mouth or pussy to pussy or mouth, then on to mouth or pussy, then on again to pussy or mouth. In that way, each would have a total of eight minutes to finish themselves off. Plenty of time, said John, bearing in mind the added stimulus of so much variety – two girls, two pussies, two mouths. If they didn't then that was just tough luck. Back they'd go to the end of the queue, where they'd have to bide their time and hope they'd be able to work their way up to the front again. Finally, anyone not hard enough to penetrate from behind would be allowed to swap places with anyone fully erect in front. Brownie points would, however, be lost. Finally, again, early comers would not be a problem. They'd be welcome, in fact, since they'd help to shorten the queues.

But first, in order to start with a bang, or rather, with several, John decided that quick introductions all round were essential. All those present, who could, would be introduced into one or other of the girls in the space of only a few minutes. Everyone would have just one minute in just one of the openings on offer. And then, once the introductions had been effected, it would be down to the serious business he'd already described – the eight-minute slot.

The introductions were successfully completed. Everyone had poked something, if only for a mere sixty seconds. The mood had been set. The girls were wet and eager and ready, and the men upright and hard. Everyone had agreed not to hold back. It was important to keep the queues moving. 'Fuck'em fast,' was the order of the day.

Off they went like rats up a drainpipe. Whilst the girls lay on their fronts, stock-still and passive, wide open fore and aft, four overstretched dicks began to race back and forth inside them, almost as if they were in competition with each other. Groins slapped hard into soft bouncy buttocks, mouths gaped open as length after length shot in and out. Fat little female bottoms began to wriggle in pleasure, and the onlookers prayed for their turn. There was no giving of head – just the taking of it.

Two minutes were up and the men switched positions, before starting to shaft once again. Now each girl was able to savour the taste of the other, combined with the distinctly different flavour of recently spent male seed. What a delightful cocktail, thought Tracie. Jean's juices mixed with Peter's. And within no more than another sixty seconds or so, the taste would be renewed all over again . . .

Then it was all change once more. Almost immediately the slow left-arm bowler was the first casualty of the evening. Having withdrawn from Tracie's mouth and then re-entered her from behind, he glanced down at the six fiery red stripes across her pouting bare bottom, and immediately started to spurt. 'Ohh!' Tracie gasped with pleasure, feeling him flooding her with a ferocity she found hard to believe.

The opening bowler, Julian Root, was next in line behind the unfortunate left-armer. 'What a feeble performance!' he muttered, pushing hard into Tracie the very second she was vacated. 'But then again, all cricketers are poofs, apart from those of us who sling down the leather as hard as we can and make the other buggers jump out of the way.'

Julian made the same mistake of staring in fascination at the plump, cruelly caned bottom, instantly suffering the fate of his predecessor. 'Fuck it!' he cried at the top of his voice.

'I intend to,' replied the next man in the queue behind him, elbowing him out of the way.

The men swapped over for the third time. Almost at once both girls were eagerly swallowing sperm. Then Tracie was implanted below the waist yet again. Seconds later, so was Jean.

Another two minutes was over, and another casualty was recorded. New recruits began to come forward frequently and fast, happily hammering themselves in and out of the sweet little passage or mouth that had become vacant. More minutes ticked by. The reserve wicket keeper was replaced in Jean's mouth by the opening bat, just as the player mounted on Tracie's bottom began to gush. Very soon the leg spin bowler had run right through Jean, his place being taken by Peter, whose dick would next be in his own wife's mouth. Jean began to gobble and swallow again, just as the man behind Tracie started to squirt. Seconds after Peter had slid out of Jean and into Tracie, Tracie's insides were splattered and splashed once more. And then, when Peter was subsequently inside there, two of the A Team bowlers simultaneously spermed Jean, top and tail.

Peter was in Jean's mouth, and he knew his eight minutes were almost up. He lifted his gaze from her plump, bouncing bottom and turned to watch Tracie at work. That did the trick. Staring intently at the long, thick organs that were servicing her front and rear, he erupted straight down Jean's throat.

Tracie groaned aloud, despite the fact that her mouth was full of the number three batsman. John was forcing himself into her lower opening. She knew it was him from his size. He was stretching her and hurting her just as he'd done on Friday night. And he still wasn't all the way home! He still had more to provide! But at least she was more than adequately lubricated.

A few minutes later, the A Team vice captain was in trouble. He was running desperately short of time. Try as he might, he just couldn't bring himself off in Jean. Any second now he'd be relegated to the back of the queue. 'I'm sorry,' he gasped to her. 'But I've got no other option. I hope you don't mind?' Of course, Jean couldn't reply – she had penis right down her throat. 'Arrgghhhh!' she tried to shriek a few seconds later, but couldn't as he vacated puzzy in favour of tight little bum.

'Gotcha at last!' the vice captain cried triumphantly, searing her anal passage with jet after jet of boiling hot seed.

Five minutes later, Jean, although securely mounted from behind, found her mouth momentarily unoccupied as a result of a mild dispute as to whose turn it was to be in there. Seizing the unexpected opportunity, she took several deep breaths and cleaned her face as best she could, licking her fingers and savouring the taste. Then she glanced sideways at Tracie, and grinned. What an incredibly sexy sight: Tracie spread across the table face down, one long gleaming dick thrashing away between the cheeks of her bottom, another sliding smoothly in and out of her mouth. And more waiting stiffly but patiently in line, both in front and behind.

Thank heavens her husband, David, was safely out of town. Whatever would he do if he could see her now? If he could see for himself how she was wallowing in the luxury of the situation, in the way she was being poked and prodded and implanted time and time again. What would he make of all that? David, her ever-loving husband who doted on her every move. David, who steadfastly refused to believe that she was capable of perpetrating even the tiniest misdemeanour. What in God's name would he feel if he were here and watching her now.

Poor David! How devastated he'd be! He'd never be able to come to terms with the fact that she was capable of behaving this way.

Jean returned her attention to the two young men standing naked and rampant in front of her. 'Haven't you two sorted it out yet? she asked with mock exaggeration. 'Surely you can agree on who's next?'

'Not really,' muttered the one to her left.

Jean reached forward with both hands, at the same time grimacing at a particularly violent thrust from behind. 'Look here,' she murmured helpfully, taking one urgently throbbing cock in each hand. 'Move forward a bit more and I'll do both of you and the same time. That will save any further argument.'

'How the hell can you manage that?'

'Just watch me!' she laughed, sucking powerfully at one and then the other. 'It's not as difficult as you think. Do you want to bet that I can't?'

'Not me,' groaned the first one, closing his eyes and throwing back his head as she sucked again.

'Nor me,' croaked the other, doing exactly the same.

She tugged them a little nearer her face. 'The waiting must have done you some good,' she giggled wickedly. 'You're both as stiff as a board. I can't waggle you at all!'

It was as well for the men that they'd declined to wager their money. Her head, masked in black silk, flew from one to the other, causing both to gasp and grimace. So fast did she work that before either of them had the chance to realise he'd been abandoned, her hot little mouth was back in place. Back and forth she beavered between them, sucking and squeezing for all she was worth, making both of them moan with pleasure, despite the fact that they had to share. At last, just as a new recruit was settling onto her upturned buttocks, she felt both men in front of her start to stiffen and jerk. Not very long now, she thought to herself, her head flying even faster than ever between them. Using her hands, she brought the two of them as close to each other as they could get, the two swollen, purplish heads stretching eagerly up at her face. Then she set to work with a vengeance, her mouth enveloping one and then the other every half second or so.

'Eureka!' she gasped happily, some thirty seconds later, as two piping hot effusions suddenly burst upon her, swamping both sides of her face before she was finally able to direct the double deluge into her mouth. These silk masks would never be the same again, she thought to herself, as she swallowed as fast as she could.

'It is Tracie!' cried the left-arm slow bowler to the man beside him. 'I've just realised that the other girl is her cousin, Jean.'

'That's right. Of course. I recognise her now. She used to hang around some of the matches last year. Do you remember what we used to call her?'

'Yes. "The Kirkley Lay"!'

'And after that, after she'd been through the first team, we used to call her the "Lay of the A". What a right little goer she was!'

'So Peter has brought his wife along to get herself fucked by all of us! Who in God's name would ever have believed it?'

'It's going to be interesting next time we see her. Perhaps she'll be coming to the match on Saturday?'

'But what the hell has got into Peter?'

Together they turned to stare at the table, where the double double-dicking was proceeding at pace. 'I don't know. But there's no doubting what's got into his wife.'

On and on went the topping and tailing: the men erupting first here, then there, penis after penis taking its turn to plunder and poke; the men fondling boobs and bottoms as they thrust, then shot and then thrust hard again; the men dispatching one load after another from front and back, taking their turns one after the other, whilst the girls wriggled and giggled and enjoyed every squirt and spurt. And still the men piled into Tracie and Jean with an unfailing energy. Groins slapped noisily against buttocks, pricks fucked and were sucked. Cream flew in profusion, and the girls came time and again. Time and again and again, one climax following another as they wriggled and writhed and squirmed and wormed with the pleasure of the gross excess. Jean's bottom was trespassed upon once again. Then Tracie suffered the same fate, twice in a row, as the idea gained support.

'Not you again!' gasped Jean, as John presented his mammoth member before her face. 'It only seems five minutes since your last go.'

'Time passes quickly when you're enjoying yourself,' he replied.

She stroked him with both hands. 'You're sure you're not cheating? I know you're directing operations.'

'If I tried something like that, I'd be torn apart by the angry mob.'

'Hey!' said the medium-paced swing bowler standing behind John. 'Is this supposed to be a blow job or a parliamentary debate?'

'Point taken,' mumbled Jean, guiding John into her mouth, just as she felt the onset of another spasm, prompted by the very brisk pace being set by whoever was mounting her from behind.

* * *

Tracie gasped as she was once again splattered simultaneously from front and rear. The men seemed to be growing in strength, she thought to herself, rather than losing their power. They seemed to ejaculate harder and in greater volume as time ticked by. And it also seemed to take less time for them to make it. She was sure that this was the third time she'd been implanted from behind in the last five minutes. She wasn't keeping an eye on the clock, but she was sure she was right, nevertheless. And she could tell from the way the newcomer was now jabbing her that he wouldn't hang around for long. You could always sense when a man was coming to the boil. Something just told you so. It had nothing to do with the speed of the coupling, it was just some sixth sense that told you he was about to blow.

And the lad in her mouth wouldn't be long, either. Perhaps she'd be treated to yet another double discharge? That was always great fun.

But eventually a halt had to be called. The girls had really worked wonders, but even for them, enough was at long last enough. The sheer physical strain had finally taken its toll. Wearily they staggered away, escorted by John, who locked the door behind them. 'Oh, my God!' Tracie groaned painfully, pulling off her mask and flopping down onto a wooden chair.

'Yes, indeed!' Jean croaked in agreement, doing the same. 'Good grief! I'm absolutely smothered from head to toe!'

Tracie licked her lips and squeezed her legs together. 'Lovely, isn't it?' she grinned. 'All those men.!'

'I'll drive you home,' said John, handing each of them a bathtowel and the coats that they'd brought with them earlier. 'I think you both deserve a rest.'

'You can say that again,' gulped Tracie. 'I think I shall sleep for a week.'

'David's away on business,' Jean pointed out to John. 'Don't you fancy a night with me?'

'You're joking!'

'Yes. I certainly am.'

Epilogue

It was the following evening, Wednesday, five days after Peter had caned his wife and transformed his marriage. He was sitting in his armchair, reading a novel. Tracie had driven off earlier to visit the supermarket, she'd said. He heard her return, but carried on reading. It was an erotic book that she'd bought him the previous Christmas. Somehow the story seemed rather tame when compared to the events of the past few days. The lounge door opened and Tracie poked her head into the room. 'Peter,' she said with a wicked grin all over her pretty face. 'Do you remember me saying that I wanted to arrange a nice little surprise for you?'

'Yes,' he replied slowly, in truth having all but forgotten her words.

'Well, here it is at last,' Tracie said brightly, ushering a tall, stunningly attractive girl into the room. 'Doesn't it look nice?'

Peter goggled in amazement at the gorgeous girl who stood there in her ultra short mini-skirt and high heels, golden blonde hair twisting and tumbling almost all the way down to her waist.

'This is my friend from work.'

'Hello,' stammered Pauline Peach, blushing as red as a beetroot and dropping her gaze to her feet. How embarrassing, she gulped to herself.

'Pauline used to do things for my former friend, George Franks,' explained Tracie. 'And now she's agreed to do them for me. Haven't you, Pauline? Just for tonight, I mean?'

'Er, well, yes . . .'

'Very interesting things she used to do, too,' Tracie continued. 'Let me show you what I mean.'

Without further ado, Tracie led Pauline to the dining recess, bent her forward over the table, and pulled her skirt up to her waist. Peter gazed in approval at the heart-stopping sight of her perfect bottom clad in the flimsiest pair of knickers imaginable. Knickers so small and skimpy that they almost didn't exist.

Before Peter could regain his senses, Tracie reached out and took hold of the frilly white knicker seat. This she pulled outwards from Pauline's upthrust buttocks, and then down just far enough to expose the plump little pussy that nestled so nicely between the tops of her thighs. Still gripping the knickers in that way, she turned towards Peter. 'Come and shag my girlfriend!' she giggled. 'I can assure you she won't object. In fact, I know she'll love every moment. She always does.'

Peter was prompt to oblige. Whilst Tracie stood by his side, the slightly displaced knickers still held in one hand, he pushed forward into Pauline with force. She was already so juicy and receptive that he slid right up her in a trice, causing her to jerk back her head and gasp in surprise.

'You can be as quick as you like,' Tracie informed him. 'This is just a very preliminary canter to get everyone pleasantly acquainted.'

Peter had no problem with that. The smooth, perfectly shaped bottom against which he was pumping, plus the incredibly hot little hole, ensured that time didn't weigh heavily upon him. Less than sixty seconds later Pauline squirmed her hips and squealed as she felt him spilling himself inside her. Almost at once her own orgasm started, prompted by the flow of white-hot seed. Together they shuddered and climaxed, with Tracie still at their side, watching happily as she continued to hold the knickers out of his way. At last he withdrew and Tracie let go with a snap.

Slowly Pauline straightened up, blushing wildly, her skirt hitched high round her waist, her little white knickers now half on and half off her pouting backside. Instinctively, she squeezed the tops of her thighs together, in order to judge how heavily she'd been implanted. There could be no complaints on that score, she told herself with a sigh. And she'd only met him less than two minutes ago!

Tracie was clearly in charge of proceedings. She told Peter to sit back in his armchair, then she sat Pauline down in the one opposite. Within seconds Pauline was professionally stripped down to her front-loading bra and high heels. 'You'll love these,' Tracie murmured to Peter, kneeling on the floor between Pauline's outstretched legs and then snapping open the bra to allow her beautiful breasts to bound happily into sight. Firm and upright as ever they were, and with long pointed nipples that poked rigidly out at Tracie in welcome. Tracie responded by taking them in her mouth, one after the other, making Pauline moan with pleasure. She sucked first one and then the other, expertly, until she could gauge that she'd brought Pauline to the brink of another climax. Then she stopped and knelt back, at the same time looking down at the sweet little opening from which her husband's fluid was starting to ooze. She lowered her head and gently ran the tip of her tongue over the wet lips and swollen clitoris. Immediately Pauline started to shiver as her orgasm returned.

Tracie slipped her tongue inside Pauline and started to lick, very delicately, relishing the delicious mixture of tastes. Very briefly she lifted her head, licking her lips. 'I'm just freshening her up for you, Peter,' she said. 'She'll soon be as spotless as any good little girl should be when her hubby isn't around.' Then her head was down between Pauline's thighs once again and the gentle licking and lapping resumed.

Pauline's head was spinning as a result of the delights afforded by Tracie's tongue. She was swooning away. Fading into oblivion. She was vaguely aware that Peter was getting to his feet and marching towards them. Her gaze was drawn to his elongated erection swaying stiffly from side to side as he moved. It was the first time she'd actually seen it, as opposed to feeling it poking her insides. And she had to admit that it was a really nice shape, long and straight and perfectly proportioned.

Tracie's short skirt had already ridden more than halfway up the cheeks of her bottom as she bent forward over Pauline's groin. Peter was no longer able to resist the sight of her scantily clad buttocks peeping cheekily out at him whilst she worked away on Pauline. He knelt on the carpet behind her and hooked a finger inside the seat of her filmy little knickers. These he drew down her thighs as far as her knees. As Pauline was forced to close her eyes with the power of the tongue-induced spasms, Peter leant forward and fed himself slowly into his wife.

'Don't use all of that up on me,' Tracie warned over her shoulder. 'This is meant to be your surprise treat,' she added, before returning her attention to Pauline's succulent opening.

Peter started to shaft her, using strokes of an even pace. 'There'll be more than enough for both of you,' he replied confidently.

Despite herself, Pauline fervently hoped he was right. This tonguing was really beautiful. But she knew from experience that after a while it led to a craving for something a great deal stiffer and more substantial. It was nice for the moment, though. It was nice just lying back here in the chair whilst Tracie licked and chewed very softly and Peter slithered slowly in and out of her. All three of them were sort of joined together.

Peter disengaged and got to his feet beside the armchair, now very damp as well as erect. Hungrily, Pauline accepted him into her mouth, instantly tasting the sweetness of Tracie as she sucked him right into her throat. She reached out, taking his testicles in both hands and then starting to pamper and pet them. She built up a rhythm with Tracie, fellating and massaging Peter at the same speed at which Tracie was eating her.

Tracie knew that Pauline was now dying to be entered by Peter. Deliberately she continued to lick as slowly and lightly as possible, making her female partner wriggle and moan with desire and frustration. For several more minutes she licked, feeling the frustration growing with every moment that passed. She'd just have to wait, Tracie said to herself. It would do her good to learn patience. It would do the randy little wench good to wait for a while. This was Peter's treat after all. This was for his benefit, not hers. So she'd make Pauline wait until she was on the point of fragmenting. Then and only then would she get Peter to feed her the hard maleness she craved.

At last Peter swapped places with Tracie and started to pole Pauline, making her writhe wildly from side to side, making her squeeze her overstretched nipples between forefingers and thumbs. Tracie whipped off her skirt and knickers and hopped onto the chair between the two of them, facing Pauline, one knee resting on each arm of the chair. Pauline opened her eyes and stared at the inviting sight of pretty pink pussy right in front of her face. 'Oh, yes, please!' she breathed fervently, pushing her tongue as far inside as she could. Whilst Peter continued to shaft Pauline, he reached forward with both hands and cupped them round his wife's bare bottom. Then he slid a fingertip from each inside the tight little hole, making her wriggle with pleasure. Now each of them was in contact with both of the others. Now all three began to heave and hump and groan.

With her bottom still being teased by Peter, Tracie started to rub her pussy up and down over Pauline's face, much to the latter's delight. Suddenly Tracie felt herself starting to spasm. At the same moment Pauline felt a further burst of Peter's seed scalding her insides. As usual, her own climax was immediately revived. Time stood still for all three of them as they shared in each other's ecstasy for what seemed an eternity.

But eventually they were through. 'Let's go to bed,' whispered Tracie, running her fingers through Pauline's long blonde curls. 'I think we've had enough foreplay.'

With Peter by her side, Tracie followed Pauline upstairs, her eyes riveted to Pauline's spectacular bare bottom as it undulated gracefully from side to side, just inches in front of her. What an appetising sight, she said to herself. That big juicy bottom, so invitingly ripe and ready for taking. Briefly she imagined what it would be like to lay Peter's cane right across the very fullest part, and almost started to climax at the thought.

Tracie reached out and took a grip on each tantalisingly plump pink cheek. 'Ouch!' Pauline giggled over her shoulder, as Tracie started to squeeze.

The cheeks were so slippery-smooth that the flesh slid right through her fingers. So she took a firmer hold and squeezed once more. 'You've got the prettiest, horniest bottom I've ever seen,' she breathed thickly, at the same time feeling herself starting to lubricate even more heavily.

'Thank you,' said Pauline, blushing slightly.

'I bet it's been shagged,' said Tracie, genuinely intrigued to know. 'I bet it's been shagged more than once.'

'Not very often,' stammered Pauline, colouring brightly at the thought of Peter hearing her admission of guilt.

Now they were inside the bedroom. 'Lie down on your front,' Tracie said to her, as they faced the king-sized bed. 'I'm going to tongue you until you come!'

Pauline gasped, for the words themselves were sufficient to provoke a sharp mini-orgasm inside her.

No sooner was Tracie finished with her, than Peter rolled Pauline over onto her back and clambered on top. Pauline was still climaxing wildly as he buried his face in her breasts and started to thrust into her. It was several seconds before she even realised he was inside her. Her whole body was still responding to the unbelievable way in which Tracie had just brought her off.

'I'm sorry?' gulped Pauline, shaking her head. 'What was that you said . . . ?'

'I said welcome back to the land of the living,' he laughed. 'I think you rather enjoyed what my wife was doing to you, didn't you?'

'Oh, yes!' she breathed with feeling, pushing up firmly against his groin in an effort to re-acclimatise herself to the more conventional form of sexual activity that was now being pressed upon her. 'I've never had that before.'

'But you have had plenty of this?'

Already she was warming to the task. 'Just once or twice,' she giggled, using her vaginal muscles to grip his penis tightly enough to make him exclaim in surprise.

Peter was taking his time. Having had her twice already that evening, he could afford to linger and luxuriate inside her snug little quim. Tracie lay on her side beside them, one hand holding Pauline's, the other stroking the back of Peter's head. After a while Pauline turned towards her. 'Don't you want a go?' she asked, smiling into the other girl's face. 'He's your husband, after all.'

'Perhaps just a few stiff lengths,' she replied. 'Just to keep in practice.'

Peter settled comfortably into his wife and started to move. She wrapped her legs round his buttocks and sighed contentedly as he worked smoothly in and out. Pauline sat up on the bed, staring in fascination at the long dripping wet member as it slithered steadily back and forth. She hadn't realised how interesting it was to watch another girl making love, how fascinating it was to sit back and take in every detail. Like the way in which Tracie's whole body was gradually growing more relaxed the longer it continued. More relaxed, but in some way more responsive to the thrusting penis. It was almost as if the penis was slowly becoming part of her. As if it was slowly becoming part of Tracie's own body, as the loving couple moved more and more rhythmically together on the bed.

After another two or three minutes, Tracie opened her eyes and looked up at Peter. 'That's fine,' she said with a mischievous grin. 'That's plenty. I think you'd better save the rest for Pauline. I think you'd better get back to her and really give her some stick. She takes quite a bit of sorting out, you know. From all I've seen and heard.'

'Tracie!' Pauline protested hotly, blushing yet again.

Peter withdrew from his wife, slowly and wetly. 'I think I can handle the job,' he said reassuringly. 'What do you think, Pauline?'

'I'm sure you can,' she murmured truthfully, opening her legs to allow him back inside. 'Ooh!' she squealed, as he suddenly started to prod her much more sharply than previously. 'Oh, dear! You've started me off all over again!'

Now, some fifteen minutes later, Peter had climaxed in Pauline for the third time that evening, hotly and profusely. Now he was lying on his back in the middle of the bed, one naked girl curled up to him on either side. 'Why don't you two look after each other for a bit?' he suggested. 'While I lie here and recover?'

Without any hesitation, Tracie rolled nimbly over him and lay on top of Pauline, her legs between her new partner's as if she was about to screw her like a man would do, in the good old-fashioned missionary position. Tenderly she kissed her with her tongue, her nipples pressing warmly against Pauline's. Then she pushed her groin into Pauline's dripping wet crotch. Backwards and forward she pushed, harder and harder, wishing – not for the first time – that she had a penis of her own. Her clitoris located Pauline's and she worked it as hard as she could, making the lovely blonde girl thrash about and groan with the need to be penetrated again – so soon after the last time.

'I wish I could fuck you!' gasped Tracie.

'I wish you could, too.' Pauline replied truthfully, before Tracie kissed her again.

More and more Tracie ground cit against clit, making both of them shudder and squeal. For several minutes they wriggled and writhed in each other's arms, kissing and stroking and squeezing, as well as fingering any hole they could find. Tracie's hot little pubic area continued to rub hard against Pauline's in an effort to achieve mutual satisfaction, but it was not to be. The more they worked on each other, the more they both yearned to be opened and stretched.

'It's no use,' Tracie panted at last, having withdrawn her tongue from Pauline's mouth. 'We'll just have to ask Peter to come to our aid.'

Both of them turned onto their stomachs: two mouth-wateringly plump little bottoms, side by side, pouting up at him and pleading for pussy to be porked. 'Come on, Peter!' groaned Tracie. 'Take both of us one after the other. As many times as you can.'

Tracie was nearest, so he mounted her buttocks and started to push. At the same time he reached out for Pauline, grabbing a generous handful of bottom and then sliding a finger inside. She squawked with pleasant surprise, then pushed up with her hips, forcing the intruding finger in as far as it would go. Slowly she began to gyrate her hips in time with the way he was working back and forth inside his wife. After a while, Peter slid over onto Pauline's back and thrust into her. Then, half a minute later, he was back on top of Tracie. Then on top of Pauline once again. And so it continued. A dozen or so strokes into one of them, and then the same into the other. From one pair of buttocks to the other, and then back to the first pair again. Thrust, thrust, thrust into Pauline, then thrust, thrust, thrust into his wife. Now Pauline, now Tracie, now Pauline, now Tracie. It was a glorious sensation for him – fresh fanny and new buttocks whenever he chose.

Tracie thrust up with her bottom and knew he was about to climax. 'Not in me!' she hissed. 'You can do that any time. She's your treat for tonight. Go and spunk her again!'

Peter pulled out of his wife and scrambled onto and then into Pauline. 'Ohhh!' she moaned a few seconds later, as his seed started to flood her for the fourth time in less than two hours. 'Oh, you're even hotter than ever!'

Tracie rolled onto his back. Now he was delightfully sandwiched between two beautiful girls, boobs and pubes pressing down into his back, and acres of soft smooth bottom squashed all around his stomach and groin. As he continued to gush, Tracie ground her groin into his bony male flanks, crushing pussy and clitoris against him. Then she, too, started to spasm, just like the two writhing bodies below her.

Peter was finished but still hard. And somehow Tracie was aware of that fact. 'Keep on fucking her, Peter!' she urged vehemently. With Tracie still on his back, he was happy to comply. Tracie pressed her groin tightly into his rump, fitting the two of them together like spoons. Now they were moving as one, up and down on Pauline's back. Now husband and wife were one, mounted together on Pauline's bottom. But Tracie was very much in control of the operation. She pushed down, and groaned with satisfaction. At last her lifelong wish had been granted. At last she was fucking a girl! Using Peter's lovely stiff tackle, she was fucking this gorgeous blonde girl. Through Peter, she was actually fucking Pauline. She could feel his penis pushing into her. She could feel it filling and stretching Pauline's little pussy, and she could feel the pussy respond. The penis was actually hers. She was actually shagging this beautiful little wench right up the full length of her cunt. Harder and harder she was screwing her, making the wench wriggle and squawk. Harder and harder and faster, pumping up and down, the moment rapidly approaching when she'd be able to implant her herself.

Peter could sense Tracie's mounting excitement, and it worked wonders on him. With one final thrust of groin into smooth bouncy bottom, he jerked back his head and let fly. 'Oh, yes!' Tracie howled gleefully, feeling herself flooding Pauline with sperm.

Tracie began hammering her groin into Peter's buttocks with all the power she could muster, forcing him further inside Pauline than ever, beating him deeper and deeper. Pauline lay there underneath, sobbing with pleasure as she felt him spurting straight into her womb. As Tracie drove him still deeper, Pauline was also struck with the sensation that it was really the girl who was swamping her. Her own climax suddenly doubled in strength with the thought, making her gasp in surprise.

Pauline twisted her head and fought for breath. She could have sworn it was Tracie who was shooting her full of this lovely thick come. The idea was so intensely exciting that she felt she was going to die.

Slap! Slap! Slap! She could feel Tracie pounding her husband's penis into the top of her vagina, even though the outpour had finally ceased. She opened her mouth and was at last able to suck in huge lungfuls of air. Now she could relax a little and start to breathe properly, despite the fact that she was still well and truly hooked from above. She wriggled her bottom, and was amazed to find that Peter was still as hard as ever. She could feel his latest torrent of fluid inside her, yet he was still rock-hard!

It was a terrible admission to have to make, Pauline thought to herself with a sigh. Really terrible. But she couldn't deny that worse things might well have happened to her. Worse things than George Franks, she meant. Worse things that George Franks and his filthy photographs . . .

Tracie groaned to herself with delight. Through Peter, she'd done it at last! And it had all been so realistic. It had felt exactly as if she, not Peter, had been delving deep inside Pauline. Was there no limit to the fulfilment he was able to give her? These past five days had definitely tended to suggest there was not. Where would they go from here? What further sexual adventures lay before them? She supposed that only time would tell. But one thing she knew for certain. From now on her sex life was going to be utterly unparalleled. From now on she'd be fucking for Peter, as opposed to behind his back. In the meantime, she'd use his lovely long dick to give this incredibly fuckable blonde girl yet another dose of what she so richly deserved.

A Message from the Publisher

Headline Delta is a unique list of erotic fiction, covering many different styles and periods and appealing to a broad readership. As such, we would be most interested to hear from you.

Did you enjoy this book? Did it turn you on – or off? Did you like the story, the characters, the setting? What did you think of the cover presentation? How did this novel compare with others you have read? In short, what's your opinion? If you care to offer it, please write to:

> The Editor
> Headline Delta
> 338 Euston Road
> London NW1 3BH

Or maybe you think you could write a better erotic novel yourself. We are always looking for new authors. If you'd like to try your hand at writing a book for possible inclusion in the Delta list, here are our basic guidelines: we are looking for novels of approximately 75,000 words whose purpose is to inspire the sexual imagination of the reader. The erotic content should not describe illegal sexual activity (pedophilia, for example). The novel should contain sympathetic and interesting characters, pace, atmosphere and an intriguing storyline.

If you would like to have a go, please submit to the Editor a sample of at least 10,000 words, clearly typed in double-lined spacing on one side of the paper only, together with a short outline of the plot. Should you wish your material returned to you, please include a stamped addressed envelope. If we like it sufficiently, we will offer you a contract for publication.

More Erotic Fiction from Headline Delta

HARD SELL

There's no holding back when it's time for the HARD SELL

Felice Ash

In the advertising game it pays to use all your assets. And Sue and Gemma certainly know how to make the most of what they've got.

Sue – she's the one with the creative ideas, both in and out of bed. Not so much an accident waiting to happen, more a sex bomb ready to explode . . .

Gemma – she likes to get down to business, using whatever it takes to get what she wants. And sometimes she wants to handle more than the client's account . . .

The bottom line is that they're both under threat from vindictive rivals, blackmailing gunmen and countless males on the make, all keen to offer their own brand of – HARD SELL

FICTION / EROTICA 0 7472 4804 4

If you enjoyed this book here is a selection of other bestselling Erotica titles from Headline

FAIR LADIES OF PEACHAM PLACE	Beryl Ambridge	£5.99 ☐
EROTICON HEAT	Anonymous	£5.99 ☐
SCANDALOUS LIAISONS	Anonymous	£5.99 ☐
FOUR PLAY	Felice Ash	£5.99 ☐
THE TRIAL	Samantha Austen	£5.99 ☐
NAKED INTENT	Becky Bell	£5.99 ☐
VIXENS OF NIGHT	Valentina Cilescu	£5.99 ☐
NEW TERM AT LECHLADE COLLEGE	Lucy Cunningham-Brown	£5.99 ☐
THE PLEASURE RING	Kit Gerrard	£5.99 ☐
SPORTING GIRLS	Faye Rossignol	£5.99 ☐

Headline books are available at your local bookshop or newsagent. Alternatively, books can be ordered direct from the publisher. Just tick the titles you want and fill in the form below. Prices and availability subject to change without notice.

Buy four books from the selection above and get free postage and packaging and delivery within 48 hours. Just send a cheque or postal order made payable to Bookpoint Ltd to the value of the total cover price of the four books. Alternatively, if you wish to buy fewer than four books the following postage and packaging applies:

UK and BFPO £4.30 for one book; £6.30 for two books; £8.30 for three books.

Overseas and Eire: £4.80 for one book; £7.10 for 2 or 3 books (surface mail)

Please enclose a cheque or postal order made payable to *Bookpoint Limited*, and send to: Headline Publishing Ltd, 39 Milton Park, Abingdon, OXON OX14 4TD, UK.
Email Address: orders@bookpoint.co.uk

If you would prefer to pay by credit card, our call team would be delighted to take your order by telephone. Our direct line 01235 400 414 (lines open 9.00 am–6.00 pm Monday to Saturday 24 hour message answering service). Alternatively you can send a fax on 01235 400 454.

Name ....

Address ....

....

....

If you would prefer to pay by credit card, please complete:
Please debit my Visa/Access/Diner's Card/American Express (delete as applicable) card number:

Signature .... Expiry Date ....